THE CHOSEN CHRONICLES

SHADOW THE PRISON

K.A. PARKINSON

Cover and title design by Deborah Bradseth
ISBN 978-1-942298-20-5

www.snowypeaksmedia.com

For Joslyn and Laura
Never stop encouraging the dreamer

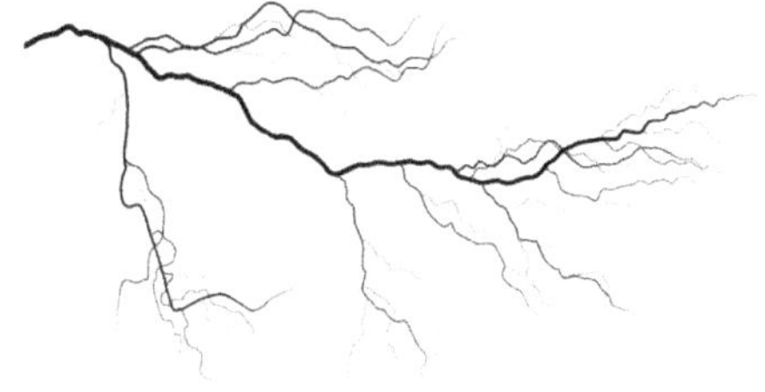

…I have promises to keep,
And miles to go before I sleep,
And miles to go before I sleep…

"Stopping by Woods on a Snowy Evening"
Robert Frost

Chapter 1

DENIED

He wasn't alone.

The feeling that someone was watching him pulled Tolen from his restless sleep. He opened his eyes to see Jonas—the ancient guardian of the camp that Tolen temporarily called home—sitting beside the cot, knobby hands folded across his cane, strange cobwebbed eyes focused intently on Tolen's face, a basket of steaming bread perched on his lap.

Tolen sat up and the blood rushed from his head, making Jonas appear blurry. He rubbed his eyes and tried to clear his scratchy throat. His mind had spun like a carousel all night, tossing garbled images and sounds around and around.

"Good morning, Tolen," Jonas whispered.

"Is it?" Tolen mumbled while rubbing his temples.

Jonas shrugged his thin shoulders. "I suppose that is up to you." He held out the basket.

Tolen took it absently and sat it on the cot beside him. He knew why Jonas was in his tent watching him sleep, and it wasn't to bring him breakfast. The bread smelled delicious and the crisp mountain air beckoned with the promise of a new beginning, but the reality of why the old man was here suppressed his appetite and slowed his feet. He leaned over and tugged on his sneakers before walking over to the metal basin beside the door. He dunked his head in the water, hoping its iciness would clear his thoughts, but he only succeeded in giving himself shivers to go along with the headache. He tugged a faded green shirt over his head, ran his fingers through his damp chocolate-colored hair, dropped back to his cot and glanced at his watch. The deep scratches on the surface made it hard to decipher the time, but told perfectly clear the reasons for his current misery. His mind flashed back over the last few weeks without his control and he buried his face in his hands, oblivious to his audience.

A freak from a small town in southern Utah, Tolen had always assumed his strange abilities were the result of some failed experiment, but the truth was far scarier. Not until Forrest Bastian—a mentor and guardian called a Watcher, the one selected to find Tolen—showed up on his doorstep did he learn the truth, at least a part of it. According to Bastian, Tolen's oddities were not a mistake, but actually *gifts* bestowed upon him at birth, so he could be a part of some elite group called the Chosen that protected mankind from monsters. Monsters—creatures of darkness—that had possibly killed his mother and best friend, and currently held his father prisoner.

For weeks he'd run from the Dark and its determination to find and destroy him. He'd tried to accept this world he was supposed to be a part of. He'd stayed in the Binithan, a series of underground caves, and trained with Doogar dwarves, learning to tap into his abilities after years of holding them back. He'd begun to find a friend in Macy, a fellow Chosen. But everything came to a crashing halt as they'd left the safety of the caves— left because Tolen wasn't strong enough to shield his powerful life force from detection by the Dark, making him a danger to himself and everyone around him.

He tried to tell himself that no one could have known what they would face once they left the Binithan and reached the surface. But the truth couldn't be ignored—he was the reason the demon wolves, the DéHool, had tracked them. He was the reason darkness found them everywhere he went. He was the reason his mother and best friend were gone. His lack of control, his weakness, his fear, was the reason Bastian was dead. And the reason why Macy now hated him.

And now...

He rubbed his forehead, trying to quiet the loud pounding in his skull. Now he had one more gigantic issue to add to the growing pile of things he didn't understand and was in no way prepared to deal with. Yesterday he'd finally learned the big secret, the terrifying mystery that everyone had been hiding from him.

The heavy weight he'd felt as Nova told him the legend of the Ninth Chosen settled back over him, and he wished for a moment he were back in Green River. As frustrating as it'd been to not know the reasons for his strangeness, at least he'd had his mother, he'd had Dane, and it didn't matter that he had no idea how to use his powers. He hadn't had a clue about a glaring destiny and no one had been counting on him. Or at least he hadn't known anyone was. Sometimes ignorance was bliss.

Jonas cleared his throat but Tolen didn't look up. "You had a difficult day yesterday."

Tolen dropped his hands to his lap clasping them into fists, keeping his eyes down, wishing they weren't going to discuss his discovery, but knowing he had no choice. As much as he didn't want to know, he *had* to know. He shrugged. "I didn't do anything hard."

"I said difficult, not hard."

He shook his head at the strange man. "Sounds the same to me."

"Gift and weapon training is hard, *difficult* is accepting what you do not understand."

"How can you accept something you don't understand?" Tolen's voice rose, he squeezed his fists tighter and looked away. *Stay calm.*

Jonas tapped his fingers on his cane. "Truth is truth whether it makes sense or not. That's why you couldn't deny what you learned, even if you didn't fully understand it."

Tolen glanced back at Jonas wanting to deny it, but he'd known Nova was talking about him, even though it made no sense. He met the old man's strange eyes and saw a hint of a twinkle behind the cobwebbed surface.

He looked back at his hands and kept his eyes down as he asked, "Bastian told me I wasn't ready to know my destiny yet, that it wasn't the right time." He heard Jonas's quiet intake of breath. "But, yesterday, Nova…I…she said some things, some things that…"

"She said some things that got your heart pounding and your mind working," Jonas prompted.

Tolen nodded.

"That was your body's response to truth. Go on." He waved his hand. Tolen could just see the tips of his fingers from his bowed position as they swished by.

"There are only eight gifts."

"Yes."

"You said something along the lines of 'the Ninth shall lead them' when I first met you."

"Yes."

"I can do a combination of things that no other Hidden or Chosen can do."

"Yes. Yes you can."

"So, my destiny…" Tolen gulped. "I-I'm supposed to be some sort of leader?"

Jonas leaned forward and Tolen looked up to see his expression was very grave. "That is a crucial *piece* of your destiny, yes, Tolen. But your duties as the Ninth Chosen encompass far, far more than that."

Tolen met the old man's gaze and tried to understand, but his insides were wriggling. How could he, a consistently dangerous failure, lead anyone? This *truth* made no sense. "Can you tell me—?"

Jonas was shaking his head before the question had completely left Tolen's lips. "No, Tolen. The Watcher is right. There is much you still need to learn before you are ready to accept the grander part of your destiny."

Tolen's stomach twisted. More secrets. His fingers started to tingle. How much worse could it be than what he'd already learned, what he'd already dealt with? He turned from the sickening thought and leaned back until his shoulders brushed the side of the tent. "How am I supposed to fulfill a destiny I don't even understand?" He tried to keep his tone calm, but his frustration and worry was obvious.

Jonas shook his head. "Your desire to know your destiny was fueled by anger and guilt, neither of which are good sources of energy to drive your intentions. You sought the information from Nova, not to really understand, but because you did not want to accept that someone else knew what was best for you. Until you want to know for the right reasons, and in the right way, the knowledge will only hurt you, and slow your progress toward the ultimate purpose of your destiny."

Tolen bit back a retort that would just prove the old man right.

"There is something I want you to understand as we move forward. You have been given a piece of information before you were ready to fully accept it. This has created a chasm in your path that is not going to be easy to navigate over, but you must find a way." The weight in the old man's words seemed to push Tolen deeper into his cot. "You know nothing of arrogance, it isn't in your nature to be so. But I fear your lack of confidence will hold you back in your purpose. You are pure in heart—."

"I'm not." Tolen held his palm up. "I wish people would stop saying that. If you only know what I'm thinking half the time, you would know what I really am." *Angry. Always angry.*

Jonas scratched his prickly chin. "You misunderstand. To be pure in heart does not mean you are perfect. It is not possible for anyone to be perfect in this dark and fallen world." He glanced over at the tent flap gently swaying in the slight morning breeze. "No. Being pure in heart simply means willing to *try*." His strange eyes stayed focused out the door and Tolen felt his words enter into his body and mind. It had been the same whenever Bastian had taught him something important. His heart started to pound and his mind whirled. Jonas had called it his body's reaction to truth.

Truth. This is how it feels to hear truth…

"Every Being on this planet has both light and darkness within them," Jonas continued. "The Balance selects the Chosen ones by seeking out those who are pure in heart—those with a life force containing great potential for light and a natural inclination to fight for what is right and true." He finally looked back at Tolen, but his eyes held an ancient sadness.

"You were created for a great purpose, as each and every Being has been, but in you the Balance has placed its hope, its need to sustain itself, its need to protect this world from the evils of the Dark, because in *you* it did find a pure heart with a deep and inherent desire to *try*…" He shook his head slowly. "And you must Tolen. You must try, even though you do not understand, even though I cannot lay it all at your feet right now. *Try*.

Try to connect with who you were born to be. Try to understand that the Light, and those who seek to serve it, only want what is best for you. Your destiny may feel like an unwelcome weight right now, but one day, I promise you one day, you will rise to it and be grateful. Of this I have no doubt."

Tolen had no idea what to say to that. He felt the truth in the old guy's words, but if it really was true, why was it so hard to believe?

He'd still be here if you weren't so weak! Macy's voice echoed through his thoughts. Bastian was dead because Tolen had been too weak to save him. How could he ever be a leader?

Jonas patted his knee. Tolen looked up to see the twinkle had returned. "There is something else you wish to speak with me about, something concerning your parents?"

"Are you a Watcher?" Tolen unconsciously slid his knee out from under Jonas's hand.

"No." Jonas chuckled. "You just have a very good one." He winked and Tolen wondered just what abilities this guy really had. "Go ahead Tolen. Ask me."

Tolen twisted his hands in his lap. Now that the moment was actually here, he wasn't sure how to ask. "Bastian—" A painful twinge twisted in his heart and he had to clear his throat to go on. "He…he said that the Light wanted me to try to save my dad from the Shadow Prison. I really think that the Dark might have my mom there too." He took a deep breath and plowed on, ignoring the regretful look forming on Jonas's face. "He said he would ask the warriors here to help me, but he's…" He swallowed. "Will you help me?"

Jonas stared back until Tolen's hands started to shake and he had to look away. "Tolen, when is your eighteenth birthday?"

Tolen's hands stopped shaking and he glanced back into Jonas's lined face with confusion. "July tenth."

Jonas nodded slowly and ran his thumb across his crinkly lips, his eyes deep in thought. Calculating. "Less than a month away."

Tolen swallowed and nodded, not daring to hope that this weird twist in conversation had something to do with helping him.

"Has anyone told you of Transcendence?"

"Transcendence?" Tolen shook his head.

Jonas nodded as if unsurprised. "Transcendence is the point at which the physical body and the metaphysical gifts of the Light fully intersect and become one. It is the time when your powers, your *gifts*, reach their peak, their strongest. This always takes place on the eighteenth birthday." He leaned forward and his next words sent a thrill of fear over Tolen. "At your Transcendence, Tolen, not even the Spheres of the citadel will be able to shield you if you don't learn enough. If you don't exercise patience, learn all you can, and master your anger, when you transcend, the Dark will take you for their own." He tapped his temple. "Work hard, Tolen, focus, discover the right fuel for your desires, and then we will help you. The journey to save your father, and possibly your mother, will be fraught with danger and much difficulty. It is not an idle task. If you are not ready to face the darkness of the Shadow Prison, if you are too close to the time of your Transcendence and your gifts are too erratic, it would be a mission destined to fail, no matter the amount of warriors who went with you."

The weight of truth settled over him and he bit his lip. He was dangerous. He knew this. Could he really expect others to follow him on a quest to save his parents when he could be the very reason they would fail? "Maybe…Maybe the Radia Warriors can go without me? Maybe they can find a way to save him—them?"

Jonas narrowed his eyes. "There is something you need to understand about your Watcher gift. You saw your father because *you* are meant to watch over him. In your visions, did you see anyone besides yourself in there with him?"

He shook his head as the nightmare filled his mind—his father on the floor, Tolen standing above him, helpless to do anything. "No. It was just the two of us."

"A Watcher sees flashes of present, possibility, and set future." Jonas pointed to Tolen's strange blue Watcher's eye, a huge contrast in more than just looks to his normal brown eye. "If the vision you beheld showed only yourself, then it is very likely that you are the only one who holds the key to his rescue. Other unseen factors *may* have played a role, but ultimately, no matter how many warriors I send, you may be the only one with the tools to succeed. I do not want to send my family into a losing battle. Tell me if your visions change, but until then, I suggest you work to make yourself ready to achieve what your visions are urging you to attempt. When I feel you are ready, when I feel you are strong enough, and in control, I will ask my warriors to go with you."

Tolen nodded. He had no argument, but the disappointment curdled in his stomach, further ruining his appetite.

If his birthday was some sort of deadline, then he wanted to get to work right away. He would prove to Jonas, and the Dominants, and everyone else who doubted him, that even though he may not be ready to learn his full destiny, he was strong enough to save his parents and not put anyone else in danger. He started to stand up but Jonas held out his hand.

"I came here this morning to first see how you were doing emotionally, and second to give you your schedule for your stay here."

Tolen sat back down and his fingers started tapping out a nervous rhythm on his knees.

"You will be awakened each morning for breakfast. Should the Dominants decide to stay, you will work with them from 6am until noon when you'll break for lunch. After lunch you will train with Incrah, other trainees, and McLacy."

Tolen tried to ignore the pang of annoyance he felt at the mention of her name.

"After supper at six, everyone retires to their tents for the one hour in ten allotted for the Light. This is a time for reflection, study, and self-evaluation. You will have free time from seven until nine pm. I know that must seem early to a teenager, but trust me, by the end of a day of training it won't feel early enough. I highly suggest you not fight the need to rest, you will need it. The next few weeks are going to be the most difficult of your life." He gave Tolen a grim nod and started to stand. Tolen jumped up to help.

He patted Tolen's arm and they walked out of the tent into the light of a new day.

ooo

Macy flipped her knife in the air, watched the sunlight flicker off the blade as it twirled, and caught the hilt before it landed point down in her lap. The hustle of early morning preparations could be heard throughout the camp. Tolen hadn't shown up for breakfast and Macy tried not to care.

After their fight, she'd packed her bags with every intention of leaving. She wanted time to mourn Bastian in her own way—fighting the Dark. She wanted to forget she'd ever met the Ninth and the confusing feelings she'd started having for him in the Binithan caves. She wanted to run away. It was the cowardly thing to do, but she was prepared to do it anyway—until she'd been stopped by Jonas just outside the camp border. She had no idea how he'd known where to find her, but when he'd stepped into her path her heart had dropped to the bottom of her boots. She couldn't leave. *Wouldn't* leave. Not yet. Not until she fulfilled her promise to Bastian. Jonas hadn't even had to say a word. He'd already said it all the day she and Tolen had arrived, and there was no way around it. No matter how angry she was. No matter how much she blamed Tolen for her Watcher's death. No matter how much she wanted to hate him.

So she stayed.

And she was miserable.

She knew the only way to get better was to get away from this place and the pain that she felt every time she looked at Tolen. But yet, here she was.

So she came up with a plan. If she had to stay, it would be on her own terms. The stories of the trainers here were legendary. Learning under real Radia Warriors could be a once in a lifetime chance. The likelihood that she'd ever have an opportunity like this again was incredibly low. She would stay. She would train. She would learn all she could. *And* avoid Tolen. There was no reason they would ever have to train together. She could make sure the others took care of his needs. Bastian said to protect him, she could do that from a distance. Then when he was ready, she could leave and go her own way, with better skills to boot. She ignored the twinge in her stomach at the thought of never seeing Tolen again.

Her Radia Shard—the source of her gifts and her connection to all Chosen—pulled her attention to the path. She looked up to see Tolen and

Jonas walking side-by-side, most likely on their way to wherever Tolen was supposed to meet the Dominants. She sheathed her knife, hurried into the gap between two tents, and waited for them to pass.

When Tolen neared her hiding spot, his head started to turn toward her and she jumped behind one of the tents, an uncomfortable feeling twisting in her gut.

You miss your friendship. Bastian's phantom voice was almost smug.

I do not! She thought bitterly. *Don't be stupid.*

She watched them pass and kept her body tight to the tent backs, her feet ghostly silent in the soft grass.

Then why are you following them?

She rolled her eyes and ignored her Watcher's imagined voice. She wasn't following Tolen. She was following Jonas. She'd only ever heard the legends of the Dominants strength in the gifts. This could be her only chance to see them in action. She followed silently, keeping to the trees when the tents became more and more sparse. She was going to watch the Dominants; this had *nothing* to do with Tolen.

Thankfully, Bastian's disembodied voice didn't retort, but no matter how much she tried to ignore it, she could tell her delusional Bastian wasn't convinced.

Chapter 2

THE DOMINANTS

Tolen and Jonas paused at the end of the row of tents where Incrah stood waiting.

"Tolen, Incrah will take you to the arena." Jonas clasped a bony hand on Tolen's shoulder. "I have some business to attend to. I will be right behind you."

Tolen nodded, but distracted by what he was sure he'd been feeling, he barely heard what Jonas said.

"Ready?"

Tolen looked up at Incrah. The huge, seven-foot tall Radia Warrior was no longer in the strange glowing armor he'd been wearing when they'd first met. Instead, he wore simple animal skin leggings and an open vest of the same material. A carved image of an elk hung from a long beaded cord around his neck. His glossy black hair was tied back in a loose ponytail. Tolen was reminded of Native Americans in old photographs.

Tolen nodded and glanced around again. His Radia shard was tugging his attention to someone nearby, and he knew exactly who. Her specific vibrations were becoming more and more familiar to him—just as Bastian had said they would. His palms started to sweat. He wasn't sure he was ready to see Macy just yet. He had no idea how they were ever going to make amends for what was said between them—if they ever could.

In the Binithan he'd begun to feel something for her, a growing flicker of attraction that went beyond their blossoming friendship. But the look of pure loathing on her face, the hatred in her voice as she'd blamed him for Bastian's death, had doused those feelings in icy water.

He closed his eyes.

"Tolen?" Incrah touched his shoulder.

His eyes snapped open. "Sorry. I'm ready." He took a deep breath and tried to look convincing as he moved into step beside Incrah.

"Jonas has informed me that you have accepted your Chosen calling."

"Yeah. I guess." He squirmed, fearing Incrah would want to talk about what happened, or demand to know why he'd run off like a coward the night before when Nova basically told him he was the Ninth Chosen instead of going with him to meet the Dominants like he was supposed to.

But Incrah surprised him when he looked Tolen up and down and asked, "Have you eaten anything?"

He shook his head. He hadn't touched the breakfast Jonas had brought to the tent with him.

"Not the best idea." Incrah rummaged in a pouch on his side. "Here. You're going to need your strength for what's coming." He handed Tolen something that resembled beef jerky.

He stuffed it in his mouth without really tasting it, too distracted by Macy's presence he could swear was tailing them, and Jonas's confusing visit. He swallowed and tried to focus on what Incrah was saying as he marched alongside him.

"Jonas asked me to prepare you a little for what is to come. The Dominants will want to test you before they decide if they will train you."

"Test me? How?" Tolen looked up at the big man beside him, his current worries briefly overshadowed.

"They'll want to see how your gifts work."

Tolen shoved his shaky hands in his pockets. "I would think they work like everyone else's do."

Incrah shook his head. "Not at all. Despite being categorized, each gift is as unique as the life force that wields it."

"So other Nature Speakers will work their abilities differently than me?" He glanced around again and swore he saw a flash of blonde hair behind a tree about a hundred yards to the left.

"Yes. The Chosen's gifts are more predictable, as they are brought out only by the power of their shard."

Tolen's attention shifted from the forest. "Why? Does it have to do with the fact that the Chosen are all human? Well, except for me."

Incrah paused and a look crossed his face. A look Tolen had learned to know well.

"You can't tell me."

Incrah stopped and faced Tolen. "That's not it at all. There is just so much we don't understand. And sometimes speaking of things we do not understand only leads to the wrong questions. The prophecy of the Ninth has been told for centuries, and for centuries the wisest of us all have studied it, and still we understand only pieces. Just pieces." He looked into Tolen's eyes and the power and majesty radiating from him made Tolen want to cower in shame.

Incrah put his hand on Tolen's shoulder. "Even the wisest of Beings don't always understand the why's of the world, but take heart, you have a difficult path ahead but you are not walking it alone. I will do all I can to help you learn who you are and become the man I can feel you will be. Do not worry about what you don't understand. Have faith. The Light is always with you. If you listen, it will guide you."

A lump rose in Tolen's throat and his heart seemed to swell with gratitude for the kindness of this stranger.

Incrah took a deep breath and started walking again. "Come. We're going to be late."

"Who *are* the Dominants?" Tolen nearly had to run to keep up with Incrah's long stride.

"They are the oldest Beings in our world, and some of the most powerful. There is no one on this planet as skilled in the gifts as they are. They have never left the citadel before, but you drew them out."

Tolen slowed down and mumbled. "You know, the more I hear about myself, the less I want to know."

Incrah chuckled once. "Come Tolen, they will be anxious to meet you. Jonas has made them wait. They aren't used to being told what to do."

Incrah led them into a walled arena topped with crisscrossed poles;

their sharp tips pointed outward in a brutal warning. Tolen had to wonder who or *what* they wanted to keep out. A heavy plank door sealed off the arena from the rest of the camp, creating an ominous, powerful feeling within the log and stone walls.

"The Dominants," Incrah whispered and Tolen looked away from the door to where Incrah pointed.

They stood in a semicircle, ancient and stooped like Jonas, wearing an assortment of colorful robes and leaning on tall, carved staffs. There was only one woman among the eight.

Eight warriors—at least as tall as Incrah, holding long rectangular brass lined shields, swords dangling from their hips, brass and steel breastplates gleaming in the summer sun—stood behind the Dominants in defensive stances, their eyes darting in every direction.

Suspicious, uncomfortable, deadly…*Bodyguards.*

Tolen had been intimidated by the just as tall Radia Warriors the first time he saw them as he'd knelt beside a bleeding and unconscious Macy three days ago. But even they, fully armored, were not nearly as alarming as the bodyguards of the Dominants.

His stomach did a nasty flip and his palms started to sweat.

Incrah motioned him forward and whispered. "You will go in front of them. I will wait over there." He pointed to a shaded area where Jonas was leading an extremely old woman wearing deep red robes and a thick sienna shawl draped loosely over her drooping shoulders to a low bench.

Tolen gulped. His legs felt like rubber as he trudged slowly to the center of the arena. He could feel all eyes on him, but he kept his own eyes on his sneakers. He hated having an audience and this had to be the scariest audience yet.

He stopped when he could see the toes of the Dominants sandaled feet then lifted his eyes and gulped again.

They stared.

The silence stretched on and Tolen's stomach started doing uncomfortable somersaults. *Say something.* "Um…I'm Tolen, Tolen Parks—er—uh, Téloran, Tolen Téloran."

Nothing.

"You wanted to see me?" Sweat trickled down his back. Were they just going to stand there and stare at him all day?

He was debating on running away when the Dominant farthest to the left took one step forward. He had a long thin face, and bleak gray eyes. He wore sweeping robes of chocolate brown and deep red. A thin gold circlet rested on his wispy gray hair. When he spoke his strange ethereal voice reminded Tolen of a stormy night.

"You look like your father." It sounded like an accusation.

Blood rushed to Tolen's face and his mouth started working before he could stop it. "Thank you for the compliment."

A few of the warriors shifted their feet, but Tolen didn't dare look at their faces.

The man who had spoken tipped his head and his eyes narrowed. "You have his defiance. Whether that will prove to serve you or hurt you, we shall see. Come forward, boy."

Tolen clenched his teeth and stepped forward. The old man raised his hand and shouted.

"*Vin'akra!*"

Instantly a whirlwind of dust spun up from the ground and surrounded Tolen's body. Dirt filled his eyes and nose. He couldn't see. He couldn't breathe. Tiny sharp rocks pelted every inch of exposed skin.

Tolen coughed and tried to shout. "What're you—?" He threw his arms up to protect his face and a big, sharp stone sliced into the back of his arm.

"STOP IT!"

The wind ceased and the dust settled.

Tolen started to wipe the grit from his eyes when someone else shouted.

"*Ma'sha!*"

An enormous eagle appeared out of nowhere and flew straight toward him. He dove to the side. The eagle came around for a second attack. Its talons sliced into his shoulder before he could roll away. It twisted in mid-air and dove toward him again. Blood seeped through his shirt and anger boiled through him. He wouldn't be bullied. No matter who these people were. As the anger built he tried to focus on the techniques Bastian and the Doogar had taught him in the Binithan, but before he could even start to recite his calming mantra, the eagle swooped low, talons out.

Tolen held his hands above his head and roared. "STOP!"

The eagle flipped direction mid-flight and twisted away.

His heart slowed for barely a beat when a female voice shouted, "*Win'tashta!*"

Tolen heard before he saw the water shoot toward him in the shape of an arrow. Water or not he knew he couldn't let it touch him or he'd be dead. He threw his hands out. "STOP!" The water splashed to the ground, inches from his face, splattering on his feet.

A deep gravelly voice cried, "*Tin'ruhl!*"

The earth cracked and rumbled beneath Tolen's feet. Walls shot up from the ground enclosing him in a prison of dirt. Sharp spikes of earth started shooting out of the ground pushing their way toward him. Panic rose in his chest for a split second until a memory of cave walls and tiny Doogar popped into his head. He reached out and pushed against one of the spikes. It crumbled at his touch. He spun around pushing on the spikes as they appeared until finally they stopped forming. He touched the remaining walls and they settled back to innocent flat ground.

"*Radi'non!*" This melodic voice rang across the arena.

Blinding light covered Tolen, engulfing him with scalding heat, but he was beginning to understand. "Stop!" He yelled before it became too much.

The light vanished.

"*Mi'no ha!*" This voice burned the air and Tolen knew what was coming for him before he saw the fireballs. He lifted his hands again. "Stop!" The fire disappeared in a trail of smoke.

Silence.

Panting, sweating, and stomach turning, Tolen dropped to his knees sucking at the air—he couldn't seem to fill his lungs. His chest burned and his head throbbed. His arms and legs were shaking so hard he couldn't stay on his knees. He dropped to all fours.

"You have passed the test."

Tolen looked up to see the man in the red and brown robes eyeing him with a calculating expression.

"We will train you."

The Dominants and their guards filed slowly from the arena without giving Tolen a second look. Jonas, and the old woman who'd been sitting beside him, followed them out.

Tolen rolled onto his back, closed his eyes, and focused on breathing. He heard footsteps crunching toward him.

"You handled that well." It was Incrah.

Tolen snorted. "*That* was the test?"

"They were making sure you are who they've been told you are."

"And I passed?"

"Yes." Incrah spoke in a tense whisper.

"Is that a bad thing?"

"Not necessarily."

Tolen pushed himself back up onto his knees—his legs felt like gobs of jelly. Incrah held out a hand and helped him stand. Tolen swayed and Incrah steadied him.

"Thanks. An introduction and a warning about what they were about to do would have been nice."

Incrah nodded with his eyes on the retreating figures. "The old ones have their own way of doing things." He turned back to Tolen. "The first man to speak to you and test you was O'shae, master of the Arwah—the wind shifters. I suppose you could call him the leader of the Dominants. The second, Took'rah, is master of the animal listeners, we call them the Animashta. The woman is Kyndras, master of the Leenwa that are the Water Callers. The fourth, Dunrath, is master of the Télora—Earth Movers. The fifth, Nephen, is master of the Lóklana, which are able to wield the Radia light. The sixth, Jun'tar, is master of your friend Macy and the other Kunamin—fire wielders." Incrah paused. "The last two on the far end, Ras'met, master of the Honitahai and Vindi, master of the Dicernan, the Unseen's, did not test you. I expect Ras'met has already heard of your exploits with Nature Speak, and Vindi's gift cannot be tested."

"I'm going to be trained to do all that?" Tolen's knees wobbled and Incrah reached over to steady him again.

"Yes."

"How? I don't know how any of this stuff works."

"Your life force knows. The knowledge was born with you. You were able to stop their gifts without even realizing what you were doing. You will do fine."

Tolen ran a hand over his eyes. "This is going to be fun."

"You have no idea. The Masters of the elements are legendary in their ways of training." Incrah smiled and shook his head. "The remainder of your training this morning will be with me——sword play. The Dominants will begin with you tomorrow. They want your gifts to be fully regenerated."

"Sounds great."

Incrah chuckled and started to walk out of the arena. "Don't sound so worried. I'll go easy on you."

A thought struck Tolen. "Incrah? Bastian told me that I also had the gift of the Dreamers, but no one tested me in that."

Incrah stopped and turned around. "The Dreamers? Are you certain?"

Tolen swallowed, "Yeah. Why? Is that bad?"

Incrah frowned. "The Dreamers are on the side of the Dark. I know of none who fight for Light."

"So that means I won't be trained in that area?"

Incrah shook his head slowly. The suspicious look was back in his eyes. He glanced at Tolen's shoulder where the blood had seeped through. "You might want to heal those." He didn't watch as Tolen struggled to focus and heal the shallow cuts on his arm and shoulder from the rock and the eagle's talons, and instead turned to leave.

It took forever to get the heat to come. Tolen wished he could just figure out his trigger, that little connection that everyone kept saying was so important in order to gain more control over his gifts, but he had to admit he'd long since realized that nothing about this world was going to be easy.

Finally, after whispering *lon'adras* at least a dozen times, he could feel the skin slowly knit back together.

He followed Incrah from the arena on trembling legs, wondering how in the world he was going to do everything that was expected of him. Being the Ninth Chosen was big, really big—what had just happened was proof of that—and he was getting more and more worried about the rest of the puzzle.

Instead of a person he was a spectacle, a tool put on display for everyone to test out, to see if it met their expectations. He stuffed his hands into his pockets, not at all ready to face the rest of the day, the rest of his life for that matter, and followed Incrah into another piece of his destiny.

CHAPTER 3

BLADES AND BONDS

"Battle skills are mostly overseen by me. Occasionally, one of the other Radia captains will take over if I have other obligations." Incrah led Tolen behind a row of tents. The clink of metal echoed off the trees as two young men, probably right around Tolen's age of seventeen, were sparring under the direction of one of the Radia Warriors he remembered meeting when they'd first arrived.

"You will learn to use not only your gifts in battle, but also several other weapons unique to our kind. I am told you have had some experience with a Shupata and Doogar blades. That'll help." Incrah handed Tolen something that resembled a small, hard hamburger patty.

Tolen hesitated, remembering Macy's warning about disgusting meat cakes. "Is that a sweetened meat cake?"

Incrah chuckled. "No, this is Sugar Tack; dried fruit and herbs. Eat it. It will help you feel better."

Tolen took a small bite. It was sweet and fruity and it did stop his knees from shaking. He popped the rest in his mouth.

"Better?"

Tolen swallowed. "Yeah, thanks."

Incrah handed him a canteen and waited until Tolen had nearly finished the whole thing before speaking.

"Now watch as the trainees incorporate Beyn's direction." He pointed to the boys in front of them and the Radia Captain, Beyn, standing off to the side occasionally shouting quick instructions.

Tolen stared transfixed. Every time the blades struck, the sound echoed like thunder. Even though it was only practice, their faces were twisted in concentration and dripping with sweat.

"Watch how they move their feet," Incrah murmured. "See how they use their back leg to hold their ground when they block and their front leg as a driving force when they strike. The placement of every part of your body, every inch of your weapon, and every piece of your surroundings plays an integral role in battle. Watch."

Tolen did.

It was amazing and horrifying. Not only did they use the blade end of their sword, but the hilt as well. Sometimes they moved so fast, the only hint at what happened was the flash of reflected sunlight off their swords and the clang as they connected.

As the youth danced about the arena, he realized that the need for skills like these meant that Raksasha and DéHool could not be, by a wide margin, the most dangerous creatures of the Dark. Raksasha would be child's play to the Radia Warriors. The DéHool, although likely a challenge, would not be as hard for these *children* to defeat as it'd been for Tolen and the others. It made the hair rise on the back of his neck.

An hour later, he stood in the arena holding a long stick instead of a sword. The other two boys had finished sparring and now stood off to the side near their captain, downing mugs of water, watching. Tolen tried to ignore them and focus on Incrah, who faced him and quietly gave instruction, but he knew he must look ridiculous. Incrah showed him where to place his feet, his hands, even where to focus his eyes. He first walked Tolen through the moves slowly increasing in speed as Tolen caught on. He scolded when Tolen got it wrong, praised when he got it right. It didn't take long before Tolen's legs and arms burned from exertion. He was grateful for the days of training with the Doogar, as some of the moves were familiar, but he was getting discouraged. With each thud of his wooden sword, he could hear Macy yelling, *"You're weak!"* With each failed jab he heard Jonas whisper, *"The Ninth shall lead them,"* and felt the judgmental eyes of the other trainees. The harder he worked to push these thoughts and feelings away, the louder they became, making him feel all the more weak and inadequate.

For two hours he waged a war with himself. Fighting to learn, improve, and ignore the glaring truth—that he was so very far behind what he should be. People began to gather around the arena to watch. Tolen could hear their voices, but didn't stop to look at them while his body screamed for a break, his mind shouted his weakness, and his heart begged him to move faster, try harder.

"Block!" Incrah kicked Tolen's legs out from under him.

"Roll!"

He rolled out of the way of Incrah's death strike barely in time.

"Up!"

Tolen jumped to his feet, knees shaking, to face an empty arena. Or what appeared to be empty.

"You're dead." Incrah's stick touched the back of Tolen's neck.

He dropped his fake sword and fought the urge to collapse on the ground. "You disappeared. How?" He placed his hands behind his head to open up his lungs, a trick he'd learned from a former gym coach, and tried to slow his breathing.

"You were distracted—I advanced."

Tolen wiped the sweat off his forehead with the hem of his shirt.

"Not bad for your first lesson." Incrah offered his hand.

Tolen shook it and applause broke out from the crowd. Even the two boys and Beyn nodded toward him in approval before turning to leave. Nova stood at the front, beaming and waving. He gave her a half-hearted smile and looked away.

"Come. It's time for lunch." Incrah patted Tolen's shoulder before leaving the arena. Instantly several of the by-standers swarmed around him, whispering and gesticulating toward Tolen.

"Here." Nova had moved in beside him. She held out a tin mug filled with water.

"Thanks." Tolen downed it in one gulp. His hands were shaking as he handed it back.

"You were incredible."

He cleared his throat. "I doubt that."

"No, really. I watch the sparring all the time. I've never seen anyone do so well in their first lesson."

"Well, it wasn't exactly my first lesson. I trained a little with the Doogar."

Nova shrugged. "Still, I was impressed."

Tolen ducked his head and pushed his hands into his pockets, uncomfortably aware that he was covered with sweat and dirt.

"Come on. I'll show you where the mess tent is. You can eat with me." Nova grinned and beckoned him to follow.

Her behavior toward him was confusing. For years he'd felt people watching him because he was different. A freak. When Nova looked at him he felt weird and self-conscious, but not for the usual reasons. When she looked at him, he felt like he should have combed his hair or checked his breath. The way she looked at him said she liked what she saw, and he wasn't exactly sure how to feel about it.

His stomach growled and he took a deep breath. It was just lunch. He fell into step beside her, not too close in case he smelled bad, and tried to smooth out his sweaty hair with his fingers.

When they entered the tent, the mouthwatering smells shifted Tolen's thoughts to his empty stomach. All he could think of was devouring everything laid out—overflowing pots of spicy meats, platters of steaming bread rolls, baskets of fresh fruit, and pans of boiled vegetables. He followed Nova through the line, piling his tray high. When they reached the end of the row of food, she motioned him to a table where three people sat in conversation.

Tolen's shard pulled his attention toward the opposite end of the tent where Macy sat at a low table with Jonas. The old man met his gaze and smiled. Macy didn't even glance in his direction. A muscle in her cheek twitched—she was still furious. That made two of them. He flexed his jaw and refocused on Nova.

"Tolen, this is my family." Nova motioned to the three elves—called Lafar—sharing their table. He set his tray down and took the seat beside her as they began introducing themselves.

"Quasar." The oldest Lafar, with long silver hair tied back into a ponytail, held out his arm. He had a long puckered scar running from his temple to the tip of his chin—a grotesque contradiction to the polite smile he gave Tolen as they shook arms.

The female by Quasar's side leaned across the table. "Nebula." She tossed her elbow length honey-colored hair behind her shoulder to grasp his arm. "Nice to meet you."

"Nice to meet you," Tolen replied.

The last Lafar wiped his mouth on a napkin. "Bolide, I'm Nova's brother," he shook Tolen's arm. "Don't let her dominate all your free time."

Nova pinched his side and he winked. He had the same ink colored hair as Nova that he too wore in a long ponytail. All three Lafar had the same strange violet eyes and surreal beauty—well, all of them except Quasar.

"So what do you think of the camp so far?" Nova lifted a forkful of beans and looked at Tolen with such rapt attention he felt his face redden.

He swallowed the mouthful of corn he'd just stuffed in his mouth and sighed. "I'm still trying to convince myself I'm not dreaming."

She chuckled. "Yes, watching trainees can be pretty intense."

Tolen thought back to the youth he had seen practicing gifts when he'd first arrived and then seeing them spar this afternoon. "I guess I just didn't realize the Radia Warriors would also have elemental gifts."

Her eyebrows lifted and Tolen realized he'd revealed even more of his ignorance.

"You really don't know much about the Hidden world, do you?" When Tolen didn't answer, she pressed, "Where did you come from? Who's your Watcher?"

Bolide pushed her shoulder. "Nova, stop being so nosy."

She slugged him back. "I'm not nosy. I'm just curious. I mean, *you* know who he is. I'm just surprised he doesn't know anything."

Tolen's cheeks flamed. He really hoped they weren't about to start talking about him being the Ninth Chosen. He was doing all he could not to think about it.

"Nova, that's enough," Quasar scolded.

As embarrassing as it was, Tolen found he really didn't mind Nova's interest, even if he was a little unaccustomed to it. Her forceful honesty was kind of a nice change from the way everyone else treated him—as if he were a bomb about to explode, or worse, like a child who couldn't be trusted with anything important. "It's fine, really."

Bolide shrugged and shook his head. "You'll change your mind in a few days." He rolled his eyes at Nova and turned back to his food.

Nova pushed her fork around her plate, no longer eating.

She looked genuinely hurt and Tolen's sympathy won out. He leaned closer and whispered. "I'm from a tiny town in Utah." She had a pleasant smell, sort of floral and sunny. Realizing he was close enough for her to smell him, and he probably didn't smell at all pleasant, he leaned back quickly.

She looked up and a small smile touched her lips. "A town? Like you lived with humans?"

The other Lafar looked up from their plates with suspicious looks.

Tolen swallowed. "Um, yeah."

Nova took a sip of her drink and eyed him up and down. He squirmed and someone behind them cleared their throat.

They spun around to see Incrah. He looked irritated. Tolen glanced at Nova to see the fear once again in her eyes. Not only could he see it, he could feel it. Nova was afraid of Incrah. Really afraid.

"When you are finished with your lunch Tolen, come to the Eighth arena for the next phase of your training." He gave Nova a pointed look and walked out of the mess tent.

The rest of the meal passed in tense silence while Tolen ate everything on his tray, puzzling over Nova's reaction to Incrah. Why was she afraid? The other Lafar hadn't reacted the same, but rather had seemed to shrink in their seats, not in fear, but as a subject would react in the presence of his king. It was odd. He glanced around and realized something he hadn't noticed at first. The other people in the mess tent sat in random groupings, laughing, chatting, socializing. A wide bubble of empty seats surrounded the little group of Lafar. The elves didn't meet the eyes of those around them, and when they did talk to one another, they did so in quiet whispers. There was obviously much more to this group than Tolen could possibly guess.

"Do you know where the Eighth arena is Tolen?" Nebula asked kindly when he stood up and looked around.

He shook his head.

Nebula smiled, her violet eyes sympathetic. "Head east, along the main path in the center of camp, until you come to what will appear to be a tall mound of earth. It will be hard to see at first, but it's there."

Tolen smiled back. "Thank you. And thank you for letting me join your table."

The Lafar all nodded and Nova offered him a small smile, the fear still visible in her eyes. "Good luck Tolen."

"Thanks." Tolen shook her arm awkwardly. He could hear Bolide teasing Nova as he left. Her overt friendliness left him feeling a little dazed, but he had bigger things to worry about. He was heading for another training session and all that food had him feeling sluggish and stupid. He shouldn't have eaten so much.

CHAPTER 4

THE EIGHTH ARENA

MACY'S ARMS SHOOK AS SHE CARRIED HER TRAY TO THE WASH BIN, HER fingers tingling as she scraped the remains of food from her plate and dipped it in the soapy water to scrub clean. *Tolen knows…* Her conversation with Jonas over lunch pounded through her head. According to him, one of the Lafar, a little elf wench called *Nova*, had spilled the beans to Tolen that he was the Ninth Chosen. Jonas had kept the full details from him, like the part that he would be *the* final hope for the entire world, that as he transcended to the height of his powers he would be responsible for every life on this planet.

But what now? How could they help him grow into the person he was to become if he was so distracted by his gigantic destiny? She clenched her teeth and the water heated up around her hands. She quickly rinsed her plate and placed it on the draining rack before rushing from the mess tent. The anger was building faster than she could hold back.

Why would the elf brat do that? Why would she go against the statute Jonas had put in place when Macy and Tolen had arrived? Bastian knew what was best. There were bigger reasons than all of them could possibly understand for keeping Tolen ignorant. She'd accepted that, everyone had accepted that, even Tolen had—for the most part. She had the overwhelming urge to find the elf and challenge her to a duel—no gifts—the Lafar had none anyway. No, sword on sword. A fierce surge of anticipation swelled within her at the thought.

"Tolen needs your help now more than ever, McLacy." Jonas had given her a sad look when he said it. He knew, somehow, her plan to stay as far from Tolen as possible. *"We have no way to foresee if this new knowledge will help or hinder him. He needs you as he transitions. You are best suited to help him."*

"Why me?"

"You are a Chosen."

He said nothing else, but she felt there was more to it than just that. If the only reason was because she was a Chosen, they could have found him another one, there were hundreds of them scattered around the world. No, it went back to what Jonas had said when they first arrived. That the Balance had brought Tolen and Macy together for a reason. *Stupid Balance.*

Macy pushed her way deeper into the trees, anger at Nova, Jonas, the Balance, and Tolen muddling her thoughts, heating her Kuna, and confusing her plans.

∘∘∘

Tolen walked slowly, shaking out his arms and legs and rolling his neck, wondering what the next phase of his training was going to be. Incrah said the Dominants weren't going to teach him until tomorrow, and the swordplay was only to finish out the morning. What were they going to do to him now? People watched him as he walked by, but he kept his eyes on the path. It wasn't long before he had left the tents far behind and all that lie ahead were thick stands of trees. The path stayed clear beneath his feet, so he continued to walk, hoping he hadn't misunderstood Nebula's instructions. Finally, through a gap in the trees, he saw what looked like a low green mountain not far ahead.

The closer he got the more he understood what he was looking at. The arena looked as if it hadn't been used for hundreds of years. The high rounded walls were made of piled gray stone and seemed at first to be nothing more than a mound of boulders held together by centuries of dirt and leaves. Only upon closer inspection could he tell that the stones were too symmetrical to have been dropped by nature. Tolen walked around the arena twice before he found the tall wooden door disguised with branches and dried leaves.

He tried to push it open, but it wouldn't budge. He shoved harder and a blast of wind knocked him onto his backside.

"State your purpose!" A woman's voice issued from the door.

"Incrah told me to come." Tolen stood up and dusted himself off.

"Name?"

"Tolen."

"Wait."

Tolen stood there staring at the door, becoming more irritated with each passing minute. Finally, he heard footsteps crunching from inside the arena.

The door swung open and there stood Incrah. A tiny wrinkled brunette, wearing a strange mixture of brightly colored silk robes, had her arm wrapped around his elbow. Tolen recognized her as the woman who'd been sitting with Jonas when he'd met the Dominants earlier.

Incrah lifted his hand and the door sealed shut with a soft hiss. He motioned Tolen to follow them to the center of the arena.

"Tolen, this is Evrah, my great-grandmother. She is the linguist for this camp. She knows every word of the ancient language."

The woman lifted her chin and Tolen took a step back. Her eyes were opaque-white—sightless.

Evrah raised her hands. "May I?" She reached toward Tolen.

"She wants to know what you look like," Incrah explained.

"Okay." Tolen leaned forward and let Evrah run her gnarled fingers along his face.

A gentle smile lifted her lined cheeks. "You are a handsome boy." She dropped her hands. Her white eyes held a depth that made Tolen feel extremely small.

She clasped her hands back around Incrah's arm. "The gifts of the Hidden are exactly that—*gifts* from the Light. We do not have magic powers or potions. Everything we are, everything we can do is because of the Light. You must remember this. Without the Light we would have nothing, be nothing."

Evrah's voice was laced with the same kind of power that Tolen had felt when Bastian and Jonas spoke; he became entranced by the words as she spoke them, lost in them.

"The elements with which we bond have their own life force. Your life force, the source of your strength, the source of who you truly are, is what connects with the elements and asks them to change their natural course."

Her white eyes seemed to bore into Tolen's soul. "The Light, the great Creator of life has given you a piece of itself, the ability to speak the language of the elements. It is a sacred gift, one that should never be used carelessly. All Chosen are given certain words of the language necessary for their particular gifts. You will be given the fullness of the language." Tolen shifted his feet, not sure why this made him uncomfortable.

Evrah went on, either ignoring or not realizing Tolen's discomfort. "Your life force will respond in ways it never has before. The language speaks to it—it connects your mortal body with the immortal gifts of the Light. It is the only way your gifts can ever reach their full potential."

She held out her hand to Tolen. The moment her fingers touched Tolen's his heart began to pound, his body filled with warmth, and his Watcher's eye dilated, pulling Evrah's face into intense focus. He could see every crisscrossed tiny vein under her thin wrinkled skin. Her misty eyes held a hint of brown.

"I am sending my knowledge to your life force Tolen. Let it listen."

Tolen had no idea how to do what she was talking about, but he closed his eyes and tried to stop resisting the strange feeling. Slowly his blue eye shifted back to normal and his heart slowed down, but the warmth didn't leave. He felt his Radia Shard heat up, pulsing against his skin. The warmth flowing from Evrah grew and grew until he felt as if he was no longer standing on the ground, but floating in a soft pocket of warm air. His mind cleared and the stress and exhaustion he had felt disappeared, replaced with a calm desire to know everything this woman had to teach him.

The language of the Hidden cannot be taught. It was Evrah's voice, but different—a hollow echo of her spoken voice, like a memory of a voice.

The language is a gift, given only to those the Light has chosen...

The Light has chosen you, Tolen Daedal Téloran. Hear the words of the Light. Remember them. They have been part of you since the day you were born...Remember...Remember....

And suddenly he did.

Thousands upon thousands of words rushed into his head as if he'd been hooked to a computer and an entire language dictionary was downloaded into his brain. He could feel his body begin to shake and Evrah's hand tightened over his. His eye went crazy, colors and images flashing so fast it made him dizzy.

She dropped his hand and he opened his eyes.

The warmth disappeared and a strange feeling of déjà vu passed over him.

Incrah watched him closely. "Are you all right?" He put a hand on Tolen's shoulder.

Tolen shook his head. "Yeah. That was wild. I feel like…like I've heard it all before."

"You have. Just not in this life." Evrah's blind eyes seemed to be watching him. She tipped her head to the side. "Your mind is a beautiful place, Tolen. I have been without sight so long I forget to appreciate the precious beauty of the feelings stirred within the heart when one looks at those whom he loves." A single tear trickled down her cheek. "Thank you."

Incrah looked back and forth from Tolen to Evrah with a confused look on his face.

Tolen's eyebrow rose. "You could see in my head?"

"The memories that are the most clear and precious to you are foremost in your mind. You love your mother so deeply…and…I had no idea Macy was such a beautiful girl. Her attitude repelled me. But seeing her through your eyes, I see I was much mistaken." *What?*

Incrah smirked.

Tolen felt his face get hot and looked away. He had no idea what the woman saw in his head concerning Macy, but he seriously doubted it could have given her a good opinion of the little *obnoxious* fireball that drove him crazy.

"Is it there? Do you know the language?" Incrah changed the subject.

Tolen nodded. "I think so."

"What do you say when you want nature to hear you?" Evrah's white eyes were still shining.

"Nit'ahai." The word came out so fast he jumped. Instantly a rush of confusing whispers filled his head.

"What do you hear?" Evrah smiled broadly and waved her hand through the air.

"Everything. It's confusing. I can hear whispering everywhere around us." Tolen rubbed his forehead. "I can't understand them though. There's too many. How do I get them to all stop talking at once?"

"You cannot. When you use the word while focused on the specific life force you want to speak with, that voice will become clearer. The other voices will still be there but you'll be able to block them out."

It was so strange. So intense. "How do I turn off their voices once I've said the word?" He didn't like the idea of hearing whispering in his head all the time.

"You use the words that mean 'be still'."

"Pench Ni'yālo?" The words spilled from his mouth fluid and perfect, and the whispering stopped. A crazy idea began to form, that this had always been his first language, he'd just forgotten. Whenever he'd repeated a word the Doogar or Bastian had taught him, it had always come out choppy and hardly flowed. Now, the words felt more familiar than English.

"Very good." Evrah smiled wider. "We will stop here today, Tolen. You have the language. You need to learn how to use it. Practice as you go about the camp. Speak the words that come to your mind, whenever they come to your mind. Let the Light guide you as you learn. You will know what you need to do. Whenever it becomes too much say 'be still'. You can say the language in your head as much as you want, for now it will not affect the elements until it is spoken aloud. Once you have mastered your focus, you will be able to project your verbalized thoughts of the language into specific actions."

Another thought crossed Tolen's mind. "Excuse me Evrah? Can I ask you something?"

She nodded.

"When I was about ten years old, I went to the river by my home to be alone and this tree started talking to me. I could hear her voice as if she were sitting right next to me—even without knowing the language. She's the only tree I've ever been able to hear like that. The whispers I just heard were slightly different. Do you know why?"

Tolen avoided looking at Incrah, not sure if this would worry him or not.

Evrah smiled softly. "Did this tree have a name?"

"Her name is Ardia. She followed me when I left my home. She stayed in the forest to protect Bastian's body from the Dark." Tolen swallowed the sudden lump in his throat.

"Ardia…" Evrah swayed a little where she stood and Incrah held her hand tighter over his arm. "There is a legend, a legend older than I, that tells of the death of the Radia Star—a great follower of Light. As Radia died, she sent her shards to Earth—the nearest planet to her held by the Light. The legend tells that although most of the shards fell to the Watchers, a few were swallowed up by the earth to spring forth as mighty trees when their power was needed."

Goosebumps rose on Tolen's arms.

"Ardia could very well be one of these trees. After all, her name means 'gift of Radia'."

A string of words flashed across Tolen's mind and, following Evrah's advice, he spoke them aloud. "*To'conchla serith hune doocrah.*"

Incrah's eyes narrowed. "Do you know what you just said?"

Tolen's heart thudded. He didn't want to say it aloud, but the way Incrah was watching him, he understood anyway. "The Ninth shall lead them."

Incrah nodded slowly, his eyes nervous and wary again. "Are you beginning to understand?"

Tolen started to shake his head, but his hands began to tremble as truth seemed to settle over him, another piece to the puzzle of his grand destiny fitting into the whole. His stomach lurched—he could do all eight gifts. He could also do other things; he could heal like the Spheres, he had the gift of the Dreamers, he had a Watcher's eye. Bastian's words came back to Tolen's mind. *It shows us whom we are responsible for.*

Am I…am I responsible for-for everyone? The whole, he gulped, *world?*

The Ninth shall lead them.

Lead who? Nova's words as she'd told him the Legend of the Ninth came back with uncomfortable clarity. *"The Ninth will…unite the Chosen, as well as all fighters for Light, in a Final Battle against the Dark, for the hope of all Beings."*

Tolen's heart twisted in his chest. *Unite the Chosen…* What? How?

"The lesson will stop here today. It's almost time for supper." Evrah's voice brought him back to the moment.

Supper? Tolen glanced at his battered watch. It was almost 6:00. Learning the language had felt like moments, but it had actually been nearly five hours. The sun had long since passed behind the walls of the arena. Only now did he notice glowing torches surrounding them that Incrah must have lit as he waited.

Evrah reached out until she found his hand. "Go back to camp. Mingle, relax, and practice when you feel like it. The Dominants will be training you in turn. The more you practice between lessons, the more prepared you will be and the easier it will come."

Unable to form a coherent sentence he stumbled away from the center of the arena only to trip over his loose shoelace at the door. Grateful for the excuse to pause and steady his breathing he knelt down to tie his shoe. Incrah and Evrah were still talking, back in the middle of the arena. A word or two met his ears. He slowed his fingers on his laces and closed his eyes, focusing on the whispers behind him.

A word echoed through his head and he whispered it aloud. *"To' konsh'la."*

Suddenly Incrah's voice became as clear as if Tolen were standing right beside him.

"…this proves it doesn't it? The legend says, 'One shall lead them with Might, and Shield…. With the breath of *Radia* so nature will yield….'"

"Yes, I believe it does give the final proof, although Jonas was already certain." Evrah sighed.

"I've never seen anyone catch onto the language so quickly." Incrah's voice sounded both awed and nervous. "And the way he passed the test with the Dominants…Even without knowing the language he was able to stop their gifts as easily as if he'd thrown up a shield. The rumors are spreading. Those who know the legend are certain. Even the younger ones know he is different. They've never seen anyone with more than one elemental gift before. His Watcher's eye makes many nervous. What should we do?"

"Let the speculation spread. They need not fear him. We do not yet know his limitations. His single Watcher's eye may not work the same as a true Watcher. He can access the elemental gifts but he has yet to discover his trigger. Only the Honitahai stays with him always. We shall all have to wait and see…" Evrah paused and Tolen could feel her blind eyes on him. "It will not be long before everyone will be looking to him. He is the one we have been waiting for—"

"—and dreading the arrival of," Incrah finished.

Tolen stood up and walked away, hoping they wouldn't notice his shaking knees. There was a reason behind the saying about eavesdroppers. He had definitely just heard something he wished he hadn't.

And the Ninth shall lead them.

Tolen barely made it to a bush before he threw up.

He staggered through the trees, the desire for food completely gone. He hardly noticed the people watching him as he escaped into the quiet of his tent, dropped onto his cot and begged for sleep.

CHAPTER 5

HIDDEN TALENTS

Tolen stood once again in the center of the Eighth arena, his empty stomach turning. He'd skipped dinner last night in the wake of his mounting destiny, and couldn't bring himself to eat breakfast this morning. Incrah had passed him another piece of sugar tack as he'd led the way back to the arena, but Tolen had only rolled it from hand to hand until finally Incrah had taken it back with a sigh, and a *you're going to be sorry later* kind of look. Jonas had been waiting for them at the door and informed him that he would be working with Took'rah, the animal guy, and Kyndras, the water lady this morning. What he hadn't mentioned was that the door to the arena was going to stay wide open. Apparently, he was going to have an audience.

Since his arrival, at least a dozen people varying in age had walked in and sat along the rim of the field. All of them kept talking behind their hands and glancing his way. He thought he understood why they were here. Incrah said the Dominants never left the citadel, that Tolen had drawn them here. The Dominants were legendary, so of course the members of this camp would be anxious to watch legends at work. It didn't stop it from being uncomfortable, especially since he was more likely to make a fool of himself than a good impression.

He scuffed his shoes in the dirt and tried unsuccessfully to pretend he was alone. His stomach growled, cursing him for skipping breakfast. He glanced at his watch. It was just after six, the sun was barely skimming the top of the arena. How long would they keep him waiting? His shard gave an increasingly familiar tug and he glanced toward the door with unease, but he couldn't see Macy anywhere in the small crowd of people pushing their way through the entrance, or among those already seated. The feeling remained even after Incrah came in, leading the two Dominants and their bodyguards, and closed the heavy door. He rolled his shoulders and hoped she was just somewhere nearby, not actually in the arena. He didn't need the distraction.

o o o

Macy kept low as she followed the crowd through the wide doorway. Tolen might sense her here through his shard, but if she stayed out of sight hopefully he'd just assume she was nearby. The group she'd followed turned to find a spot to sit along the rim, and she ducked behind a dirty wooden barrel. A quick glance around the arena showed it wasn't going to be easy to find a hiding spot that would allow her to watch and stay hidden at the same time.

Finally, about fifty feet from where she hid, she noticed a tall woodpile, likely used to fill the many fire-barrels surrounding the arena, supplying heat in the winter. If she could get to the pile, she should be able to sit behind it, remove a log or two, and watch through the gap. She waited until Tolen was distracted by the arrival of Incrah, the Dominants and their Protectors, before sprinting to the pile and sliding behind it.

She could hear them talking while she maneuvered the wood, creating a suitable peephole. Through some of the cracks, she also had a decent view of the surrounding crowd. She situated her legs beneath her and waited for the action to start. She caught a glimpse of Tolen's face. He looked terrible. He hadn't shown up for dinner last night or breakfast that morning, but she'd figured he was getting special treatment and had eaten in his tent or with his trainers. By the looks of him, she'd been wrong. Dark circles stood out against his pale skin. His extreme nervousness evident in the way his eyes darted about, the way he kept mussing his hair, and fidgeting with his shirt hem.

Before she could stop it, a tiny glimmer of pity twisted her heart into a painful knot. He clearly wasn't handling the news of being the Ninth well at all. Jonas had said Tolen needed her help now more than ever. Guilt wriggled in her stomach, but she pushed it aside as Kyndras moved to the center of the arena and raised her arms for silence. What could she do about it now anyway? An image of her fist connecting with Nova's jaw flashed across her mind and a smug smile pulled at her lips. Her palms tingled in anticipation and her heart pounded. The elf brat was going to seriously regret going against Bastian's wishes.

I told you, you care. Bastian's voice whispered.

About you, not Tolen. Now, shut up. I want to watch without you inter-rupting. Macy focused on the scene unfolding in front of her, ignoring all other thoughts—real or imagined.

○ ○ ○

Chills ran down Tolen's back as he watched Kyndras lift her hands for silence. He felt all eyes turn toward them and stay there.

She stood there aged and stooped, yet filled with power and majesty. Her thick blue and white robes billowed out from her body, fluttering in the breeze. Her silver hair hung in a long braid down her back that brushed the ground, her deep brown eyes full of dignity. "We have wel-comed you here today to participate in this momentous occasion," her voice showed her age—thick and scratchy, yet firm and loud. "You are allowed to observe, but you are to remain silent. This is an opportunity for you to learn by watchful care. If you disrupt these proceedings in any way, our Protectors will escort you out."

The Dominants' guards, their *Protectors,* glanced around the group and Tolen could sense the nervousness of the spectators. Tolen remembered Bastian saying Daedal Téloran, his father, had been a Protector of legend. Could any of these men have known him? As he surveyed their confident stance, their overall demeanor of power, he couldn't help but feel a surge of pride for the man his father must have once been. A tiny flicker of hope filled his heart. Surely if his father had been this powerful once, it would take a lot for the Dark to break him. Then his mind pulled up the image of the broken, dying man on the floor in his nightmares, and completely snuffed the hope.

Kyndras snapped her fingers and Tolen's attention returned to her. A short middle-aged man with long wispy gray hair rolled a barrel over next to her and stood it up. Tolen could hear sloshing from inside and his suspicions were confirmed when the man pried off a lid to show clear water inside before tapping the lid back on. Kyndras snapped again and another man, this one far younger, with piercing blue eyes and jet-black hair, stalked forward carrying a small wooden cage. Tolen couldn't see what was inside, but the growling and hissing coming from it didn't suggest a cuddly creature rested within. His sweating increased and his heart pumped louder.

*Just pretend you're alone…Just pretend…*He swallowed back his nervousness and tried to think of this as just another video game with Dane. He would learn the moves and win the game. That's all it was. Just a game. The creature hissed again and for a second his charade faltered. He stood on trembling legs and waited for it to begin.

Took'rah stepped forward—his long white hair tied back in a smooth ponytail, his black and yellow-gold robes hanging long and loose over his body—and put his hand on Tolen's forehead, his pale, hazel gaze mesmerizing. "The Animashta people are a quiet, gentle group." His voice was barely a whisper, thin and soft. Tolen noticed several of the crowd lean forward to hear.

"Our gift is not the ability to command the animals to do our bidding, but to share one another's burdens. To make light those trials that beset both our worlds. Together we are whole, apart we are as a bird with only one wing—flightless, powerless, unable to fill the measure of our creation. You will only succeed in tapping into your Animashta gift when you recognize the partnership, the purpose being to complete one another."

He tipped his head. "This is far more difficult than you can imagine. It is the natural tendency of man to believe they are above the animals, that they are the masters. This is not true. As you try to listen, you *will* try to force this creature to do your bidding." He waved his hand toward the cage. "This will not go well for you." His lips turned down as he surveyed Tolen through narrowed eyes.

Tolen wiped a trickle of sweat off his upper lip.

Took'rah opened the cage and whispered something Tolen couldn't hear. The tip of a tiny black nose appeared, followed slowly by sharp black eyes set in a black and white face, a thick furry body, carried by tiny feet ending in menacing claws. A badger.

Unfortunately, Tolen understood this animal well. It happened to be one of those seemingly cute creatures which were severely underestimated. Although they could be quite unassuming if they were cornered or felt threatened in any way, they fought ruthlessly. He'd heard the farmers talk about them often in Green River. He even remembered one story about a badger sow taking on a whole pack of coyotes that were trying to get to her cubs-and she won.

He seriously hoped Took'rah wasn't going to expect him to pick the thing up.

Took'rah whispered again and the badger turned and waddled back into the cage, but he left the door open. "Coax her out." He said to Tolen.

"What?"

"Come over here and coax her out."

Tolen took two steps forward and the badger made a strange sort of chirping growl. He paused and looked up at Took'rah.

"You need to sense her mind. What word should you say?"

"Ma'sha?" He asked it as a question, but as soon as the word left his mouth he could suddenly hear the chaotic, he wouldn't call them thoughts, but rather feelings of the badger. She was a young female. Nervous, and scared of the strange smells and sounds. She felt a kinship toward Took'rah, as if he were just another badger. She'd sensed Tolen's movement toward her and her instinctual need to defend her burrow, which was just a cage, had overtaken her fears. She was pushed back against the rear of the cage, waiting for him to come near enough to strike. Tolen stepped back.

"She's waiting for me so she can attack."

Took'rah nodded. "You need to send her your intent. Let her know you are not an enemy."

"Um, okay?" Tolen could feel the eyes on him like burning lasers. He knew he looked like an idiot. In his haste to prove himself he stepped forward again *before* trying to send his thoughts to the badger. A short leg with long claws shot out of the opening, ripped through his jeans, and grazed his ankle. He jumped back with a shocked gasp, and the badger advanced out the mouth of the cage, swatting and growling.

Pench Ni'yālo, he thought, but the badger kept coming, angrier than before. He shuffled backwards wracking his brain. He'd told her to be still, but she wasn't interested in heeding his command. He jumped onto the water-barrel to avoid another swipe of claws and heard several in the crowd snicker. Kyndras raised her hand and they cut off.

He could feel warmth filling his sock as he tried to think. How could he get this creature to know he had no intention of hurting it, or forcing it to do his will? He simply wanted to get it to stop trying to attack him. His eyes flicked to a woodpile off to his left and for a split second, he could have sworn he saw a flash of blonde hair. Macy?

His Radia shard warmed against his chest and a small tingle started in his hands. He looked at the badger swatting and growling at him and suddenly knew what he needed to do. They were equals. He was not greater than this tiny creature. He met the badger's fierce gaze for a brief moment and whispered quickly, focusing with all his might. *"Ma'sha. Y'na da'bay."* Hear me. I am friend.

As soon as he said the word *da'bay,* friend, the badger stopped growling and looked up at him, her head slightly tilted, listening. Tolen took it as a good sign and started to lower one foot. The badger growled in her throat and Tolen lifted his foot back up. *Okay…* He bit his lip. He'd told her he was a friend. He needed to prove it. But how? He looked around the arena, ignoring the watching crowd. His eyes passed over the woodpile again, but the vegetation growing around the edge of the field caught his attention. He noticed a small berry bush pushing its way through the cracks in one of the stone walls. *"Nit'ahai."* The bush shook, and the branches containing the few remaining berries left this late in the season, moved to the front.

Now what? He couldn't get off this barrel. *Think!* He tapped his fingers against the barrel in frustration. He could feel the cool water beneath the lid and a crazy thought popped into his head. He had no idea if he could even get it to work, but he knew the word, it came to him as easily as snapping his fingers. "*Win'tashta.*" He focused on what he wanted to take place then directed his energy at the water barrel beneath him. It took a few tries before anything happened. Sweat drenched his body and the effort to concentrate made his arms shake. Finally, a trickle of water lifted up in a thin stream from the edge of the lid of the barrel. Tolen focused, trying to hold it in a sphere, but it stayed in a stream, as if it wanted to go back into the barrel. He was fighting against gravity. He started panting.

"Connect with the water, Tolen," Kyndras encouraged softly, her eyes bright. "It is an element of this earth that is also a part of you. You cannot survive without it in more ways than just one. Give in to your need."

Lights popped in front of Tolen's eyes and he realized he'd been holding his breath in concentration. He let out his breath in a loud whoosh and the water splashed back into the barrel. He took a slow deep breath back in, "*Win'tashta. Ke'ay mea chan'ta?*" *Help me please?* He focused again on a mental picture of the water rising from the barrel and becoming a sphere. He had no idea how long it took for the mere cupful of water to rise out and form a dangling sphere, but the badger's growling had increased by the time the ball of water made it to the bush, and Tolen called it back, the berries floating inside. He lowered the sphere to the badger who looked up at Tolen, seemed to know it was a gift, placed her mouth to the water, and began to drink. As soon as the water was gone, the berries fell to the ground and she began to eat.

Mah' ne. Tolen heard the word in his mind, not as a voice speaking, but as—he didn't know how to describe it—a feeling? He looked up at Took'rah in confusion.

"She is telling you her name. She has…accepted you." He seemed almost shocked.

Tolen slowly lowered himself off the barrel, and sat beside the badger with his legs folded beneath him as she finished the berries. "Your name is Journey?"

She looked up from her meal, the fur around her lips tinged purple, and nuzzled her face against his leg. Tolen reached down with shaky fingers and scratched between her ears. "Well Journey, it's nice to meet you."

The crowd burst into applause and Journey scrambled into his lap, burrowing her head under his leg.

ooo

Macy pressed her forehead against the woodpile, her heart pounding as the applause faded. Those Dominants had set him up to fail. Took'rah had barely explained anything and Kyndras hadn't explained at all, and yet he'd succeeded. It was a small test for sure, but as she'd studied their faces she knew they were surprised at how well Tolen had done.

For the next four hours she watched entranced as Tolen was faced with more and more challenges, and every time, despite his obvious exhaustion, he didn't just succeed, he surpassed the expectations of the Dominants, the crowd, and—she grudgingly admitted—herself.

When they brought in a mountain lion, she had to hold onto the woodpile to keep from jumping in to protect him, a stupid inclination that made her angry. However, just minutes into the exercise, the mountain lion was following him around like an overgrown, friendly, house cat. It was freaky cool.

The longer she watched the more she believed the Chosen really *could* use someone with his skills—if he could stay focused and continue to learn how to use them right. He was great in a closed arena, with a Sphere protecting him and Dominants to correct him when he got it wrong, but what would he do when faced with a real-life situation? Would he be able to call on his gifts as he did now, or royally screw up like he did with the DéHool?

She wasn't sure she was ready to trust him like the rest of the crowd seemed to. They watched transfixed, their expressions hungry and full of hope.

She'd caught glimpses of Jonas a time or two, sitting beside Incrah and Evrah, heads bent together, deep in discussion. Twice he'd looked at her hiding place, and she was fairly certain he knew she was there. Both times had been right after Tolen had looked her way, and she'd pulled back from the peephole to see Jonas staring toward her woodpile.

The action came to a stop and more clapping ensued.

Tolen now had a whole zoo around him—the badger at his heels, the mountain lion brushing against his leg, a falcon perched on his shoulder, and a company of squirrels scampering around his feet, the badger nipping at them if they got too close to her.

Kyndras raised her hands again for silence. "Thank you for your attendance. We hope you all learned something today. It is time to adjourn. Tolen will return to the arena again tomorrow, at which time you are welcome to attend once again, if your studies allow." She waved her hands and the crowd slowly dispersed, all chatter and smiles.

Macy sat back against the wood, determined to wait for everyone to leave before sneaking out. She jumped nearly a mile high when a shadow appeared above her. She looked up to see Jonas standing above her with a smirk.

"Good morning McLacy. Would you care to join me? I have something I need to discuss with Tolen and it would be prudent for you to be present."

Feeling stupid and angry, Macy stood up and dusted off her jeans. She bit her lip and motioned for him to lead the way.

o o o

Tolen stood beside a water barrel, drinking cup after cup of water that sloshed in his empty stomach, watching Took'rah lead the animals away, all except for Journey who stayed by his side. He seemed to have made a new friend. Three times he'd noticed her try to come out and help him as he'd tamed the mountain lion, calmed the falcon, and befriended the squirrels, but Took'rah kept her back, explaining to her that it was important for Tolen to go through this. It had been strange, sensing her thoughts as he'd worked with the other animals. It was as if their minds were now connected, she shared everything with him. It was oddly comforting, and he actually found himself welcoming the companionship—even if it was with an animal.

Journey growled and Tolen turned to see Jonas, Incrah, and Macy walking toward him from the direction of the woodpile. So she *had* been watching him. He'd guessed as much, but had hoped to be wrong. Journey settled lower and growled louder. He sent his thoughts toward her, telling her the newcomers were friends, but Journey seemed to sense his animosity toward Macy and wouldn't allow her any closer.

Macy glared at Tolen, but stayed farther back than the others. Tolen held back a smirk.

"You did very well, Tolen." Jonas shook Tolen's arm. "We were all very impressed."

"Um, thanks." Tolen cleared his throat. "It was …," he couldn't think of the right word—*incredible* sounded cocky, and *confusing* made him sound stupid, "weird."

Jonas's mouth lifted in an understanding smile. "I can imagine." He glanced at Incrah who gave him a slow nod. "I came to tell you, your afternoon training will be slightly different than planned." His eyes flicked to Macy who still stood three feet back. "You will not train *with* the Radia Warriors. Incrah will direct the training, but it will be McLacy that you will spar with."

"What?" Macy blurted, stepping forward. Journey growled again and she stopped, fury flowing from her eyes.

Tolen's stomach dropped and he met the old man's eyes. Had Jonas noticed what Tolen had? Had he noticed each time Tolen looked to where he suspected Macy was hiding, his gifts had gotten stronger, that he suddenly knew what to do? Had he begun to suspect the same thing Tolen did? That as crazy impossible as it seemed, *Macy* might actually be his trigger?

Jonas watched the play of emotions cross Tolen's face with his eyes narrowed.

Yes, yes he did.

CHAPTER 6

TO FIGHT OR NOT TO FIGHT

MACY PACED THE LENGTH OF THE SMALL SPARRING ARENA, TAKING LONG deep breaths, searching for the calm she knew was never going to come. How could Jonas do this? The old guy was a Sphere, which meant he was super close to the Balance, he would know beyond any doubt the not-so-nice feelings she and Tolen had for each other. Why in the heck would he have them train together? How did he know she wouldn't run her sword through Tolen's big head?

She glanced up at the sound of approaching feet, but it was just a couple of wandering kids. She went back to pacing, staring at the dirt, and fuming. She should've just left. Packed up and went. Forgot all about what the old guy wanted. Let them worry about showing the Ninth how to fulfill his chosen destiny.

She kicked a rock with a little more force than necessary. It skipped across the ground and slammed into a nearby tent. The owner poked his head out and looked around. She ignored him and resumed carving a path into the dirt.

She'd gone straight to her tent after the session and avoided the mess tent at lunch, choosing rather to eat jerky in solitude. She'd tried to pack and leave, but her mind kept replaying the events of the morning. Tolen really was the Ninth Chosen and if he kept it up, he was going to be amazing. She'd picked up her pack twice only to drop it down again, empty. She couldn't forgive Tolen for his involvement in Bastian's death, but she couldn't deny the slice of guilt she felt when she thought of leaving, how it would break her promise to her Watcher, and how Jonas was counting on her now. She said she would protect Tolen. If she left now, without sharing her knowledge and experience of the Chosen with him, without figuring out why the Balance put them together, would it weaken his protection, slow his progress? Or worse, weaken their chances in the Final Battle?

These questions stayed her feet and solidified her resolve—or so she'd thought. She did not want to be here, but she wouldn't betray her Watcher's final plea. She'd stalked to the arena determined, only to start pacing five minutes after her arrival, plagued with the same doubts and frustration.

Movement from the corner of her eye had her turning toward the rows of wooden benches for spectators. Nova was situating herself on the front row. Macy's eyes narrowed and her feet pulled her toward the elf before she could think through what she was about to do. She vaulted the low pole fence surrounding the arena and landed in front of Nova. The elf slid back on the bench and looked up at Macy, her expression shifting from surprise to fear as she caught the look on Macy's face.

She could feel the tingle in her palms and with enormous effort held the heat in her chest, but her hand still shot forward, grabbing Nova's wrist. Hard.

Nova stared up at Macy, trying to wriggle out of her grasp, her eyes livid.

"You picked the wrong person to make an enemy of, Little Miss Elf," Macy growled, pulling Nova so close she was forced off the bench. "If you hurt him in any way, even if it's just sharing information that isn't yours to give, you will answer to me. Got it?"

"Macy!" Tolen's arms wrapped around her shoulders, pulling her back. She let go of Nova who dropped to her backside with a huff, a shiny red burn blossoming on her wrist. She cast Macy a murderous glare before scrambling up off the ground and racing off into the trees.

Macy wrenched out of Tolen's grasp, but before she could walk away, he grabbed her arm and forced her to face him.

"What the heck are you doing?" He shouted in her face.

"Nothing!" She pulled free and folded her arms across her chest, embarrassment flaming her anger.

"Bull crap!" His hands shook. "You just attacked her for no reason!"

"I had my reasons!"

His fingers curled into fists. "Not good ones! I heard your so-called reason! Just because she shared something *you* could have told me ages ago doesn't give you the right to hurt her. She hasn't done anything to you! You can't treat people like that."

Macy stood on her toes and met his glare, her heart thundering in her chest, the heat returning. "She's not a person. She's not like us. You have no idea what *her kind* have done. And her interference with your destiny just adds to the list! You barely even understand the Hidden world. Everything kept from you was to protect you. Bastian felt that knowing would be too much to take when you'd barely discovered your true race!"

"Fine! In the beginning I wasn't ready to know, I'll accept that. But I've come a long way since then! Why was it still kept from me? In the Binithan we—You could have told me!"

People were starting to gather and Macy fought to control her Kuna, afraid of embarrassing herself further. "I promised Bastian I wouldn't! And I know you're an idiot if you try to mess with the Balance. Bastian and Jonas both felt that there was a bigger reason why you didn't know that went beyond your mother's deception. They didn't know what that reason was, but in my experience, you don't argue with those who know a heck of a lot more than you do. Nova was told not to talk to you about legends and lore, that was to be left to Jonas, and she purposely ignored his instructions!"

"You had no right to hurt her."

Macy's temper flared and a tiny stream of smoke escaped her palm. "She had no right to do what she did!"

Tolen backed up and ran a hand over his face. He looked around at the gathering crowd and lowered his voice. "Did you agree with it? With not telling me?"

Macy's hands clenched into fists. The anguish behind his words zapped the anger right out of her heart.

"Well?" His voice rose to a rough whisper. "*Did* you agree that keeping the truth from me was a good idea, no matter what excuses they gave?"

Macy shook her head. "No. No I didn't. Okay?"

Tolen's eyes hardened. "I'm not sure if that deserves a thank you or not."

"It doesn't." She shook her head and rammed her hands in her back pockets. "But I had to trust in those smarter than me, even if I disagreed with it. Nova should have done the same." Her heart began a chaotic drumroll in her chest as she watched the fight leave Tolen's eyes. All her hatred toward him seemed to be seeping out of her body. Pity, remorse, fear, and confused longing fighting to take its place. She clenched her teeth, jumped back over the fence, and stalked toward Incrah who stood watching from the center of the arena. *Tolen's the reason Bastian is dead, remember that.*

Macy… Bastian's phantom reprimand cut into her conscience.

I told you to stop!

o o o

Tolen hopped the fence and followed Macy, wanting to be angry with her for her treatment of Nova, but failing. She'd been defending him. She hated him, yet she defended him. All through lunch he'd thought about the way his abilities reacted when he looked her direction while with the Dominants. Now being near her again, despite the anger between them, he couldn't deny the way his shard zinged with energy, or the surge of power he felt in his fingertips when he looked at her. How could she be his trigger? They could barely stand each other. A tiny voice in his mind argued this statement and brought back how it felt to touch her hand in the Binithan. He shook his head and noticed Jonas stood off to the side, his expression thoughtful. Jonas was likely wondering about Tolen's trigger too, hence this little experiment. Tolen hoped it didn't end up backfiring on them all.

Incrah started to speak and he tried to focus on what the warrior was saying. "This will be a Victory Match. Each round will be fifteen minutes long, with five-minute breaks to consult with your team. The match ends after the third round, the winner being the fighter with the most amount of points, or with the yield of an opponent."

Tolen heard Macy's low scoff. Apparently, she had no intention of surrendering. He squared his shoulders. Well, neither did he.

"You each have six teammates. You will have ten minutes to consult with your team before the match begins." He nodded toward Macy who stomped to the other side of the arena, where the warrior Kapha waited with two others Tolen had seen sparring, plus two females and one male Tolen didn't recognize.

Tolen followed Incrah to the fence, his nerves beginning to tingle in anticipation.

"Tolen, I will be your captain. Meet your teammates." He waved his hand. "Quasar and Bolide you've met." Tolen wondered if they knew about Macy's confrontation with Nova and the greeting he was about to offer stuck in his throat.

"The Lafar are brilliant strategists." A muscle in Incrah's jaw twitched. "They will be watching Macy's moves and coming up with strategy for you." His tone seemed to imply he wasn't exactly thrilled with them being here.

"My sister, Ingrid, will be your weapons specialist." Incrah pointed to the young woman on Tolen's right who looked to be around twenty years old, with soft brown hair tied back in a waist-length ponytail, large gentle brown eyes, and a warm smile. She reminded Tolen of one of the motherly clerks at Grange Grocery. But she shook his arm with roughness that didn't fit her gentle look, and her voice was a lot deeper than he expected when she spoke. "Good to meet you."

"Janu is a genius at grappling and sparring moves." Incrah pointed to the short, thickly muscled, stocky young man standing beside Ingrid. He reminded Tolen of the wrestlers at school. His thick black hair hung in loose dreadlocks down his back. When he smiled, it was clear he had lost more teeth than he had left. His eyes were bright and mischievous. He didn't speak, just nodded as he shook Tolen's arm.

"Bey, son of the warrior Beyn, is good at everything. He sees what no one else does." The last young man looked no older than eleven or twelve.

His round pink face, broad smile, freckles, and flaming red hair hinted at a merriment that his eyes contradicted. His eyes were like Evrah's. White. Sightless. Empty. Tolen looked up at Incrah in surprise. The others all chuckled.

The boy tapped Tolen's shoulder. "It doesn't necessarily take eyes to see."

Tolen could see his reflection in Bey's white eyes. It was a little creepy. He shook the kid's arm and stepped back to look at the arena, ignoring the wriggling in his stomach when his eyes passed over Macy's group, where they appeared to be helping her into her gear.

He looked back to see Quasar holding out what looked like a coat of sticks.

Tolen lifted it up to see at least a dozen leather straps.

"Here." Quasar took it back and helped him put it over his head. Bolide came over, and between the two of them, they had it tied around his chest in a matter of seconds.

Ingrid handed him a long, crude looking metal sword. Guess he'd made it past the wooden sticks.

Incrah laced a scabbard around Tolen's thigh and tapped the wood vest. "The breastplate is made of strips of blessed oak. It won't stop a real blade, but it will deflect these duller practice blades. Don't get overconfident; even a dull blade can cause significant damage. Remember to protect your vital areas, watch her moves so you can counter correctly, and be aware of your surroundings."

Bolide slid a knife into the scabbard and glanced at Macy's team. "The girl is too feisty. This will cause her to make rash moves the angrier she gets. Keep her busy and frustrated. It will work to your advantage."

Bey knelt and touched the ground, his eyebrows furrowed. "She's light, but I'll still be able to feel her moves. I'll let you know her weaknesses by first break." He stood up and Incrah motioned for Tolen to follow him.

"You have a good team, but so does Macy. Don't underestimate her."

Tolen shook his head. "I won't. I've seen her fight."

"Good." Incrah paused before they reached the middle of the arena. "This *is* a mock fight Tolen. It isn't real, but I urge you to stay focused. The best way to learn is to treat every training session as if your life depends on it. The reason we use methods such as Victory Matches is not for sport, it is to teach you how to react to an opponent."

Tolen swallowed.

"That being said, in the heat of the moment remember that your opponent in the arena is not your enemy, do not kill each other." There was no humor in his tone. Tolen met his eyes and his stomach tightened. "If there comes a moment when you feel your anger is getting out of control, and the methods you learned with the Doogar are not helping, signal me and I will step in and stop the match."

Tolen took a deep breath and nodded, grateful, but slightly ashamed that Incrah felt it was necessary to give the warning. He had felt in control of his anger fairly well lately. Having a goal helped, but sparring with Macy would likely bring up a lot of unresolved feelings. Losing control of his anger was a distinct possibility. He rolled his shoulders, adjusted the heavy breastplate, checked his knife, and gripped the sword more firmly in his right hand.

Incrah squeezed his shoulder. "Good luck." He turned and headed back to the team waiting just outside the fence. Bey sat on the ground again, legs folded beneath him, both palms in the dirt. The others stood back, arms folded across their chests, focused.

Tolen looked back to the center of the arena to see Macy walking toward him, wearing similar garb. While he was sure he looked awkward and clunky, Macy looked tough. He reminded himself to focus. He wouldn't give Incrah a reason to stop the match, and he wasn't about to give Macy the satisfaction of beating him.

Tolen raised his sword and waited for Macy to do the same. They touched the edges together and waited for Incrah to signal the beginning of the match.

Incrah's loud voice echoed across the arena. "This is a no gift match. Swords only. The use of gifts docks your points and counts as a penalty. Three penalties result in automatic forfeit. Penalties are also given for underhanded or dishonorable conduct. We do not fight like the Dark. We fight with honor." He whistled and Macy drew her sword back so fast

Tolen stumbled forward a step. Her snicker quickly turned into a scowl when he recovered quickly and moved in.

For the first few minutes, they only seemed to be testing each other's moves and abilities. Tolen tried not to feel smug when he was able to block and counter most of Macy's attacks. Five minutes before the round was to end, he noticed their scores were tied.

Sweat dripped off Macy's nose and Tolen's chin. The oak breastplate felt hot and heavy, but Tolen realized he was actually enjoying himself. Macy was good, really good, and as he countered her moves, he learned better how to strike.

Incrah whistled, signaling the end of the first round. Tolen gave Macy a mock bow, but she simply returned to her team. Tolen walked back to his side, gratefully taking the water jug Bolide held out, and after drinking his fill, poured the rest over his head.

"You're doing alright." Incrah stepped over and handed his sword to Ingrid who started cleaning the blade.

"Alright? We're tied in points." Tolen folded his arms across the breast-plate. "She's had years of practice, I've had weeks. She's frustrated that I'm keeping up. I'm learning her tactics. I think that's pretty good."

Janu snorted and Bey laughed.

"What?" Tolen pushed his wet hair off his face in irritation.

"You're *enjoying* the fight." Janu shook his head.

Bey laughed again. "This isn't a game. Until you feel like you want it to end so bad you are almost ready to surrender, it's not a real fight. It's child's play. You're not giving your all. If you were, you would have already won. You're holding back."

Tolen raised his hands. "Of course I am. Incrah told me not to kill her!"

Janu and Bey shook their heads.

Bolide walked over and handed Tolen a tiny piece of jerky. "For strength."

He'd ate his fill at lunch, but could feel his body weakening fast. Probably had something to do with missing two meals and not sleeping well. He gratefully popped the jerky in his mouth, relishing the instant surge of energy.

Bolide waited for him to swallow and handed him more water. "What they mean is you won't grow into a real warrior until you look at matches like this as you would a real fight. Macy is. She is fighting you with strategy. She's getting frustrated as you said, but you have not coaxed the most out of her yet. She still has greater skills to bring to this fight. You were not the only one learning in this round. She suspects you are weak on your left side. You leave it unprotected too often. Your jabs are too slow, leaving her room to counter easily."

Bey broke in. "She's swift on her feet. She gets in faster than you do, but this can be exploited to your advantage."

For the remaining three minutes of the break, Tolen made mental notes on the advice and tips of his team, realizing he had done exactly what Incrah told him not to. He'd become overconfident. The first had been a learning round. Yeah, he hadn't made it easy for Macy to beat him, instead he'd given her all the information she'd need to take him out in the next round. He shook out his arms, rolled his neck, and took several deep breaths before gripping his sword and walking back out into the arena.

The look on Macy's face as she marched back into the arena told Tolen his teammates were right. She was ready for the second round, armed with knowledge of Tolen's weaknesses, and prepared to defeat him. He thought of what Bey said about her speed and focused hard as she moved for the first strike at the whistle.

It came like a snake, so fast Tolen barely saw a flash of the blade. He countered quickly, stepping to the side so her strike would carry her too far into his circle, but she spun and pushed her body against his shoulder knocking him sideways. Warmth tingled down his arms into his fingers from the touch, and Tolen was reminded of the thrill of joy that passed through his body when he'd first held her hand in the Binithan. The urge he'd felt to run his fingers through her long hair to see how soft it was. The constant desire to make her laugh just so he could see the dimple beside her lips.

In his moment of distraction, Macy struck and Tolen barely parried in time so the blade just grazed his arm. The dull edge still managed to cut through the first layer of skin on his bicep. He stepped back, taking on a defensive stance, ready for her next move, but something had changed. The warmth that had surged into him from thinking of Macy in the Binithan hadn't left. In fact it seemed to be working its way through his whole body. The word *lon'adras* barely entered his mind before his arm started to heal. He heard Incrah's two trill whistle, and he realized he'd just been penalized for using a gift, but it had happened instinctively.

His Watcher's eye shifted and focused on Macy's face. There was no hint of a dimple showing, but the image Tolen saw as he watched her wasn't the angry face she wore now, it was her smiling and laughing with him as they'd talked in the Binithan, and the warmth in his body increased.

Macy jumped forward, but Tolen's eye was faster. He saw her moves before she made them, countered them almost before she started them.

Macy's my trigger. As soon as the thought completed, Tolen's heart felt like it would burst with heat. Before the idea had appalled him, now it intrigued him.

Why her? It makes no sense.

The ferocity in the fight increased, Macy's frustration caused her to make more and more mistakes. Anger creased her brow, and Tolen fought harder. *Why? What is it about you?* He thought as he struck, jabbed, parried, literally danced, around Macy. He knew he could end the fight. Win right now, but he was too entranced by the truth, too preoccupied by the feeling, to make the final move. *Why?*

Macy screamed and ran forward. "You killed him!" she brought her sword down.

Trance broken, Tolen dropped and rolled out of the way.

She rushed forward and he barely had time to jump to his feet. Incrah blew the whistle to end the round, but Macy kept coming. Tolen blocked her jabs over and over again, the anger rolling off her was tinged with despair, her eyes wild and filled with pain.

Bastian. She's talking about Bastian. Here he'd been focusing on himself, the connection to *his* life force, *his* destiny, *his* trigger, and she was in pain. He was such a hypocrite.

Tolen's heart sank to the bottom of his shoes. With painful clarity, as if he were once again sitting in the cave beside her, he saw the moment after he'd touched her hand in the Binithan. At that moment, he'd felt something shift powerfully in his feelings for her and he'd forgiven her for her coarse attitude, accepted that she had her own way of dealing with pain. Yet when Bastian was gone and she'd screamed at him, he'd thrown her pain back in her face. When in reality, he was more angry with the fact that there was truth to what she'd said—he *was* weak—than he was with her. Yes, her way of dealing with grief was terrible, but was he any better? Look at the way he'd treated Bastian and Macy as he'd grieved for his mother and best friend. Look at the way he dealt with everything. Anger, always anger.

Suddenly every angry, hateful feeling he had toward her dissolved to dust. Despite all she'd said and done to him, he realized with a pain so severe it took his breath, that he had never actually hated her. Whether the realization that she was his trigger had brought this on or not didn't matter. He'd been selfish and he regretted it.

Macy moved in for another strike. Tolen dropped to his knees and laid back. Macy's blade skimmed the top of his head. He reached out as she passed and knocked her legs out from under her. She landed on her back with a huff. Tolen dove onto her legs and held her arms by her sides, squeezing her wrist until she dropped her sword. He could smell the light floral and mint scent she gave off when she was about to release her gift.

The fear and resentment in her eyes nearly did him in, and he almost didn't say what he knew he had to say.

"I'm sorry, Macy. I'm so sorry," he breathed, his heart pounding, and eyes stinging from her pain. "It *is* my fault Bastian died and Dane died, and my mom is missing. I will carry the burden of that truth for the rest of my life. I can't fix the past." The words burned in his throat. "But I promise, I *am* going to do all I can to be stronger for the future."

A mix of emotions played across her face. Anger, embarrassment, grief. She opened her mouth, but Incrah whistled again and this time the teams rushed the arena. For the first instant since entering the fight, Tolen felt angry. Not anger he could not control—disappointed anger that their moment had been interrupted. Macy wriggled beneath him, and he rolled off her legs to allow one of her teammates to help her up. She met his eyes once before turning to her team, but the look was so fleeting that Tolen couldn't guess what she might be thinking.

Incrah pulled him to his feet and raised his arm in the air. "Winner!"

Tolen pulled his arm away, tugged off his breastplate as he walked, leaving it and his weapons at the gate. He turned toward the forest, wanting more than anything just to be alone.

CHAPTER 7

MOVING FORWARD

MACY WATCHED TOLEN LEAVE AS HER TEAMMATES HELPED HER REMOVE the gear. She hadn't meant to shout at him. It just came out. Her Kuna had rushed to her palms and as she fought against it, trying to hold it in, the real source of her anger flew from her lips. She'd rushed forward wanting to hurt him, wanting him to feel her pain, wanting him to *pay*. In that moment, the Dark desire for revenge filled her heart.

Looking back, she was incredibly grateful he'd knocked her down and forced the sword from her hand, grateful that the anguish in his expression as he apologized shoved the darkness out of her heart. She'd never been so filled with hate and bloodlust, not once in the last ten years of destroying Dark creatures had she ever wanted to inflict a painful death on another Being. Quick and merciful was the Light's way. It horrified her that she had fed the darkness inside her and let it have its moment. She shuddered to think what could have happened if Tolen hadn't realized his trigger and read her moves the way he had.

She could sense the moment his connection with his life force solidified. His moves went from clunky and rehearsed to graceful, lithe, and perfectly maneuvered. Which could only have come about if Tolen had discovered his trigger and connected to his life force on a conscious level. Part of her wondered what his trigger was, but the bigger part felt mortified. Tolen had apologized and every cell in her body recognized the truth and depth to his apology. As she witnessed *his* pain for pain he'd inadvertently caused her, she felt humbled to her core. The battle inside she'd been fighting to keep hold of her anger ended as if a white flag had been waved and both sides had given up. She couldn't even try to bring the hate back. What happened to Bastian was tragic and unfair, but laying blame, feeding hurt and anger, would not bring him back. Instead, it fed the darkness within her until she'd tarnished Bastian's memory by taking it out on the one person he'd begged her to protect.

Even as the guilt threatened to consume her, in a corner of her mind, she pictured Bastian with a satisfied smile on his face.

This doesn't mean I like him. She shook out of the armor and handed it back to Kapha with a nod of gratitude. *I just don't hate him anymore… Ugh, I can't hate him.* She thought with a frustrated sigh.

"You fought well McLacy," Kapha said while her other teammates nodded. She shook all their arms and thanked them each in turn for their advice. They really were good trainers, but she was preoccupied, and right now, all she wanted to do was escape the arena and be alone with her thoughts.

She'd hardly taken two steps out of the arena however, when Jonas seemed to materialize out of nowhere by her side. Incrah and the rest of Tolen's team were farther up ahead, but Tolen wasn't with them.

"That was an interesting match."

Macy slowed her steps to the old guy's pace. "I guess you could say that."

Jonas nodded. "It would seem Tolen has discovered his trigger."

Macy blew a hair out of her face. "It would seem."

"It would seem you discovered something out there as well."

Macy felt Jonas's eyes on her, but she kept her own on the path and didn't answer.

"If I might leave you with one piece of advice, McLacy," he paused and she glanced up. "Don't fight what you know you must do. You need to make things right with Tolen. He is not responsible for Bastian's death. Remember what I said before. The Balance brought the two of you together for a reason. This is bigger than any of us can possibly understand or explain. Do not resist the desires of the Light. There is purpose in everything."

Macy swallowed and paused to look out toward the forest where more than just her shard was tugging her to go.

"He is alone. So very alone. You can heal much of his pain, McLacy." He patted her hand and continued down the path back to the heart of camp. He did not look back. He was leaving it up to her. She could follow him, or she could follow her heart.

What about my pain? She shook her head at the thought. Her pain was different, a grief that would heal in time—this she knew from experience. Bastian was in a good place, she understood this, and although the ache for him would never truly leave, she knew one day she would survive despite it, just as she'd learned to live without her parents after they were killed by the Shadow Wraiths. She would take all she had gained from her Watcher and be stronger because of him. She sighed, she could no longer argue that Bastian's death was all Tolen's fault either. Maybe a little, but not all.

Yes, her pain would fade, but Tolen's? Tolen was facing a future more terrifying and overwhelming than any one person should have to face. Especially alone. She sighed again and stared into the trees. Why was it so hard to do the right thing?

Because humility requires opening our hearts, LaUnahi. You have guarded yours for a long time.

Macy gritted her teeth.

Do not be angry my little bird. I am not chastising you. You have had good reason to protect yourself, but I think it is time you start to let others in again. Jonas is right. You are needed so very much. You can heal not just Tolen, but so many others with your beauty.

Beauty? Macy snorted and glanced around, hoping no one had noticed her standing here having internal conversations with a dead guy.

Beauty is more than skin deep, LaUnahi. Surely I have taught you that much.

Macy sighed. "Why me, Bastian?"

Only you can answer that little bird. Only you… His voice faded out and she knew her delusion was leaving her alone to decide, just as Jonas had.

Finding Tolen and talking to him would require her to apologize and admit she was wrong in her behavior toward him. It would also mean committing herself to spend more time helping him. Despite what her delusional Bastian tried to imply, admitting her mistakes was about as fun to her as eating dirt. And a tiny part of her she fought hard to silence, feared what would happen if she let them be friends. She didn't know *how* to be a friend. She didn't know how to let people in.

○ ○ ○

Tolen felt her coming before he heard her.

He leaned back into the tree he sat behind and dropped his head against the bark.

Macy was the last person he'd expected to come looking for him. He wasn't sure if he was glad it was her or not. He was both embarrassed and afraid of what he'd felt as he'd sat above her and apologized.

What was it about her that did such strange things to him? He had left the arena with a vow to work harder than ever to be worthy of this great destiny, to be a strength to the Hidden world, not a liability. What was it about her that made *her* of all things, his trigger, the glue that connected him to his life force, his abil—his…his gifts?

They *were* gifts. He could see that now.

The moment he connected to them, he could no longer see them as a curse. They were as much a part of him as his arms and legs. With them, he could *become*…Without them, he would never be enough; he was broken, incomplete. So if Macy was the trigger to his gifts…He stopped that thought in its tracks.

Macy paused on the other side of the tree. He closed his eyes and took a deep breath.

"Hi," she whispered. "Can I…can I join you?"

Tolen was reminded of all the times he'd asked her the same question. He let the breath out slowly and opened his eyes. "Sure."

She moved in front of him, sat down against a tree about three feet away, pulled her knees to her chest, and stared over her shoulder into the trees.

Tolen felt a strange burning sensation on his right ankle. He tugged his sock down, but saw nothing. He tilted his head and looked at Macy's ankle. "Did I hurt you?"

Macy followed his gaze and lifted up her pant leg to reveal a long bloody scratch. "Hmm. Weird. I don't remember that happening."

Tolen swallowed, leaned forward, and paused only briefly before putting his hand gently above the cut. "*Lon'adras,*" he whispered. The warmth surged from his fingers so fast Macy jumped. "Sorry."

She tugged her leg back to look at the perfectly healed skin. "No. It's fine. It sort of tickled." She looked back up and he could see chagrin in her eyes. "Tolen, I—"

He held up his hand. "Don't, Macy. Please. You have nothing to apologize for."

She was shaking her head before he'd finished. "Yes I do. I *need* to or it's going to eat me alive."

He watched her with his heart pounding in his chest as she struggled for words, her dimple barely visible as she bit her lip in concentration.

One day you will see the whole Macy and it will change your life. Tolen suddenly remembered Bastian's words in the Binithan. Had the Watcher suspected then that his wards were connected in a bigger way than just Chosen? That Macy was his trigger? As he watched her try to form an apology, he saw a side Bastian had tried to explain.

She was a far, far better person than he'd given her credit for. She'd been raised outside the human life she'd been born into. She never went to school dances, out on dates, or had girlfriends to hang out with. Instead she sacrificed every day of her life to protect the race she belonged to—but never actually got to be a part of—never expecting reward for her sacrifice. She did it because it was the right thing to do. But she did do a *really* good job of convincing everyone around her that she was selfish and out of control. Bastian knew the real Macy and he wanted Tolen to as well. Right now, he wanted to, he really, really wanted to, but he was terrified of the damage he'd already done. How could she ever let him in when he'd been the cause of so much pain?

Trust you thoughtful heart. Chills ran down Tolen's arms. This wasn't Bastian's remembered voice from the moment before he died. This was *his* voice, repeating in Tolen's mind what he'd begged for as he'd left this life. Tolen hadn't thought about it since. So much had happened. She finally started to speak and a tingle ran across Tolen's shoulders as if confirming the thought.

"First of all I guess I—I mean I know, I shouldn't have punched you after Bastian's farewell. I was—"

"You're forgiven. I was being a jerk with wounded pride."

Macy shrugged, allowing that. "I guess. But you were right at least about one thing. Bastian wouldn't want me to live a life of anger and pain. That's not the Light's way. I guess I didn't realize it until we were fighting and I let the dark feelings take me. I—I wanted to k-kill you."

Tolen swallowed. "I'm sorry I caused you enough pain that it drove you to feel like that."

"Stop apologizing." Her eyes flashed and he had to bite back a grin.

"Sorry." He ducked as she tossed a stick at his head.

"Jerk." She didn't smile, but the dimple became more pronounced.

A chuckle escaped Tolen's lips. "Sorry."

Macy picked up a handful of leaves and tossed them his way, but he directed his thoughts to the wind and blew them back in her face. She stood up sputtering, and war ensued. She threw leaves, sticks, and anything else she could grab, while he blew them back at her.

Macy dodged behind a tree and Tolen followed, grabbing her around the waist. They fell laughing to the ground. Tolen rolled up on his side and propped himself up on one arm, his side aching from laughing so hard.

Macy lay back chuckling—hair spread out around her head and full of leaves, dirt smudged on her face and arms—never looking more beautiful. Her eyes literally sparkled, and her full smile was irresistible. His hand was touching her cheek before he could think to pull it back. His fingers burned with pleasurable warmth where they brushed her skin. He moved a strand of hair off her forehead, and found himself leaning toward her. Their eyes met and for a single second he thought he saw mirrored there the same longing he felt growing within himself, but she cleared her throat and rolled away with another chuckle.

"You're a cheater." She jumped up and dusted herself off, keeping her eyes on the ground.

Tolen tried to slow his pounding heart and hide his embarrassment as he stood up to remove the forest floor from his jeans. Had he actually thought of kissing her? He wasn't sure if he'd actually thought of anything. Felt joyfully compelled, was more like it. As in the Binithan when he couldn't *not* touch her, this time he wanted so much to kiss her.

Put on the breaks dufus, he chastised himself. They had barely made up and started to mend their precarious friendship. He'd scared her off in the Binithan just by trying to hold her hand. He needed to be careful. Her heart was a precious thing. He couldn't *break* down the walls or climb them like some burglar. He needed to find the key.

"We'd better get back or we won't be getting any dinner." Tolen pushed his hands in his back pockets.

Macy looked relieved as she met his eyes. "Sounds good." Her cheek lifted in a mischievous half smile. "Rematch later? No gifts this time."

Tolen grinned. "You're on."

ooo

"So, do you miss it?" Macy asked between bites of mashed potato. She sat so close to Tolen she could swear she could feel his body heat. She resisted the urge to close the tiny gap between them and push her leg against his.

Tolen looked at her quizzically and she clarified. "The human world? Being oblivious?"

He met her eyes, and for a quick second she saw the same fire burning in them she'd noticed when he'd almost kissed her back in the woods. Well, at least that's what it seemed like he was thinking of doing. She really couldn't be sure, since no one had ever tried to kiss her before. It was more of a guess. She shook off the thought and took another bite of potato, fighting to act and feel normal, while she waited for him to answer.

He shrugged, but waited for a group of children to walk past their table before he answered. "I miss a few things." He sniffed his arm. "Real showers for one thing, root beer floats, stuff like that."

Macy nodded. "I had one of those once. It was great."

"What? A shower?"

Macy pushed his shoulder and a tiny thrill ran through her body, kinda like when she blasted a dark creature, but better. "No. A root beer float."

"Oh, so you've never had a shower before?"

She slugged his arm.

He grinned. Crap, he was cute when he goofed off.

His eyebrows raised and her cheeks warmed. She really hoped he hadn't sensed that thought. She turned back to her food and thankfully he followed. She looked around to avoid his eyes. It felt so freeing, yet slightly confusing, not to be angry with him anymore. She still missed Bastian desperately, but somehow, incredibly enough, Tolen—the last person she would have expected—seemed to be finding his way into the empty space Bastian left behind.

The mess tent had been overflowing when they'd arrived and got in line. Now there were only a few people left. Jonas had given her a knowing smile when they'd walked in, and a few people had come to congratulate them on their match. Macy had teased that Tolen had only won because he'd used his Watcher ability, but no one agreed.

Macy could tell by their faces that he'd gained more than a few fans in the last couple of days. He hardly seemed to notice the attention. Even when the gorgeous, annoying, Nova, came to fawn all over him while throwing harsh looks at Macy, he hardly said two words to her. Macy knew it was wrong, but a tiny part of her liked seeing the red burn just visible on Nova's wrist as she'd stalked off.

It wasn't like she was trying to stake a claim or anything. Tolen was free to like and spend time with whomever he wanted, but Nova was dangerous and untrustworthy. As were most Lafar. She'd heard the legends. She didn't care if Jonas trusted this little band. She didn't, and she needed to make Tolen see that too.

Tolen wiped his hands on a napkin. "Well, it looks like they're getting ready to close up. Are you finished?"

Macy nodded. "Yep."

"Here, let me take that." Tolen balanced her tray on top of his own and piled their cotton napkins on top.

She followed him to the counter where they washed their own dishes. Tolen held his hand out to stop her from washing hers. "I'll do it. Why don't you take the napkins to the wash basket?"

Macy took the thin cotton napkins and walked away chewing on her lip. He was acting the gentleman, doing what Bastian used to do when she was a little girl. She hadn't let anyone do anything for her in a long time. Bastian had always demanded she let him treat her like a lady, let her in the door first, open car doors—if they weren't running for their lives—so that she would always know what it meant to be in the presence of a real gentleman. He always said that just because she was probably tougher than most guys out there, it didn't mean she wasn't still a lady, and deserved to be treated as such. But as she'd gotten older and he'd gotten weaker, she'd made sure to do everything before he could try.

She wasn't sure what to make of Tolen's behavior, or if she should encourage it. She didn't want to give him the wrong idea. Yes, she was finding forgiveness—for the most part. Yes, she would try to fulfill her promise to Bastian, and yes, she wanted to see Tolen become who he was meant to become, for the good of the whole world. But that was all. They could be friends, nothing more.

She dropped the napkins in the basket, and turned to walk slowly toward where Tolen stood with his back to her, scrubbing dishes. His light green shirt could use a good washing—or a trip to the garbage. Several holes were starting to appear around the seams, and the worn-thin fabric clung to his broad shoulders, showing just how much muscle he'd gained over the last month. His lean arms were becoming more defined, the veins starting to stand out. When they'd first met he'd walked sort of hunched, trying to be invisible. Now he stood taller, not necessarily more confident, but with purpose. He really was trying hard to live up to what was expected of him.

You can help…Jonas and Bastian had both said, but this life was too complicated and crazy for stupid teenage drama. She bit the side of her lip. He was the Ninth *and* he was Hidden-kind. Once he realized this, he would know they could never be anything more than Chosen acquaintances, so encouraging his over-friendliness would just come back to hurt them both later.

She paused behind him, suddenly very, very tired. He turned back to look at her and she forced a smile. He smiled back, but it seemed strained, as if he'd heard everything she'd just been thinking. It bothered her a little, especially if he'd heard her thoughts on his looks, but maybe it was for the best that he know it would never work between them.

"Thanks for washing my dishes." She tried to sound casual, but she knew he could hear the hint of gloom in her tone.

He dried his hands on a towel and led the way out of the mess tent. "I did the dishes a lot growing up. I don't mind it."

"You like doing dishes?" Macy paused just outside the door.

"I said I don't mind it. I don't necessarily *like* it." He grinned as she fell back into step beside him. "I have a hard time imagining anyone likes to do dishes, but it's just one of those things that has to be done, right? So you can either do it and not whine about it, or think about how bad you hate it the whole time and make it a lot worse."

Macy glanced at him out the corner of her eye. "That seems to be your philosophy with life too."

He slowed his steps and tugged a hand through his hair. "I *try* to think that way. I still whine more than I should."

"I'm sorry, Tolen."

"Like you said, life isn't fair, right?"

"Right."

He took a deep breath and looked up at the sky. "It's a beautiful night. Wanna take a walk before lights out?"

She bit her lip, unsure.

"Just as friends?" He met her eyes and she knew. He *had* heard her thoughts, and for the first time he was aware of it. He was trying to let her know he would go forward on her terms. Friends only. She didn't think this thought should be making her as sad as it did.

She grinned. "If you can beat me to that tree." She pointed to a large pine about a hundred yards away.

"No gifts?" He smiled and held out his hand.

She shook it once, ignoring the tingle in her fingers, and pushed off, not sure if she was really racing or running from the boy beside her.

Chapter 8

Balanced Truth and Lies

Macy took a mock bow. "I win."

"We tied!"

"Whatever, my finger brushed the bark first."

"Only because you knocked my hand out of the way." Tolen's eyes danced, revealing the smile he was trying to hide.

"You only said no gifts," Macy shrugged.

"I assumed 'no cheating' was implied."

"You implied wrong, but I'll still go for a walk with you."

"Hmm, sounds like you feel guilty for cheating."

She shrugged again. Really, she should be heading straight for her tent, not giving Tolen any ideas, but she couldn't fight the desire to be with him just a little longer. As friends. She led the way along the less traveled side path through the trees toward the river. The path was narrow enough that occasionally their fingers brushed against each other. Every time it happened a funny zing shot up her arm, and she found herself repeating the word *friends* over and over in her mind. Both hoping that he could sense her desire that they stay just friends, and worrying that he could also sense the strange rush of feelings when they touched. It didn't matter what she felt, what mattered was what was true.

They walked in silence until they reached the bank of the river. Macy sat down on a large boulder at the water's edge, kicked off her boots, tucked her socks inside, and dangled her toes in the cool swirling current.

"I take it you've been here before?" Tolen paused beside the rock and looked over his shoulder at her.

She nodded. "It's a quiet spot." *I should invite him to sit down.*

"You don't have to." Tolen cast her a quick glance then turned his attention to the river.

Macy swallowed. "You heard me?"

He bit his lip and looked away. "I hear a lot of things now, but…" he knelt down and dipped his fingers in the river.

"But?" Her heart started to pound, she wasn't sure if she really wanted him to answer.

He stood back up and turned to look her in the eye. "But, your voice is the clearest. Louder than any other voice, clearer than any other thought I sense."

She couldn't look away from his gaze. It felt as if her face was locked in an iron vise, forcing her to stay focused. A quiet thought, getting louder each second, whispered she really didn't want to look away, nothing was forcing her, except confusing need. Without realizing what she was doing, she slid over and patted the rock beside her.

Tolen looked hesitant for half a second before joining her, their legs brushing against each other. He reached over and grabbed her hand, but this time the Kuna didn't rush to her palms to burn him, it stayed in her heart, warming, consuming, distracting. He traced his thumb back and forth over her knuckle, his fingers trembling.

Friends, friends, friends… she chanted, but he continued to hold her hand. She kept her eyes on the ground, fighting the need. *It can't work!*

Tolen squeezed her hand. "Why?" When she didn't respond he used his other hand to touch her chin and gently tugged until she looked up at him. "I'm not trying to push you into anything Macy, but I can feel what you're feeling. I feel it too. This—this pull, this need to be near you, I can't help but think it's more than just that we're supposed to fight together. It feels…I don't know, different, apart."

Macy shook her head. "You don't understand how the Balance works Tolen. You don't understand enough about the Hidden world to really know what you're thinking." His face fell and she rushed to explain, not wanting to hurt him, but he had to understand. "The way I went from hating you to wanting to…to be near you," she felt her face redden and looked out into the forest. "It's not normal. Jonas believes the Balance put us together for a reason. It makes sense that once the irrational hatred, the dark feelings I had toward you, were removed, the stronger ones relating to the will of the Balance—that we be a team—would take over. Drawing us together, to be a *team*, nothing…nothing more." She looked down at their entwined fingers. "This…this is nothing but adolescent hormones running crazy, confusing duty with attraction." Even as she said it, she didn't want him to let go. Messed up feelings or not, it *felt* nice. But feelings were deceptive.

He didn't let go, he held tighter. "But, it's so *strong*. Macy I *want* to be with you." The sincerity of his words felt like a serrated knife twisting in her heart. Coming here had been a mistake.

"That's how the Balance works, Tolen. It's not what you think." She pulled her hand free, leaned over to pick up her boots, and walked away without looking back.

○○○

A full moon lit the concealed pathway as the cloaked figure crept through the deserted forest. The only sound was the slight whisper of wind through the trees.

An owl hooted in the distance, the figure pressed against a tree and waited. On one side of the shrouded face, a trickle of sweat mirrored the moonlight.

Silence.

The figure quickened its pace.

Twenty feet, ten feet, and finally the cave came into view. The false face that hid it glowed blue at the touch of one hand. With a glance behind, the figure stepped inside the cold darkness and shivered.

"You're late." A voice reverberated through the small space and the cloaked figure fell to its knees.

"I am sorry, Master Daemon. The Old One has been suspicious. It is getting more difficult to avoid the guards."

Daemon growled. "You need to be more careful. There should be no reason for suspicion."

"Yes, Master. I am sorry. I will try harder."

"What news do you bring me? Will we be able to continue?"

"Yes, Master, but there is a slight complication. The—the Dominants are here. They are training him." The figure flinched as the sound of grating metal keened throughout the cave.

"Curse them! The more the boy learns the more difficult it will be to break him. You must follow through sooner than planned." His anger left no room for argument.

The figure swallowed and shivered again. "Yes, Master."

"Good."

The figure pulled the cloak tighter and waited.

"I will give you two days. They will be ready by then. Go now. Do what I ask, and all shall be forgiven."

"Yes, Master."

The cloaked figure hurried from the cave, touched the false door, and watched the opening disappear before hurrying silently along the hidden path to the protection of the Old One.

CHAPTER 9

LEGEND AND DESTINY

MACY SAT UP AND THREW HER LEGS OVER THE EDGE OF THE COT. SHE fought all night against the noisy, gnawing guilt so she could sleep—but it ended up a battle sorely lost. The sun had not quite risen, the air still felt chilly and damp. It had started raining around 3 AM. The incessant pounding against the tent roof hadn't helped her insomnia. It seemed to be twisting and repeating her mantra, but instead of saying *friends*, it shouted *liar, liar, liar…*

She tugged her fingers through her tangled hair. She hadn't lied to Tolen *exactly*. More like bent the truth so he could get rid of his ridiculous ideas and get his head in the game. So much was at stake. No, the Balance wouldn't ever take away your freedom to choose, nor did it send false romantic ideas into a person's head, but it did draw people together if their fates were entwined somehow. Like Watchers and their wards. And Tolen was a Watcher over everyone. Whether Tolen's *romantic* feelings really were legitimate—a thought that sent the guilt wriggling through her stomach again—was not the point. A relationship like that between them couldn't happen. They were too different. Their responsibility too important for the distraction it would become. Why couldn't he just see that? Why did she have to keep pointing it out?

She'd done the only thing she could; used his lack of knowledge of the Hidden world against him. And she felt terrible for it. She rubbed her fists against her eyes and laid back down, trying to ignore the gentle tapping of the rain—now barely a drizzle—that seemed to be whispering *liar, liar, liar.*

But the most troubling question plagued her: who was she lying to? Tolen, or herself?

○○○

Tolen opened the flap of his tent and took a deep breath. Wisps of cloud slashed across a purple sky quickly turning to vivid blue as the sun crept higher. The rain last night had cleaned the air, leaving behind the invigorating scent of pine resin, damp leaves, and wildflowers. He hoped it could help clear his head. He'd slept terribly. His dreams had been random and strange, jumping from vivid pictures of walking with Macy through the lush green forest, to awful nightmares about a demon with yellow eyes, blood-red skin, and black pointed teeth, directing an army of the foulest creatures imaginable. The dreams had but one thing in common; at the end of each, Incrah stood above Tolen with a spear in his hand, a look of pure loathing on his face.

He shivered at the memory. The image did not fit his feelings about Incrah at all, but he couldn't shake the thought that they were more than just dreams. For one thing, he would swear he'd seen the demon creature before, even though he knew it couldn't be true. Yet he'd not only looked, but *felt* familiar too.

He wished he could have continued the dreams with Macy in them—at least in his dreams she wasn't trying to convince him he was imagining his feelings for her. When he'd first heard her thoughts while washing their dishes he'd almost turned around, certain she'd spoken, but he'd known she was across the room. It started out disjointed, but once he'd focused they became really clear, without even having to use the hidden word. The fact that she found him attractive made his hands shake so much he'd dropped the fork he'd been washing twice. But as they'd talked by the river she'd completely disregarded any chance of them ever being more than friends. The bitter disappointment felt like a sword running through his gut.

The things she'd said about the Balance lurked in his mind like a dirty sock left out in the sun. You didn't want to touch it, but the smell kept bringing it to your attention. Yes, the Balance wanted them together for a reason. Yes, she was human and he was Hidden-kind. Yes, she was his trigger—something she didn't even know about—and that could be one more thing drawing him to her. But there *had* to be another reason he felt this way. Something that was more than the Balance wanting them to be a team.

But what could he do about it now? She firmly believed a relationship was out of the question and he had to admit, she was right about one thing for sure, he *didn't* understand the Balance or the Hidden world well enough to be one hundred percent sure he was feeling what he thought he was feeling.

He pushed his hands in his pockets, walked slowly past the six small canvas tents that separated his and Macy's tents, and resolved he would just be her friend—at least for now. They would work together as a Chosen team. But he wouldn't entirely give up. There was more to their relationship, and he was going to figure it out.

His shard gave a familiar tug and he looked up to see Macy standing in the door of her tent. She was looking down at her feet, but Tolen knew she could feel him walking toward her, just as sure as he could feel her. He couldn't have held back the smile that pulled at his lips if he'd wanted to. He bridged the gap between them in four long strides. It took more effort than he thought it should not to pull her in for a bear hug. Could this really just be because she was his trigger, because of the Balance? It felt like so much more. As he'd said to her last night…other. Apart. He couldn't describe it. He wished he had the time to think about it, but the first words out of Macy's mouth reminded him of a bigger worry.

"Jonas stopped by to tell me to make sure you eat breakfast before you train with the Dominants this time." She looked tired.

He tried to sense her thoughts then felt guilty for searching without her permission and asked instead. "So you're going to babysit me?"

She finally looked at him and a hint of a smile touched her lips. "I doubt you can afford my fee."

"Well, I'm dirt poor so I guess I'll have to find another form of payment." He whispered a Hidden phrase through his teeth and turned to gather a bouquet of the wildflowers that he'd just caused to grow outside her tent.

Her mouth turned down and she tilted her head.

Tolen's hands started to sweat. "Too tacky?"

She chuckled. "No. Um, thanks?" She took the flowers and glanced around. "Let me just stick these in my tent and then we'll get you to breakfast."

Tolen stood outside her tent, feeling stupid. Why was he even thinking of a relationship when he was supposed to be trying to save his parents, and oh yeah, the whole *freaking* world?

He watched her arrange the flowers in a water jug beside her bed, with a strange look on her face. When she came back to join him on the path, her expression was blank.

"Will you be watching this morning again?" He wasn't sure if he wanted her there or not. He needed to focus on the real issues and her presence muddled his thoughts.

"Yes."

His stomach lurched and he tugged on a strand of her hair. "From behind a wood pile, or from a seat this time?"

She slugged his shoulder and warmth shot down his arm. She took a breath as if she were about to say something, shook her head, and led the way to the mess tent.

They walked silently while Macy chewed on her lip and Tolen fidgeted with his shard, his mind going a million miles an hour.

ooo

Macy tried and failed to get Tolen out of her head. Why did he have to give her stupid flowers! Ugh! She thought she'd made it perfectly clear where they stood.

She tried to think of something to say as they loaded their trays, but couldn't come up with anything. She should have felt relieved when Incrah and the other Radia captains invited them to join their table. She should have been glad that they demanded Tolen's attention so she wouldn't have to explain to him, again, that he wasn't feeling what he thought he was. But as Tolen talked and laughed with the others she felt only loneliness.

"You okay?" Tolen asked as they left the tent half an hour later. He nudged her arm and goosebumps rose on her skin. She stepped a little farther from him. He noticed and his eyebrows scrunched together.

She cleared her throat. "Yeah, just thinking. Jonas wanted me to tell you a little about the Kunamin gifts before you train with Jun'tar. Sort of a heads-up."

"Okay." He took a deep breath. She'd hurt his feelings. It was only going to get worse.

She paused just outside the arena and met his eyes. He had to understand. This couldn't continue. "Tolen, you've got to get your head in the game. You've got to focus on what really matters. Whatever you think is going on between us, stop thinking it. The Balance put us together—"

He put his hand gently over her mouth. "Don't Macy. You don't have to say it again." His eyes were so sad it made her stomach hurt. "I know what you think. How you feel. And I understand. You're right I need to stay focused and…" He paused and continued in a lowered voice his eyes barely meeting hers. "The flowers were supposed to be a truce, *friend* flowers, not make you uncomfortable."

Macy's skin heated where his fingers brushed her cheeks. She stepped back and he dropped his hand. She could see he was telling the truth, and it hurt like heck. "Okay…" She pushed back the ache and tried to focus on turning the conversation. "So Kuna is one of the most difficult gifts to control." She picked at a vine dangling on the side of the arena, unable to meet his eyes. "Bastian was constantly beating that into my head. All your gifts are emotionally driven as you've learned, but Kuna is a constant fire burning in your chest. Whenever your emotions are heightened, it's like throwing gasoline on the fire. It's going to be ten times harder for you to control your Kuna if you don't keep your head straight."

Tolen watched the crowd spilling into the arena. At all those people who knew, or suspected, that he was a child of prophecy meant to be their hero, waiting for him to come in and give them hope. Macy worried when his shoulders seemed to droop.

He looked back, their eyes met briefly and he tried for a smile. "I'm fine. You're right. Head in the game."

She tried to think of something, anything to offer him comfort, but he spoke first.

"So, being Kunamin, do you feel that burn in your chest all the time?"

She nodded, mimicked his change in tone, going along with the switch in subject, hoping it was what he really needed, and placed a hand over her heart. "Yep. Gives new meaning to the term heartburn." She forced a grin.

He smiled back, but it didn't quite touch his eyes, and shoved his hands into his pockets. "That's why when you get upset your palms start to smoke."

"Yep."

"Is there a reason it smells sort of floral and minty?"

"Roses and eucalyptus…" she chuckled softly. "No, every Kunamin thrower has his or her own unique smell. I'm not sure how or why that's true." She shrugged and kicked at one of the rocks forming the arena wall.

"Is getting angry the only way to use Kuna?"

"No. Quite the opposite in fact," said a strange harsh voice and they both turned to look.

The ancient Dominant, Jun'tar, walked up to stand beside them, his bald head glistening in the sun, his fire red robes coated with ash, his red-brown eyes staring them down beneath bushy black eyebrows. "Anger *will* produce results with Kuna. However, positive emotion—love, joy, peace, contentment—will feed the heat with far greater outcomes." He stepped around Tolen and reached toward her.

She gripped the top of his arm, resisting the urge to wipe her hands on her jeans when she let go. "Jun'tar."

Tolen seemed to sense her not-so-nice feelings toward Jun'tar and gave her a funny look.

"I have heard about your talents, McLacy. You are a very gifted Kunamin. I have to wonder though if your abilities would increase if *you* could learn to use love, rather than anger to feed your Kuna. Perhaps you will absorb something from today's training as well."

Jun'tar turned around and she wondered if he could feel the glare she was throwing at his back.

The Dominant spoke as he walked away. "Come Tolen, it is time to begin."

As Macy watched Tolen walk into the center of the arena with Jun'tar, she lifted Bastian's crystal from beneath her shirt.

It can't happen. Even he realizes it now. So why does it hurt so much?

The large shard pulsed gently as she twisted it between her fingers.

You didn't prepare me for this Bastian. You said protect him. Jonas said the Balance put us together for a reason. I know I shouldn't feel like this. I'm not supposed to feel this way about him. Am I?

LaUnahi, everything will come together soon. Trust Jonas, my little bird, he can guide you. You will be all right. I promise. Bastian's voice—the faint echo, the product of her imagination that she'd been hearing since his death. It wasn't right and it wasn't healthy, but right now, she'd take a little advice, any advice, even if it was just an illusion.

She wasn't stupid. She knew the legend. She knew that as the Ninth trained it increased their chances of victory in the Final Battle. But that didn't mean it had anything to with her—so what if the Balance gave them both the same Watcher? That was between Tolen and Bastian. Maybe Jonas was wrong.

Tolen needs you.

Knock it off. Stupid hallucinations. What about her needs, huh? Didn't anyone care what she wanted?

What do you want, LaUnahi?

Macy tugged her hair off her shoulders and quickly wove it into a loose braid. *I want to end this conversation right now.* She wrapped a rubber band around the end of her hair and stalked into the arena to stand next to Jun'tar. She'd show the old fart just how much her anger worked with *her* Kuna.

He paused in his oration to give her a scathing look.

She hadn't even listened to a word he'd been saying. In truth, she hadn't even noticed he *was* speaking; she'd been too involved with her own internal conversation. If she kept up these little delusions, she was going to end up in a psyche evaluation with the Houseman. She ignored Jun'tar's scowl and started rubbing her palms together.

"Tolen, we've allowed McLacy to come today to show you what an experienced thrower can do—albeit one who still has a lot to learn." He raised an eyebrow at her, daring her to argue.

Allowed me to come today? Still has a lot to learn? I'll show you, geezer man.

Tolen snorted, quickly turned it into a cough, and met her eyes with the hint of a grin, before focusing back on Jun'tar.

"...The art of the Kunamin requires tremendous focus. Fire can be unwieldy once you have given it life and set it free. It devours the air around it, sucking in the particles, and moving them so fast they burn. Kunamin are like the fire they create, clumsy and unruly, until they learn to discipline their gift, hone it, channel the riotous energy in the correct way, and with the correct emotions."

He cast a wry glance at Macy before giving his full attention back to Tolen. She had to fight the urge to flick something at the back of his head. "You have used your Kuna before, without meaning to. It is a far different thing to call it in to being on purpose, and with a predetermined purpose. Up until now, you have seen your fire come to life following only the whim of your emotions. Today you are going to give it life for a specific reason." He motioned for Macy to come beside him. "Create a flower."

Macy tried not to roll her eyes. *A baby could do this.* She called the heat that constantly simmered in her chest and let it roll down into her palms. The calming scent of eucalyptus and roses seeped from her hands, giving her the balance she relied on to keep the flame under control. Bastian always believed the reason for the combination of strong spicy and soft floral was the symbol of balance between the ferocity of her gift and her gentle heart—keeping the gift balanced and her heart protected. She saw it a little differently. Fire was warmth and peace, but it could also be deadly. An unguarded heart was exactly the same.

She called the first spark to life softly, a gentle, tiny flame, like the flicker of a candle. She felt the surge of relief that came whenever she began to release the heat, but she held it back, ignoring the pain, and twisted her fingers, guiding the flicker into the air in front of her, pushing more and more heat in tiny little bursts, adding petals to the flower. It looked like a time-lapse film of a fire-rose in bloom. She heard the ooh's, and ahh's of the crowd, but she kept her eyes on the flower. Pretty soon she had a dozen different species of flowers blossoming in the air in front of them. She was showing off—just a little.

Jun'tar grunted and she held back a smirk. Apparently, he couldn't argue with the results. "Enough."

Macy closed her fists and the flowers disappeared, leaving nothing but a trail of smoke and a burst of light behind her eyelids each time she blinked. Jun'tar leaned close to her ear and whispered so only she could hear. "Your arrogance will be your undoing if you are not careful."

Macy glanced at Tolen, but he was still staring where the flowers had disappeared. She bit back a retort and ignored the chills running down her back at the man's words.

"You are excused. I will call you back if needed." Jun'tar pointed to the side of the arena where Jonas sat on a spindly chair.

She looked right in his crazy red-brown eyes and shrugged, putting as much indifference in the motion as she could, nodded at Tolen, and walked off amidst soft snickers from the crowd to take the seat beside Jonas.

Chapter 10

THE KUNAMIN WAY

Once seated she could no longer hear what Jun'tar was telling Tolen. She saw him nod, send a tiny smile in her direction, and with a slight furrow to his brow, hold his hand in front of him and create a dancing flame in his palm. His eyes never left her face as he manipulated the flame into a dozen different shapes. A flower like the one she created, an eagle in flight, a burst of sparks that fell like snow, a prowling lion. It was incredible, mesmerizing, almost terrifying. He never once looked at what he was creating, his eyes stayed on her face. Her heart thundered in her chest at the look in his eyes—a look she couldn't explain, but that held her gaze, just as it had last night, a look that filled her with strange longing.

She found herself wanting desperately to know what he was thinking about. He tilted his head, gave her a lopsided grin and somehow she knew. He was thinking about *her*. Good or bad, right or wrong, he was thinking about her.

It felt almost physically painful to force her gaze away and look at the crowd.

Hope lit their faces. It was obvious that they were starting to believe they might actually stand a chance in the Final Battle with him on their side. But as Macy watched them, she felt something else—deepening sorrow.

The power and sense of purpose as a Chosen had given meaning to her life. She had always known she was important. Maybe it was arrogance as Jun'tar had suggested, but it got the job done. As she surveyed the reactions of the crowd, the sheer courage and faith in the future Tolen gave them just by being himself—not just his gifts, but the kind of person he was—she couldn't help but wonder if she'd been missing something. She'd had pride and power. It was a total rush, destroying creatures of Darkness, but it was a job, a responsibility. Tolen had something else that she never thought mattered.

Compassion. Pure, selfless, compassion.

Not just sacrificing everything to fight *for* people, which was a noble cause, yes, but not nearly as powerful as sacrificing everything because you actually *cared* about those you fought for. Wanting to succeed for them, for their lives and happiness, not just for self-satisfaction and praise. Jonas had tried to tell her that she cared more for others than she did for herself, but she still didn't believe it. She liked praise and outside validation much more than she knew she should.

She only remembered truly loving and caring about three people in her life; her parents and Bastian—although she'd never showed that love to him like she wished she would have. Had she ever cared for anyone else that much? Had she allowed herself to care deeply about *anything*? No. It was dangerous to love—something she'd learned the hard way.

"He's doing incredibly well."

Macy jumped. She'd totally forgotten about Jonas sitting beside her. Maybe she really was going crazy. She glanced over, but his eyes were on Tolen, his gnarled fingers folded over the top of his cane, his crinkly chin resting on the back of his hands.

"Yeah. Yeah he is." She swallowed the painful lump growing in her throat.

Jonas nodded and sniffed. "Smells like cloves and earth. Is that Tolen or Jun'tar?"

"Tolen, I think. It doesn't feel like *Jun'tar* has released anything yet."

"You do not like the Master of the Kunamin?"

Macy shrugged again.

Jonas nodded. "They can be slightly arrogant."

"Slightly?" She cringed. Was she any different?

"You did very well with your display. I'm sure *your* arrogance was warranted on this occasion."

On this occasion. She held back a snort. "Maybe."

Jonas sighed. "Thank you for trying with Tolen. I can see he is doing much better already." He took a slow breath. "He seems to be taking the knowledge of the Ninth in stride."

"I guess so. I think he's ignoring it more than dealing with it."

He nodded slowly, watching Tolen toss two balls of flame at a target fifty feet in front of him, and twist his fingers until the target disintegrated into a pile of smoking ash. "I hear you confronted Nova."

"Um, yeah." She didn't meet his eyes.

"Although your anger was justified, it was also unnecessary. Nova will pay the price for interfering with the flow in the Balance."

She turned to study Jonas' face. "But Tolen figured it out on his own. Technically, she didn't tell him."

"Yes, that is true. But she broke the decree. The Balance will hold her accountable."

Macy nodded, feeling smug, yet a little confused. "But you never had any intention of telling him. You said that fate had another plan. Couldn't that plan have involved Nova telling him?"

"It very well could have. That is yet to be seen. But whether or not that is the case, she still went against my statute and she *will* face judgment for that—I cannot change the laws of the Balance."

Macy felt no remorse for Nova, but it still seemed unfair. "It doesn't seem right."

Jonas turned his odd eyes toward her and one of his bushy eyebrows lifted. "So you believe that only certain wrong acts are to be punished? That justice should only be met under certain circumstances?"

"No, I just meant that it didn't seem like such a bad thing. You know…just telling someone something." She squirmed as she realized the real problem. *She* wanted to be the one who got to tell Tolen the truth.

"Even when that something was restricted by law?"

She frowned. "Was the law right though?" Her cheeks reddened. Here she'd been telling Tolen it was best to do what those smarter than her requested and yet she was arguing with Jonas about the same thing.

"Maybe, maybe not." Jonas half smiled. "I simply went the direction I felt prompted to take."

Macy recognized the rebuke. Jonas was a strong follower of Light with immense power and belief. He was closer to the Light *and* the Balance than anyone here; she had no right to question his decisions.

She looked away. "I'm sorry. I've been trying to take Bastian's advice and think before I speak, but I'm not succeeding."

Jonas patted her arm and she glanced back to see him smiling. "It's alright. I like you McLacy. You entertain me. You are who you are. By the way, the Movan managed to squeeze a few more hours out of our electricity last night so Incrah charged the battery in your music thing." Jonas pulled out her MP3 player and handed it over with a smile and a shake of his head. "He also put in your tent a large bag of the purple suckers you favor over the Meat Cakes and Sugar Tack."

"Thanks." Macy's face reddened again as she placed the ear-buds around her neck. "That was really nice of them." She flicked a speck of dirt off the screen before tucking the MP3 in her pocket. "I know it's stupid, but music helps me drown everything out so I can fall asleep."

"It's not stupid." He looked back at Tolen. "Everyone has something that brings them comfort. Your mother loves classical music and the color purple. You love your mother."

"My mom loved classical music and *everything* purple," Macy mumbled.

Jonas shook his head again, this time with sadness. "Oh, McLacy, so much you do not understand. Those who pass into the next world are not erased, they are not *gone*. They are continuing their existence in a much better place. Do you think your mother loves you any less where she is?"

She shrugged. "No, I guess not."

"Do you think she now hates classical music where she is?"

"No."

"You see?" He tipped his head. "Remember what I told you during Forrest Bastian's Farewell? Those who have left through Light's Door should not be spoken of in the past tense. They are still themselves, their likes, dislikes and the love they have is the same; their bodies are simply in a far more glorious state. They have been able to shed mortality and exchange it for immortality in the form they began in; the beautiful form that the physical body tries to mirror, but can never quite match in its exquisiteness, its perfection. Your mother is glorious and happy and very much herself where she is."

Macy looked away, past the crowds, past Tolen, and into the forest.

"Thanks Jonas. I—well. I guess I knew that, but I needed the reminder."

He patted her arm again. "It is hard to remember truth in matters of our own pain. Love is a complicated emotion. It is the only one I know of that can cause such powerful, yet completely opposite feelings—unexplainable joy and crippling pain."

Her shard pulsed and drew her attention back to Tolen and Jun'tar. Tolen's dark hair glistened in the sun; sweat was beginning to run down his face and neck. His eyes were no longer on her, but focused on the task. She watched his hands as he manipulated the fireballs in mid-air, twisting and turning his fingers gracefully, naturally—and remembered how it had felt when he'd touched her in the Binithan. How it felt to have his hands on her waist as he'd pulled her down into the leaves, the shimmer of pleasure as he'd brushed her hair from her face, the confusing thrill when she realized he was leaning in, possibly to kiss her. The feel of his fingers entwined with hers as they'd sat by the river and she'd told him the truth. That it could never be.

A painful ache settled just below her heart. Whether they were meant to be more than friends or not he was finding a way in. Her mind repeated what Jonas just said. *Love is a complicated emotion. It is the only one I know of that can cause such powerful, yet completely opposite feelings—unexplainable joy and crippling pain.* Joy and pain—he'd only been talking about her parents, and Bastian, hadn't he? She didn't *love* Tolen, that was ridiculous, she just cared about what happened to him.

"It's been an interesting week wouldn't you say?" Jonas asked, thankfully interrupting her thoughts.

Macy nodded, not trusting her voice.

"Tolen has come far in a short time. He has accepted the gift of the language of the Hidden. It flows flawlessly from his mouth and everything he speaks to does his bidding instantly. His sparring with you produced amazing results as well." His tone turned calculating. "I wish we had the means to give him everything he needs, but some things will have to wait until he reaches the citadel."

Macy's head snapped up. "The citadel?"

"Of course. He will need to be introduced at the Guardian Court."

"Right, Bastian told me that." A sick knot formed in the pit of her stomach. Tolen would go to the Guardians and she would take up her life as a Chosen once more. How many years would it be before he was ready for them to be a team and fulfill whatever mission the Balance had for them? How long would it be before she saw him again? Why did she have to care? "When will he go?"

"I have not decided yet. The idea of letting him leave the protection of my shield is frightening now that the Dark knows his identity, but I cannot go with him and leave the camp unprotected." He frowned gently. "I can feel his power growing. He has not yet mastered the art of shielding himself and it is getting more difficult for me to shield him as his knowledge increases. Bastian and I share the same fear."

Macy took a deep breath, unsure if she really wanted to know the answer to the question she was about to ask. "What's that?"

Jonas looked down at her with a grave expression. "That by the time Tolen has the power that will come when he accepts his destiny *and* transcends at the human age of eighteen, not even the Spheres at the citadel will be able to hide him." He trailed off with a shake of his head.

Macy shivered.

Tolen sent a volley of fireballs into the sky, twisted his hands to combine them midair, and the resulting explosion sent waves of heat across their faces and bent the nearest branches of the trees. He was so powerful now. What would he be like when he transcended and reached the pinnacle of his gifts?

Macy absently rolled Bastian's shard between her fingers. Where would the next phase of their lives take them? Would Tolen be able to eventually try to save his father—or would his duty override his family, just as being a Chosen had taken away hers?

She looked at the ground, her heart aching for Tolen. "How're you going to get him to the citadel before he turns eighteen? Or will you have him transcend here?"

"I am still working on that. We do not have a Capka set up here for Transcendence, and the closest settlement that does have one powerful enough to protect him during the process is too far from here to attempt with his shield so faulty. He could transcend at the citadel, but the Guardians are leery of releasing the location of their door. They don't want Tolen leading anyone from the Dark to them unintentionally." He fell silent, his wise eyes filled with uncertainty.

The pull from her own shard toward Tolen had increased as they talked about him. "I've heard of direct links to the citadel being opened before, inter-dimensional doorways. Couldn't we open one of those, can't the Guardians?"

Jonas shook his head sadly. "Opening doorways, or links, creates huge ripples in the Balance. There is no way to shield the action from the Dark. We can open com links, as they only create minor wrinkles, I can shield those. But the citadel is in the Light Realm, and is vastly protected. Links can only be opened from their side and they won't do it with Tolen's life force—"

"Acting like a beacon to the Dark." She sighed.

"Correct. The Dark has been close by since you left the Binithan. My shield prevents them from knowing Tolen's exact location, but they are near enough that should we attempt to open a door, the possibility they could ambush the link and storm the Light Realm is very real."

Macy's eyes narrowed. "I thought the Dark couldn't survive in the Light Realm. It's impossible."

Jonas took a deep breath. "There are forces at work that I have never seen before. The Guardians are worried. It is a risk they are unwilling to take."

Macy thought back over the events of the last month. Kreydawn miners acting weird in the desert, the Balance restoring Bastian's youth, the arrival of the Ninth, the awakening of the Shadows, the appearance of DéHool. Yes, things were changing. She rubbed the chills from her arms.

Tolen manipulated another fireball, letting it grow bigger and bigger, just like her fear for him. How were they going to protect him if his Transcendence put everyone around him in mortal danger?

You can help him, LaUnahi.

She twisted the end of her braid between her fingers. *How? I'm no Sphere. I can't block him. Heck, no one will be able to, and I can't fight off a whole army of Dark creatures by myself.*

Tolen suddenly closed his fist—the fireball he'd been enlarging went out in a puff a smoke—and looked over at them with an almost angry expression.

Her stomach dropped. His Watcher's eye. *Oh crap, crap, crap!* Had he been listening to their whole conversation?

Tolen dropped his hands to his sides. "Jun'tar? Would it be alright if I spoke to Jonas for a moment?"

Jun'tar bowed and waved his hand. Tolen walked toward them and Macy's heart slammed in her chest.

He didn't even glance in her direction; his focus was entirely on Jonas. "Jonas?"

"Yes, boy?"

Tolen's eyes flicked to Macy for a split second. "My gift of empathy, m-my thoughtful heart, it's my Watcher's eye isn't it? Bastian said it'll allow me to sense the thoughts of those I'm meant to watch over, is that right?"

Jonas cleared his throat. "Most likely."

"Since I'm the Ninth, that's pretty much everyone then, isn't it?" His jaw clenched and Macy knew. He'd heard everything.

Jonas sighed, the look on his face and the tone of his voice when he answered said he knew as well. "Yes."

"Okay." He took a deep breath. "Okay…" Tolen's eyes flicked to Macy's again. Without another word, he turned and went back to the center of the arena, his hands smoking slightly.

Jonas watched Tolen walk away with an odd gleam in his eye. "Every time the puzzle seems complete another section is added; the pieces continue to accumulate. What will it look like when it's finished?" he whispered.

Macy spun on her heel and stalked out of the arena, not sure if she was embarrassed, worried, horrified, angry, or all of the above.

She passed Nova on the way back to her tent. Their eyes met and Nova smirked, her surreal beauty overpowering despite her sneer.

Macy's hands shook and smoke drifted from her palms. "*Mi'no ha!*" She aimed the fireball just above Nova's head, who dove for cover. She twisted her fingers sending the fireball into a small cook-fire in front of someone's tent where it slammed dead center, shooting flames five feet in the air.

"Hey!" a man shouted angrily, but Macy was already running into the safety and silence of the trees.

C H A P T E R 11

CONFUSION

MACY ATE HER LUNCH BY THE RIVER. WELL, PICKED AT IT ANYWAY. SHE was supposed to spar with Tolen in twenty minutes, but she couldn't force herself up from the rock. Her feet glided through the chilly water, a little higher on her ankles from the rain, while her head went over and over her conversation with Jonas. How much had Tolen overheard? Which part upset him the most? Was it the fact that she thought it ridiculous to love him, or fear of his growing power? Was it fear for the danger he would put everyone in, or the idea that they wouldn't see each other for a long time, years possibly? She knew she shouldn't care, shouldn't feel like she needed to know what he was feeling, but she did. She really, really did, it was exasperating, and exhausting. The desire to leave had come back, but this time it wasn't because she hated Tolen so much she couldn't stand to be near him. This time what she felt was much more powerful, and way more terrifying.

ooo

Tolen sat at the edge of the arena twisting the small Fire Stone between his fingers. Jun'tar had given it to him as a reward for his hard work. It didn't do anything special that he could see, aside from being a few degrees warmer than his skin and strangely beautiful—the red and gold swirls along its surface seemed to shimmer and move like flames when the light hit it. Jun'tar did say the warmth from the stone could help to calm one's thoughts. He lifted it up and traced the swirls within the stone with his finger—he definitely needed to calm his thoughts.

Macy never showed up for lunch. He'd gone to her tent, but she wasn't there. He'd felt the pull from her shard toward the forest, but when he'd set off to find her, Jonas stopped him and said she needed to be left alone; she was "choosing which piece to be." Whatever that meant.

He knew he could have asked Jonas about what he'd heard in their conversation. In fact, he'd sensed the old guy wanted to talk to him when he was telling him the puzzle thing, but Tolen didn't want to hear it from Jonas, he wanted to hear it from Macy. There was a lot in that conversation that frightened him, angered him, and confused him.

Just as in the Binithan, Tolen felt dirty, tainted, a problem to be dealt with. He'd been trying so hard to become what he needed to be in order to not be a risk, and be good enough to go after his parents, but apparently, he hadn't been shielding himself at all. Jonas was taking that burden as Tolen got stronger.

Along with the anger and disappointment, he felt afraid and excited from the feeling he sensed growing in Macy's thoughts. It had been there as they'd talked by the river, but weaker, quieter. She'd been feeling for him the same growing attraction he felt for her. An attraction that felt soul deep and incredible. A choice, a path they could take together if they wanted to that was exciting and scary at the same time. But her words had canceled it out. He'd decided to let it be. Remain her friend and nothing more. Because it didn't matter what someone felt if they never acted on it, right?

But today, as he'd listened, well heard in his thoughts, her conversation with Jonas, the feeling was still there, getting stronger. She did feel for him what he felt for her. A feeling outside their Chosen connection. She just didn't recognize it for exactly what it was, having lived a life with a guarded heart, but he did. His destiny may make it seem to her that it could never work between them, and maybe they would be separated for years as he trained, but that didn't stop it from being right. They could make it work out somehow if they really wanted it to. Right?

He rubbed the stone between his fingers and decided to try an experiment. One way to know for sure he was hearing thoughts, and really sensing Macy's feelings for him, would be to try it out on someone else. He squirmed a little at the idea of entering someone's mind without their permission, but he told himself it was just an experiment. If he was really supposed to *watch* for everyone he needed to understand this gift, and Bastian had never had the chance to teach him. He gulped. But how?

Maybe he just had to think of someone and say the word? Yeah, that sounded like a good place to start. Who? Incrah? Jonas? He tugged on his hair. No, not them.

Dirt walked by carrying a basket of bread. He was a good place to start. Just a normal guy.

He closed his eyes, licked his lips, and feeling foolish, thought of the chubby old guy and said, "*Iy'hika.*" *To watch.*

Colors flashed behind his closed eyes in odd patterns. Dirt's thoughts *were* on the basket he carried and where he was heading with it, but another part of his mind was occupied with his family, another on the happenings at camp and the Ninth Chosen and what it meant to have Tolen here. He was afraid for his loved ones, but there was hope there too.

He could see why Bastian had said it was being *aware* of thoughts, not actually reading a mind like a book. Thoughts weren't words—people didn't think in sentences. More like rushes of images and feelings that had to be sorted out like a puzzle in order to deduce specifics of what a person was actually thinking. The way that Bastian could do it almost word for word had to come from years of practice and really understanding peoples' reactions.

He pulled out of Dirt's head and compared it to what he experienced with Macy. It was similar but different enough that he was unsure if it was something else entirely, something deeper. He wasn't an outside observer watching the workings of her mind. It was more like their thoughts were connected. He shook his head. It made no sense. Maybe it had to do with the fact that she was his trigger. But why did her thoughts jump into his head without him even thinking about it, or saying the hidden word, as if she had put them there herself?

Could it be that he really *wasn't* entering her mind, she was entering his, by her own subconscious choice?

Tolen shifted and the old wooden seat creaked beneath him. It was so confusing.

"Where's Macy?" Incrah asked.

"What?" Tolen jumped and looked around. "Oh, I dunno. She's supposed to be here." He felt warmth in his cheeks and avoided Incrah's eyes.

"Jun'tar gave you a Fire Stone huh?"

Tolen nodded and tucked it in his pocket.

"He must have been very impressed. That's a rare gift."

Tolen nodded again, distracted, and only half paying attention. It was getting ridiculous. Macy was right, no matter what he was or wasn't feeling, he had to get his head in the game. He had a big destiny, a job to do, and had he forgotten about his parents? They could be in that prison suffering and he was worrying about girl trouble. Chagrin filled him and he determined again to focus on what really mattered. He needed to learn, he needed to train, and then maybe, just maybe, he wouldn't be as dangerous as Jonas and the others feared and they would help him. The Macy business could wait. It *had* to wait.

"Well, we don't want to lose any training time so why don't you start out with Janu?"

Janu nodded from across the arena, his dreadlocks bobbing, his toothless mouth pulled into a mischievous grin.

Tolen walked over so Quasar and Bolide could help him into his gear. Ingrid handed him a sword. Bey sat quietly on the ground, his eyes closed.

"Looks like you get to fight a real warrior." Janu slugged his shoulder.

"Don't get too excited, Janu," Bey said from the ground. "Macy's here." His eyes were open and he pointed across the arena where Macy was walking toward her team.

Now that he was paying attention, Tolen felt the tug from his shard, but he moved his gaze back to his team, reigning in the emotions. The fact that she was his trigger would make it hard to maintain the right focus, but he would do it, he *must* do it…for his parents.

∘∘∘

Macy watched Tolen walk toward her. They raised their swords and when they touched to start the match, she glanced in his eyes. Something had changed since that morning. His eyes were harder, more focused, less warm and open. It tugged at her heart.

It's for the best. She said this over and over as she felt him pulling away, his focus on the fight, the moves, the training, not on her the way it had been as he'd practiced with his Kuna. He was becoming the Ninth, becoming who he was supposed to be, fulfilling the role. And it shouldn't hurt. *I won't let it hurt.* She pushed the thought into her moves, countering his attacks, learning with him. He was good, but she had more experience, he could read her moves in her thoughts, but not if she allowed instinct to take over, pushed the emotion out and let years of training take over.

Sweat blossomed on Tolen's brow as her technique began to succeed.

ooo

Tolen fluffed the lumpy pillow on his cot, and closed his eyes, trying not to go over the entire day, but failing miserably. After the fight, he and Macy had shook hands and she left quickly. They ate dinner on opposite ends of the mess tent. He found himself again with the Lafar, Nova pounding him with questions on the fight through the entire meal. What moves did he think were his strongest, why did he do this or that, which of his trainers were his favorite, what were the Dominants like. He hadn't even known she'd been one of the spectators until she'd brought it up. Macy had sat with Jonas. They didn't make eye contact once, and although he felt really good about what he'd learned today, and how it would help him in his quest to save his parents, he couldn't deny the sadness he felt from pulling away from Macy. *It was for the best.*

He turned on the cot and tried to empty his mind…

Thick oily blackness fell over him. Tolen shivered so hard his teeth rattled. The paralyzing darkness pushed down, sucking the life from him. He could barely breathe. His eyes couldn't focus through the gloom.

An eerie flickering blue light appeared from somewhere above in the windowless room. He looked up and saw a dripping torch hung high on the wall. The wall itself seeped with black liquid that trailed down and disappeared somewhere in the darkness.

He shuddered, his pulse sped, and sweat ran down his face.

"Tolen…" A gravelly whisper sounded from the ground beside his feet.

Daedal was on his knees, patches of white scalp showed through his elbow length hair.

He lifted a skeletal hand and reached out to Tolen. "Tolen…Tolen, help me." He took a shuddering breath and collapsed.

"No!" Tolen threw his arms out to catch his father and fell off his cot.

He stared into the darkness, breathing slowly, trying to pull his head out of the nightmare and not throw up. Why did he dream it now after so long? Could it be because he was running out of time? Or was it a product of his own imagination brought on by his guilt?

He stood up, walked to the water basin, and washed the sweat from his face and neck. The image of his father flashed across his mind and he threw the towel across the tent.

"I can't let him die!"

Tolen already knew what Jonas would say. He *wasn't* strong enough yet, and his destiny was too important to risk his life to save just one man, blah, blah.

But it isn't just any man. He's my father and he's calling for my help.

Tolen sat back on the bed. He'd talk to Jonas in the morning, try and get him to understand he couldn't wait any longer, no matter what might happen…*and if he doesn't agree?*

The answer came in a flash. *I'll beg Macy for her help.*

Surely all those years with Bastian had given her something that would help him. He wouldn't ask her to go with him and face the Shadows, he wouldn't do that to her, but maybe she'd tell *him* how to do it.

He looked at his pillow. There was no way he could go back to sleep. The nightmare was too fresh and real. He leaned over and tugged on his sneakers. Beneath the scratches on his watch it showed it was just after two in the morning. He tugged a shirt over his head and smoothed out his tangled hair.

He'd take a walk. No one would be out except the guards. It was past lights out, and technically he wasn't supposed to be out wandering, but the guards would most likely ignore him as long as he wasn't causing trouble.

The air was chilly and moist when he unzipped the tent flap. The sky overcast—no stars visible.

He shivered. The darkness felt too much like his dream.

He shook his arms, rolled his neck and stepped into the night, focusing only on the sounds around him—the chirping of crickets, the soft hoot of owls, the light breeze through the leaves, and the crunch of the dirt beneath his shoes.

He reached the end of the row of tents and turned into the forest, asking his eyes to pull in more light. Without consciously deciding to go there, he found himself on the path he'd taken with Macy that led to the river. He plopped onto their rock on the bank and kicked at the dead leaves, and watched the gentle rippling current, counting the hours until sunrise and fighting the growing dread in his heart.

CHAPTER 12

NOVA'S STORY

"Hey, Tolen. What are you doing here?"

Tolen jumped, looked to his left, and noticed Nova just a few feet down river. Soft white light flickered from her hands.

A tremor of disappointment passed through him. He'd really hoped to be alone. He wasn't really in the mood for Nova's chipper attitude. "Hi, Nova. I couldn't sleep."

She nodded. "I like to walk at night too when I can't sleep. It's quiet and no one watches you." She glanced up into the trees, "well no one noticeable anyway."

Tolen thought about the guards stationed all over and sighed. "Yeah, I guess you're never really alone around here."

"Nope." She sounded much more subdued than her usual self, and Tolen felt a stab of pity. "So, what are you doing?"

Nova glanced back at her glowing hands. "Picking Kornikye. I usually collect them during the day, but sometimes it's fun to catch them in the middle of the night—it's the only time they glow."

"That light is from something alive?"

"Come here, I'll show you. They're incredible." She motioned him over with a tip of her head.

Tolen stood up, dusted off his jeans, and walked over to look in her hands. "What exactly are they?" He stared at what looked like tiny, glowing, white flowers.

"They're a plant raised by Linessa. When they are above water and exposed to light they sing until they are spent. Then I bring the tired Kornikye back here and the Linessa rejuvenate them."

"What are Linessa?"

"Given you were raised with humans, I guess the closest comparison would be a Water Sprite."

"Oh."

Nova laughed and her violet eyes sparkled in the light from the Kornikye. "I read a lot of human books—the way they twist the truth into legends fascinates me. Do you not like to read fantasy?"

"Actually I've read quite a bit. It sometimes made more sense than reality." He smirked. "It's just that in most of the stories, Sprites aren't exactly cast in the best light."

"They can be a pain, that's for sure. But they are the only creatures who can raise Kornikye, and Jonas needs their restoring powers in order to maintain his shield for such long periods. There are only a handful of Linessa settlements capable of raising Kornikye left in the United States. Jonas picked this area because of them."

"It's hard to imagine anything being difficult for Jonas."

"Oh, his life force is powerful enough to cast his shield easily, it's just his body is weakening. He's really, really old."

"How old?"

"No one knows. But Evrah is something like fifteen-hundred and he's older than her."

"Wow, and I thought Bastian was old."

Nova nodded. "I've heard the legends of the Watcher, Forrest Bastian. I would've loved to meet him."

Tolen cleared his throat.

"I'm sorry, Tolen, I didn't mean to bring up a hard subject. Here." She filled a small jar with water, wrapped it in a piece of leather, and handed it to him. "Hold this. I'll hand you the Kornikye when the Linessa hand them up. You have to put them in the jar really fast and tie the leather shut so they won't waste any of their song before Jonas needs them."

Tolen watched Nova's hands as she worked. She was so gentle and loving, like a mother to the Kornikye as she lifted them from the tiny hands of the Linessa. The Lafar had been nothing but kind to him. It made him curious. "Nova? Can I ask why you and your family seem to…avoid the rest of the people here?"

Nova's face drooped.

"I'm sorry. It's none of my business."

"No, it's okay Tolen." She cleared her throat. "I know you'll understand."

She looked so sad Tolen set the jar on the ground and motioned for her to sit on the boulder he'd just vacated.

She played nervously with the ends of her hair for a full minute before she spoke. "People don't like us because of…" she paused and licked her lips, "the Daklafar." Her voice trembled so much on the last word that Tolen could barely understand what she said.

"Sorry?" He bent over and she pulled him down onto the rock beside her.

"The Daklafar." She whispered in his ear.

He leaned away and looked in her eyes. "Who?"

She nodded as if she wasn't surprised he'd never heard of them. "They were once Lafar, but now they're ugly, filthy creatures who live to serve the Dark. They loved their beauty and power more than the Light. The Dark seduced them—told them they could be immortal, have elemental gifts, be even more powerful than they already were. Instead, their beauty was replaced by repulsiveness, but they couldn't go back. They had bound themselves to the Dark in their greed." She closed her eyes. "People in the Hidden world no longer trusted the Lafar after that."

It seemed an unfair reason not to trust someone. Hidden-kind obviously struggled with some of the same prejudices as humans. "Why are you here then if they don't trust you? Instead of with your own people?"

Tolen leaned closer to hear as she continued in a whisper. "Twenty-five years ago my parents were sent with a group of eight hundred Lafar—nearly all of our kind—to try and reclaim the lives of their friends and family. After all, *surely* those who had listened to the Dark now regretted their choice." Nova shook her head sadly and then leaned it on Tolen's shoulder. He put his arm behind her on the rock. He wanted to offer her comfort, he could feel that this story was not going to have a happy ending, but he didn't want to give her the wrong idea either.

"It was a pointless effort, a stupid plan," Nova continued. "Once you make a promise to the Dark you are bound to that promise. You can't change *anything*." Her shoulders trembled. "Those who had chosen the Dark were no longer our friends and family—their hearts had been altered forever.

"When my parents left they begged their good friends, Quasar and Nebula, to hide Bolide and I and care for us should anything happen to them. Quasar had been badly injured in a battle and Nebula was expecting their first child. Our parents were high captains in the Lafar army. They couldn't stay behind. The rest of the Lafar children were sent to the clans in Europe to wait for parents that would never return. All eight hundred Lafar were captured or killed. I was six months old. Six years ago Quasar's son was killed and he brought us here—he felt we'd be safer under Jonas's care. Safer maybe, but not happier." She sniffed and a tear trickled down her cheek. When she raised her hand to wipe it away, the moon highlighted the scabbed burn Macy had put on her wrist.

"I'm so sorry Nova. I shouldn't have asked." He lifted his hand and placed it over the injury, knowing the deeper injury, the one in her heart, he could do nothing for. He whispered "*Lon'adras*" and she glanced up through wet lashes to give him a sad smile.

"It's just part of life in the Hidden world, isn't it?"

He shook his head. "I wish it wasn't."

He made to move his hand away but before he could, she put her hand over his, closed the narrow gap between them and brushed her lips against his mouth. He pulled back without returning the kiss and was about to explain to her that he didn't feel that way when the smell of eucalyptus and roses filled his nose.

His heart slammed to the pit of his stomach, he pushed Nova away— nearly knocking her off the rock, and jumped up to look behind him into the trees. "Macy?"

Macy stepped out, her face livid, arms shaking, her hands billowing smoke, her fingertips lit with tiny flames.

His entire body tensed—she'd seen Nova kiss him, he could see it in every angry line on her face, and she wouldn't know, couldn't know that he hadn't kissed her back, that he hadn't wanted any of it.

Macy clenched her teeth. "I'm so sick and tired of worrying about you—of trying to fulfill my *promise* to Bastian."

Nova shifted on the rock and Macy shot her a fiery glare.

Tolen stepped forward. "What are you talking about?"

"I'm talking about being your babysitter—about the fact that my life was fine until we had to come looking for you." She pointed a finger in his direction and a flame shot toward him.

"*Win'tashta!*" Tolen lifted his hands; water flew from the river and doused Macy from head to toe.

"*Mi'no ha!*" Fire flew from her hands.

Nova dove out of the way but Tolen threw up a wall of water and the flame went out with a sizzle. "Knock it off! Let me explain! It's not what you think!"

"Oh really?" Macy shouted shrilly. "Do you think I'm blind? It's disgusting. Kissing someone years older than you and not even your species! That's a little hard up, don't you think?"

"Oh get over yourself," Nova spat. She stood up and dusted herself off. "You're just jealous that you're such a beast *no* species would take you."

"Nova. *Don't.*" Tolen put his hand on her arm.

Macy looked at his hand and her eyes filled with moisture. "I don't care who you are. I'm not going to deal with you anymore."

"Fine!" Tolen threw his hands in the air. "Truthfully, I'm sick of putting up with your crap too!"

"I hate you." Macy growled.

Tolen gritted his teeth and clenched his hands into fists. He could smell a hint of cloves and earth and the words shot from his mouth before he could call them back. "Then go! Leave like you've wanted to from the very beginning. I *don't* need you."

Macy's face fell and her lip trembled. She turned and ran back into the forest.

"Macy! Macy, wait!" Tolen moved to go after her and Nova grabbed his arm to stop him.

"Tolen, don't go after her."

He wrestled out of her grasp. "Nova, enough. There's nothing between us, okay? I'm leaving." His heels spun in the dirt and he took three strides in Macy's direction before Nova's icy tone stopped him cold.

"You're going to get her killed."

Tolen turned back to Nova, his teeth clenched, hands still smoking. "What are you talking about?"

"I know your destiny Tolen Téloran. You're a danger to everyone here. *Especially* her." The fury in her eyes pushed the heat stronger into Tolen's hands.

"Nova, you have three seconds to tell me what the crap you're talking about or I'm going to light you on fire, whether on accident or on purpose I haven't decided." He could feel Macy getting farther and farther away. He needed to find her before she took off. It couldn't end like this.

Nova stood up and lifted her chin. "There's a reason no one here likes me. I'm a snoop. I eavesdrop. I hate it here. I hate all these people who don't really care about me or my family. If it wasn't for Bolide I would have run away a long time ago, but my brother needs me. He's the real reason Quasar brought us here. He still has nightmares about our parents. The Kornikye helps him, and Jonas protects his mind. He's happy here, even if I'm not." Her hands clenched into fists. "I heard them talking about you the day you came. I heard how dangerous you are to us all, but they think we needed you, so I watched you, and I could see the truth to that."

Tolen became lost in her words. Her sickly sweet pretense had totally crumbled. Gone was the bubbly flirtatious act—the one that made people think she was an air-headed flake and not a threat—and in its place was a bitter, lonely girl who was miserably callous.

"The world does need you Tolen, but you need to leave before you are responsible for getting everyone here killed." Her violet eyes meet his own and he could see the truth mirrored back at him. She truly believed this.

Tolen swallowed. The concerns Jonas had shared with Macy—that Tolen was getting harder to shield, that the Dark was always near him—came rushing forward.

Nova stood up and backed away from him, her next words confirming his worst fears. "The Dark is coming. They are testing the borders of Jonas's shield even now. It won't be long before they find a way through. Incrah and the other captains have been going on patrols—haven't you noticed how they are never all together anymore?"

Tolen looked around feeling hollow and afraid. He *hadn't* noticed, but now that she mentioned it, he realized he hadn't seen all the Radia Warriors together since that first day he and Macy arrived here.

"A few days ago, shimmers indicating a transport link trying to open from the Shadow Realm was spotted just north of here." She continued to back away, but her eyes never left his face. "Incrah and Jonas think the Dark is getting ready to attack."

"What can I possibly do?" He wasn't really asking her, he wasn't sure who he was asking. He saw no way to help, no way to stop what was coming. Another terrible event that would be all his fault.

Nova paused and leaned forward, her angry eyes boring into his own. "Leave, Tolen. Leave tonight. I can show you a way that the guards will never see you. You can spare the people here. You can go after your destiny. You can save your father."

"How do you know about that?"

She tipped her head and her eyes narrowed. "I know a lot more than that." Her jaw flexed. "I know it's your fault your mother and best friend died. I know it was your actions that caused Forrest Bastian's death. I know who you are. You *don't* belong here. Stop letting others sacrifice for you. Go. Do what you are meant to do." Her eyes were cold and distant, not a single hint of the attraction she'd shown as she'd flirted with him the last few days or forced her kiss upon him.

He shook his head and looked away. He couldn't believe he was actually considering what she was saying. But wasn't it the truth? He'd heard Jonas say about as much, just not as bluntly. Could things really be that bad, but they didn't want to tell him. Could they right now be plotting how to protect him at the expense of the camp? It wouldn't be the first time they'd hid the truth from him. How much did Macy know?

He looked down at his trembling hands and turned his palms up. He was dangerous. He'd always known this. He'd led the Dark to his home and they'd taken his mother and killed his best friend, he'd led them to the Binithan and Elryn and Bastian had paid the price. Now the Dark was on its way here. His heart plummeted. *Macy…* If she left she could be headed right into the hands of the Dark.

He saw no alternative. No other choice. He wouldn't lead the Dark here. He would lead them away. He would leave. Tonight.

Where would he go? His heart thundered in his chest. What if there really was a link to the Shadow Realm opening up not too far away? Tolen's vision had showed him in his father's cell in the Shadow Prison alone, no one there to help. Jonas said this meant he was the only one with the key to get in, whatever that key may be—determination, or a willingness to sacrifice himself to save someone he cared about, he didn't know, but it was time to try. He might not know enough about his gifts, maybe he would be like a lamb going *willingly* to be slaughtered, in order to save another, but did that make it wrong?

If he was going to do it, he had to do it now. When he'd woke up from the nightmare he'd determined to ask Macy for help, but he knew now that she couldn't know what he was doing. He wouldn't put her in that kind of danger. Maybe, if he survived, he could find her and prove to her that what she saw wasn't what she'd thought, that he hadn't meant the harsh words he'd said. But right now he had to get away to protect her and everyone else.

"Show me the path."

Nova's eyes gleamed in the darkness. "Wait here and give me ten minutes to gather supplies and deliver the Kornikye. We don't have much time until the camp starts waking up. We need to hurry." She jumped up, grabbed her jars, and took off.

Tolen watched her run away and a burst of inspiration hit him. He searched the night for Journey's thoughts. She was sleeping near Took'rah, but woke as soon as she sensed Tolen's need. He whispered his desire from his mind to hers, not knowing if it would work without her here in front of him, but he felt her intentions and knew the badger would do as he asked.

The next ten minutes flew by in a blur of thought and anticipation. This was it, he was going in, nothing could stop him this time. To death or victory he did not know, but he felt eerily calm about his decision and ready, although grossly unprepared, to face whatever lay ahead.

Nova stepped through the trees, determination on her face, her eyes deep indigo in the darkness. She had a large backpack over her shoulder and her black hair bounced in a tight braid down her back. "Ready?"

He swallowed and nodded once.

She turned, led him across the river and into the thick forest. A hundred yards in she stopped. "Take off your Radia Shard."

"What?" Of everything she'd said, this shocked him most.

"If you don't, Macy will be able to track you."

A jolt of nerves ran through him. He fingered the shard around his neck as it pulsed a warning. Bastian had cautioned him to never take it off. Horrible things would happen if the Dark got their hands on it.

"We don't have time for this." With a flash of silver Nova cut the shard from his neck. He watched it swirl toward the ground and felt as if a piece of himself was falling with it. He sent his will to the nearest tree while glaring at Nova.

Keep the shard safe. Don't let anyone besides Macy have it. He sent an image of Macy's face to the tree.

The tree wrapped a vine around the necklace and pulled it higher until it rested in the fork of two thick branches. It twisted more vines and smaller branches covered with leaves around the shard until it was barely visible. It would be perfectly camouflaged unless someone knew what to look for.

Thank you.

Nova took off and he followed her away from the camp and toward another piece of his destiny.

Chapter 13

PROMISES AND LEGENDS

Macy picked her half-filled pack off the floor and threw it across the tent. Clothes, notebooks, discarded sucker wrappers, and socks flew everywhere. Smoke curled from her hands, but the scent offered no comfort, no balance to the war raging in her heart.

She stalked over to her cot, flipped it over, ripped the wrappers off two suckers from the bag on the floor, and stuck them both in her mouth.

She tugged her MP3 player off the wash table, crammed the headphones in her ears and set the volume to max, begging the soothing beat of the classical music to drown out her thoughts.

But they couldn't be silenced.

Just finish packing and go! She yelled at herself. Over and over the scene of Tolen kissing Nova replayed in her head. The smoke became thicker and colors swam before her eyes. Tiny plumes of fire flickered from her fingertips. *He can kiss whoever he wants to! Just go, leave, right now! He doesn't need you, he said so himself!* She bit into the suckers, crunching them into tiny shards.

Shards. The fire on her fingers went out leaving only a faint trail of smoke.

She lifted the Radia Shards out of her shirt—Bastian's longer heavier shard and her smaller lighter one. She felt nothing but emptiness from

Bastian's shard, but the pull from her own was strong toward the forest. She grabbed at the cords, determined to throw the stupid things as far as she could.

Macy, NO!

Bastian's deep tenor voice echoed so clear and loud through her mind that she grabbed the sides of her head. This was not her imagination.

Tolen needs you! You need him! He growled.

She twisted her fingers in her hair. *He doesn't. He said so himself!*

He did not mean it.

Yes he does!

No, he does not. Let go of your pride, Macy. Let him in. Stop lying to him. Stop lying to yourself.

I don't need someone to take care of me, Bastian.

No, you do not, but everyone *needs someone to care about them.*

Pain shot through her chest. *He doesn't care about me. It's* her *he likes.*

Stop focusing on what you saw, your eyes can deceive you. What did you feel that went beyond your own jealousy?

Jealousy? She scoffed and the hallucination sighed. *I was mad, not jealous.*

Without consciously meaning to bring it back, the scene began to replay in her mind. The anger flared again as the images returned—Tolen with his hand on Nova's neck, Nova's lips brushing his. But this time she noticed something else, he was leaning away, and he *didn't* return the kiss. Her breath caught when she noticed something far worse, something in the elf's eyes that made her blood turn to ice.

Nova does not care for him… Bastian clarified her feeling.

A sick knot of fear clenched in her chest. *She's playing with him.* The fear morphed into growing dread. *Why?*

She hadn't trusted Nova from the first day they'd met. It wasn't jealousy like her hallucination said. It was more, deeper, a feeling she'd learned to trust over the years.

No matter what was going on between her and Tolen, could she stand by and let Nova hurt him?

She squeezed her shard in her fist until the edges cut into her fingers.

She needed to really *listen*. Focus on that part of her that knew how to recognize the Dark, no matter how hard it tried to hide.

She ripped the headphones from her ears, tossed the MP3 player onto the cot, closed her eyes, slowed her breathing, and thought about what she really needed to understand, to know.

She pushed the sounds of the night from her ears and wiped the tears from her face. She had to concentrate. Too much was at stake. She needed to look at *everything*. Not just Nova and all the confusion this night had brought with it, but all the things she'd avoided thinking about since the day Bastian received Tolen's shard. She fought against her personal feelings, shoving them aside. It was time to think as a Chosen. This was what she was made for. She pressed her palms together and let the Kuna push just to her fingertips, the scent calmed her frayed nerves, and allowed her to focus on the questions and answers she most needed to understand *right now*.

Her Watcher was picked to find the Ninth when Tolen's Watcher—for whatever reason—couldn't fulfill his duty. *But why?*

The Balance could have chosen any Watcher; it did not have to be Bastian. It could have sent the Dominants to find the Ninth—they were powerful enough, and their bodyguards formidable enough that they could have reached him *and* gotten him to the citadel without a problem. A Protector could have been sent for him…The possibilities were numerous.

Bastian told Macy the day her parents were killed that she had a greater purpose than the rest of the Chosen. He claimed not to know what that purpose might be, but the strength of her life force *was* such that it had shifted the Balance enough that the Dark had taken notice and—always on the watch for the shift that meant the Ninth had been chosen—awakened the Shadows.

Jonas had also told her she had a purpose—a purpose "far greater than being a Chosen protector for humankind," he'd said. He said that she needed to find that purpose, that she couldn't let her parents' and Bastian's loving sacrifices be for nothing. She had a job to do.

Her mind replayed the scene. Jonas had come to her tent. She was angry—he was reminding her of her promise to Bastian.

"The Balance put you together for a reason."

"Oh yeah? Well I'm sick of the Balance messing with my life. Why the crap did the Light have to choose me anyway?"

"That is a very good question, and only you can find the answer."

Macy pulled her hands apart to rip the mutilated sucker sticks from her mouth and toss them to the floor. She began to pace, the scent of eucalyptus and roses still strong in the air. The Balance had put her and Tolen together for a reason. Bastian and Jonas both believed this. She'd argued with Tolen about it. She'd lied to him and said that was the only reason they were drawn to each other—but was it a lie? What if the reason Bastian had to become his Watcher, the reason the Balance needed them together was like End of the World big, and if they didn't stay together, if they didn't find a way to find the purpose together, the success of the Ninth, of the whole world, would be in jeopardy?

Wow, that's arrogant Macy. She chastised herself, but at the same time it *felt* true. Like, scary true.

Another memory surfaced, something she'd barely acknowledged at the time. Tolen's mother, Areen, filled with anger as she'd said, *"You put too much faith in your little group of Chosen children who have no idea of the real truth behind their selection."* Areen was bitter and angry and what she said could mean nothing at all, but Macy had to wonder if she knew there was more to the Balance's choices. That maybe there was a deeper destiny for them all.

Why did *the Balance choose me? Why did the Shadows come after me when I was chosen? It's obvious they would feel the shift of the Ninth and would come for him, but what is it about me that threatened them? Why were Tolen and I tossed together? Why are we so drawn to each other?*

And then she felt it. The separation between the *Balance's* need she felt to be with Tolen, and the *other* need that Tolen had tried to explain. They *were* separate. One was a need to fulfill a duty, a purpose, the *other* was …it was a need of the heart. Both she and Tolen had felt it. As two souls filled with pain they'd found solace in one another—but despite recognizing it, she knew it *couldn't* be, they were too different. It was just a reaction to their situation, the needs of their broken hearts. It wasn't real. Her chest constricted and the heat in her palms increased.

Understanding seemed to be filling her brain like a flash flood. A piece of the old legend suddenly crashed into her mind, a piece she'd never really paid attention to before, but with the force of a tidal wave the memory of the terrible night her parents died, the night that Bastian told her the Legend of the Ninth, came back with painful clarity.

It was her sixth birthday. There was a huge thunderstorm. She could remember the cake, the candles, how for some strange reason she felt the desire to reach out and touch the flame.

Just before her fingers met the tiny wick, a bright blue orb had burst into the kitchen and Macy caught her Radia Shard in her tiny hands.

Her mother had screamed—probably thinking the bright light came from the burning candles, that her daughter had touched the flame. Her father snatched her up in his arms checking her fingers for burns.

When he saw the shard his eyes opened in fear.

And then…Macy's head pounded…and then…*they* came…

Raksasha smashed through the kitchen window. Everyone was yelling. Her father held her tightly against him and shoved her mother behind him. He could not see what was after them, but he knew his daughter could.

Her father knew. Somehow he'd known, how had she forgotten this?

Of course. She'd blocked the entire night out of her memory—because what happened next was too horrible for any child to deal with.

Thick and black like ash the Shadow Wraiths' mist crept through the broken window until it filled the whole kitchen. Macy was paralyzed with fear. Her father dropped her and fell to the floor. Her mother grabbed her hand.

They were going to die.

Suddenly, a huge white-haired man jumped through the fog and killed the Raksasha.

A loud thundering scream rent the air and shook the kitchen. Arms wrapped around Macy and lifted her off the floor. Warm light engulfed her.

"Daddy?" she mumbled.

"What are you doing?" Her father held onto her arm, struggling to tug her back toward him. He looked up into the man's face and his grip slackened. "She has been Chosen?"

"You know—?" the stranger whispered.

"Yes. Go. Take her. We'll distract them. Go!" Her father rolled away from them. More screaming…blood-curdling screams.

The next thing she remembered she was lying on the back seat of an ancient car. The white-haired man said his name was Bastian and he tried to calm her, but she was crying, sobbing, begging for her parents.

"There is much to be explained young one and you must listen. It will calm your fears and speak to your heart. You will not understand all that I tell you now, but you will. Day by day the importance of your destiny will become clearer and clearer…."

She remembered Bastian's voice being soothing, pulling her from the horrors of what had just happened, and creating a new horror, a horror she would soon spend every day of her life trying to stop.

He talked of the job of the Chosen ones. He told of the legend, of how the day would come that Dark would be near to taking over the entire world, when creatures worse than the Raksasha and Shadows would roam free and without number.

Bastian knew the prophecy of the Ninth, word for word. *"Eight there are and the Ninth shall lead them with Light's Aid beside…"* She could still hear his deep voice as he spoke the words.

This was it. The piece, the vital clue that she'd never paid attention to before.

Her father had somehow known things about the Hidden. Macy's eyes widened. Her great-grandmother was of Native American descent and often the old tribes passed down stories for generations that came incredibly close to the truth.

McLacy Allicandra.

Her father had chosen her name. He said it meant 'helper of light' in an ancient language. Macy's mother had liked it, but had taken to calling her Macy for short.

Helper of light? Light's Aid…?

Holy shifters! Was *she* actually a part of the prophecy?

Her hands shook. Was that her purpose? The reason the Balance put them together? To stand alongside the Ninth as he united the Chosen and to help him lead the Final Battle?

Bastian, did you know the whole time? Am I—am I, Light's Aid?

A tiny whisper grew in her heart until her life force suddenly soared with the truth of it.

Her knees knocked together and she dropped to the floor. She covered her head with her arms and cried.

∘∘∘

Tolen followed Nova's shadow through the trees. His nerves charged as a live wire, his fingers tingling, his arms trembling. He could feel his gifts building within his body, preparing him, reacting to his stress, but he maintained his purpose forefront of his mind, kept an image of Macy close—activating his trigger. This was it. This was what he was supposed to do. *You are the master of your fate, you are the captain of your soul…*

He did not need to repeat the mantra he'd come up with in the Binithan to stay in control of his anger—he didn't even feel the tiniest bit angry. His mind had called it up for the reassurance and the hope that filled him because of memories of his mother. It wasn't his own voice he heard, it was the comforting sound of her voice that played over and over in his mind as she'd recited the poem night after night, her eyes focused on the evening sky. Only now did he fully understand why she loved it so much. It spoke of hardship and pain, death, and fear—but it also spoke of courage in the face of trial, the power within one's self to carry them through—of an unconquerable soul. This was his mother. She'd faced a difficult life because she'd given in to her fear, but she'd also fought with courage and bravery to protect what she loved most. It was also his father. Who knew how long he'd been tortured by the Dark, but they had yet to conquer his spirit. It could be Tolen—if he was strong enough. He repeated it now to assuage his doubts, to calm his misgivings by thinking of his parents and their shared strength.

Nova slowed down, put a finger to her lips, and pointed above them. "Guards." She mouthed, and then put her lips next to his ear. "We're about to leave Jonas's protection. Can you shield yourself? We need to be able to sneak past the guards and keep anything out there from discovering us before we reach the link."

Tolen rubbed a hand over his eyes. "I'm not very good at it."

"You're going to have to be or we won't make it. Once we're out of Jonas' shield you will shift the Balance and *everything* Dark near here will come after us." She blew out a quiet, frustrated breath, and glanced around. "Do the best you can. I just hope you run fast if you fail."

Tolen hadn't had to think much about what the Doogar had taught him in the Shield Room since getting under the protection of Jonas. He thought back on his time with Kiad, Elryn and Deegan. He'd learned why a shield was so important. It protected not just himself, but also those around him from being harmed because of the Dark he unconsciously led in. He thought of Macy and the possibility of his faulty shield putting her and everyone here in immediate danger—the idea horrified him—and he felt the warmth begin. It was working. He remembered Deegan describing how a shield is like hiding behind pictures, feelings or other vibrations, and he concentrated on hiding his presence behind the vibes surrounding him from the trees and wildlife.

He didn't need Nova's curt nod to know he'd succeeded. For the first time he felt almost perfectly in control of his shield. Macy's face flashed across his vision and his heart clenched painfully in his chest and he wondered briefly if he'd ever get the chance to tell her *she* was his trigger. He pushed the thought aside as Nova pointed to an almost invisible path beside the river.

"We'll follow the river until it branches off. Stay close behind me. These guards are really good."

Tolen nodded and tried to mimic her light footsteps, but he knew his big feet were leaving prints behind. He just hoped by leaving his shard it would take them a lot longer to figure out which way they'd gone and by then it would be too late to follow. Once they were far enough, he would drop his shield a couple times to draw the Dark away from the camp, but he'd have to do it just right, he didn't want them to find him before he had a chance to attempt the door into their realm.

○ ○ ○

Macy jumped to her feet and wiped her face on her sleeve. Bastian's shard began to glow brightly, intensifying the pull from her own shard toward Tolen. "Tolen, what in the heck are you doing?" She glanced out of the tent door and nearly jumped out of her skin when she looked down to see a fat badger pacing outside.

"Journey?" The badger stomped its feet and took off in the direction Macy could feel the fade of Tolen's shard. There were only two things that would make a shard fade—death or taking it off.

She knew he wasn't dead—how she knew she wasn't sure—but she knew.

He'd taken off his Radia Shard. The only reason he would take it off would be to keep her from being linked to him. He was leaving.

Go after him! Bastian's concern cut through her musing.

She took a step through the door.

Take supplies!

She didn't take the time to question the voice, the urgency left no room for doubt. Imagined warning or not she obeyed, running frantically around the tent, stuffing everything her hands touched back into her pack. She paused as her fingers brushed Bastian's bag where it lay beneath her overturned cot. She hadn't looked in it once since she'd carried it here.

Her fingers shook as she slid open the zipper. She swallowed the lump in her throat, searching through the pack until she found Bastian's emergency stash of non-perishable food and cash. She shoved the stash into her own pack, stood up, tied her belt around her waist, did a cursory check of the pouches, threw on her sleeveless jacket, pulled the hood over her hair, and flew through the tent flap.

She rushed to catch up with Journey, her hands smoking by the time she reached the forest's edge.

Five minutes into the forest she felt a shift in the Balance and cursed Tolen under her breath. *Where are you going, you freaking idiot?*

She pushed her feet faster.

The guards were stationed not far up ahead. She enhanced her eyes— Tolen's shard was almost completely hidden in the branches of a tree nearby. If she hadn't been so focused, she never would have seen the tiny reflection of the pale moonlight sparkling off its surface. She ran to it, tried to tug it from the branch, but the tree curled its branches tighter around. "Come on." She whispered. "Give it to me. I can't leave it here." She tugged again and it almost disappeared.

She stepped back and tapped her foot anxiously. She didn't have time for tug of war. She looked up into the tree. "Give it to me, please?"

Nothing.

She shoved the hood off her head and reached for her knife, determined to cut it out of the tree. The second her face was visible, the tree unfurled and lowered the shard into her hands. *It was waiting for me.* Huh. *You're still an idiot Tolen.*

She tugged it over her neck. When the three shards touched, they glowed so brightly she had to put her hand over her shirt to hide the light. A sense of joyous reunion flowed through her from the shards, and for the first time she felt a real connection to Bastian's shard as well. It was distant, quiet, but it matched the joy she felt from her own.

Her heart thudded in her throat. Tolen was gone. He'd left Jonas' shield, he'd left the only link she had to him behind. She was furious.

What the crap am I supposed to do now?

Going back for Jonas or one of the Radia warriors seemed like a good idea. She took a step back toward the camp but stopped when she felt something that made her palms tingle.

Far outside the safety of Jonas' shield, something had been growing. They'd all sensed it, discussed it, but something about it had just changed. A tiny shift in the Balance, so tiny if her senses hadn't been heightened she probably wouldn't have felt it.

Whatever was out there was making its first move.

Macy looked at the ground, picking out Tolen's huge footprints. She searched nearby and her stomach lurched. A smaller set of barely visible footprints were in line with Tolen's. Only Lafar were light enough on their feet to leave so small a trace.

Nova!

Nova was with Tolen. She was leading him away from the camp, away from safety.

Nova does not care for him.

Heat surged in her chest—the scent of eucalyptus and roses filled the air. She tugged three pouches from her belt. It was time to figure out exactly what that elf was up to.

Nova thinks she's something special. Well, she's about to see what it's like to be hunted by a Chosen.

She poured herbs from the pouches into her hand before returning them to her belt. "Journey go back to camp. Get help."

The little badger snorted and glanced toward the forest. "Go now! Please!" The badger snorted once more and took off back toward the camp. Macy closed her eyes briefly, took a deep breath, and ran. When she passed the guards all they felt was a swift breeze, all they saw was the flutter of leaves tossed up by her racing feet.

CHAPTER 14

THE DOOR TO THE SHADOW REALM

Tolen felt the immense vulnerability the instant they passed through the safety of Jonas' shield; he hadn't even realized the extent of the protection and safety he'd been subconsciously aware of until it was no longer there. His own shield became heavier, harder to hold. His imagination called up an image of himself, holding a heavy iron shield above his body as he ran, getting lower and lower, pressed upon by a wall of darkness determined to crush him.

"Nova. Nova, wait. Stop. I need a minute."

She paused and turned around, her eyes angry. "We don't have a minute." She pointed at the faint light of dawn barely visible in the night sky.

"It's a lot harder than I thought," he panted. "Holding my shield." Tolen shook his head as little lights popped before his eyes. They were only about a mile from camp, maybe he could let it go for a minute. He took a slow breath, trying to fill his lungs and calm his racing heart at the same time. Was he crazy to think he could actually do this?

Nova glanced around and walked up to stand next to him. "The link is only about another half mile. I guess we can rest for a few minutes." She handed him a canteen.

He took it gratefully and drank nearly every drop. "Will there be guards at the link? How do I find the prison once I get inside?" He was starting to see gaping holes in his not-very-well-thought-out-plan. He was still determined to go through with it, but he needed as much information as she could give him.

Nova took the canteen and hung it back on her pack. "Dark Links are almost always guarded by Ookra—small, but fierce creatures, and Kreydawn—stupid, mindless, demon slaves controlled by Suppressors. There will be a lot of them, but I'll keep them distracted at the link while you sneak inside. I've never been in the Dark Realm before, but the legends of the Shadow Prison make it sound like it's pretty huge. I'm sure you'll know it when you see it. You're going to have to figure the rest out on your own," she added without remorse. It was amazing how much her cruel new attitude marred her beauty.

Tolen looked away from her hate-filled eyes, squared his shoulders, and dropped his shield. It was almost as if someone had turned off the sun, his eyes went dark and he could hardly breathe.

"What are you doing?" Nova shouted.

Her voice sounded far away. Tolen fought to pull air into his lungs, fought to bring back his shield. He had no idea how long it took before he felt it fall back into place, and for the light to return, but Nova looked furious when he could focus on her again.

"That was stupid," she said through her teeth.

"No, it was necessary." He waved his hand. "Let's go."

ooo

Macy lifted a clump of leaves to her nose and closed her eyes.

Tolen and Nova had followed the river until it reached the fork and then…her eyes snapped open. They turned northwest. Toward the coast. Toward the darkness they'd all felt growing.

Jonas would send someone after them as soon as he discovered they were gone. Hopefully Journey had understood Macy's plea and would speed up that process even more.

She'd left her jacket in the spot where Nova and Tolen had crossed the river a little ways back, and using some of her crushed herbs, burned the Kunamin symbol into the ground beside it. Now she dropped more herbs, set them on fire, and watched until they burned the symbol into the soft undergrowth next to the bank, signaling whoever might be following that their path had changed. She took a drink from her canteen and started to run again.

ooo

"How did you find this place?" Tolen asked as their steps slowed and he could feel the evil growing. They were getting close.

"I try to escape the camp whenever I can get away with it. I followed Incrah out here once."

Tolen remembered his strange dreams where Incrah stood over him with a look of hatred on his face. He shook his head. It was a dream. He knew Incrah's character, but he was starting to wonder about Nova. Was she really leading him here because she just wanted him away from the camp, away from her family? Or was it something else? He paused when the hairs on his neck stood up.

She looked back at him. "What now?"

"Whose side are you on Nova?"

Her eyes narrowed. "What are you talking about?"

"What's the real reason you brought me out here?" He took a step back. Yes, he was meant to go in there and try to save his father, but not by walking right into a trap.

"Tolen, knock it off." She watched his feet and talked fast, a hint of panic in her tone. "If I was on the side of the Dark, you'd know. I'd look like the Daklafar. I'm just trying to protect my family."

Tolen paused with his foot in the air. If what she'd said about the Daklafar was true…He lowered his foot, bumped into a tree and side-stepped, keeping his eyes on Nova. "You may not look like the Daklafar, but you do have a reason to make a deal with the Dark. What's going to be waiting for me on the other side of that link, Nova?"

"I—I don't—"

Ty'hika, " he said, his eyes locked on hers. Suddenly her horrifying plan fell into his mind. He saw her kneeling at the feet of the creature that had haunted his nightmares—the red-skinned, yellow-eyed demon, who had seemed so familiar. "You offered me as trade for your parents." Tolen's blue eye dilated, zooming in on Nova's face as her eyes widened in shock.

Her knees trembled. "How-How do you know?"

He pointed to his blue eye. "I'm the Ninth Chosen, remember?"

"Tolen, I—"

He saw something else in her thoughts. Despair. She truly did want to protect her family. She did want to save her parents. Her motives were pure, but her methods were terrifyingly flawed. "Nova, come back with me. Jonas can help you."

"You don't understand!" She grabbed handfuls of her hair, ripping it loose from the braid. "I can't go back. I told you about the promises to the Dark. I made the promise before I knew you. Before I saw that maybe, just maybe, you really could save us. I followed Incrah and a few other warriors here the day after you came. Jonas had felt a shift in the Balance, and told them a door was being opened to the Shadow Realm and he wanted them to find where it was. I wanted to know, I *needed* to know what happened to my parents, but no one would help me. No one here trusts us. No one cares what we've been through. I'm so tired of the nightmares and never knowing the truth…" She took a deep shuddering breath and Tolen realized everything she'd said about her brother was actually about herself. She was the reason her guardians had brought her here. They were trying to help *her*.

"I snuck back to the link that night—it wasn't open yet, just a blue shimmer in the rocks, but the Demon Master sensed me there and forced his way into my head. He hurt me. He…showed me my parents. They were slaves. Tortured, beaten. He said he would forgive them and give them back their lives if I helped him. I had to, Tolen!" Her voice was shrill, wild. "Can't you see I had to?"

She stretched out her hands, fingers curved like claws. "After I saw how powerful you were becoming I wanted to take it back, see if *you* would help me save them, but I was in too deep. I want my family back!"

Tolen glanced over Nova's head. Any minute this place could be crawling with Dark servants. "You have no idea how much I understand your desire to save your parents, but you've made a huge mistake." He looked over her head again and held out his hand. "Come on, let's get back to Jonas. We'll figure this out."

She thrashed her head side to side. "I tried to get Jonas to help me. I tried to get my brother, Quasar, and Nebula to help me, but they wouldn't. They definitely won't help me now, not after what I've done. I will be tried as a traitor and sentenced to death if I go back."

Tolen clenched his teeth. "Not if I can help it. Come on. I promise I'll help you." He stepped back a few more feet and motioned with his hand.

Her face crumpled. "I can't." She grabbed the sides of her head, and fell to her side on the ground.

Tolen rushed to her side. "Nova?"

"Tolen, go! Run! They're here!" She screamed in pain and her arms and legs started to shake. Tolen tried to hold onto her but she kicked him away.

The side of a large pile of boulders fifty feet ahead began to glow bright blue—the blue of Tolen's nightmares. A shimmering crack appeared, sending a cascade of broken stone across the ground, and thick black mist seeped out. Screams and anguished cries emanated out of the mist as it curled along the dirt toward him. Piercing cold sank straight into his heart. Strength left his body, darkness covered his eyes, and all sound left his ears.

Shadow Wraiths.

This was nothing like what he'd felt as they'd ran from them to the Binithan. This was death—this was what it felt like to die.

Pain, so much pain.

Tolen called heat to his palms, the air swirled with the scent of cloves and earth, but the effort to hold the heat made him stagger. He shot two fireballs toward the approaching mist, but it had no effect. As soon as the flame hit the mist, it went out with a sizzle.

He called up huge swarms of rocks and willed them toward the fissure, trying to seal it off, but as soon as they hit the opening, they crumbled to dust.

His breath came in gasps and he fell to his knees. The effort to maintain his shield and use his gifts against the prevailing evil was too much. He felt his shield drop and suddenly it was as if he were on fire and a thousand knives were being shoved into his burning flesh, and his mind, his mind….

Black thoughts and dark dreams ran like a looped film over and over: his mother's sacrifice; Dane's death; Elryn's death; Bastian dying; and the image of his father's emaciated and lifeless body.

Every fear he ever had flowed through his thoughts, crippling him, stealing away every good memory. He exerted every effort, every thought, to the trees surrounding him. *Help me!* A trio of branches lowered and Tolen tried to climb on, but he had no strength. He rolled over and the branches curled under him. He could feel the tree trying to pull him out of the mist, but the branches creaked and cracked with exertion. The force of evil was too much for the tree.

A cruel harsh voice rang through Tolen's mind and he gripped the sides of his head against the excruciating pain. *I know who you are Tolen Daedal Téloran. You may be the Ninth Chosen, but you cannot defeat me. You cannot save a world so filled with evil—and why would you even want to try?*

Images of heinous crimes committed by humans filled his head and bile rose in Tolen's throat.

The humans are a dreadful, disgusting people; they do not deserve this world. Join me and you will see the world I can create. Fight against me and you will soon realize that I am everything…I know everything…

I know your fears…I can destroy you….

Image after image of the people Tolen loved and cared for flashed across his mind's eye. They were all dead. His mother, his father, Dane, Bastian…*Macy.*

"No!" He screamed, and the tree began to thrash its remaining branches at the mist, but the images only came faster and faster. His father rotting in the Shadow Prison, his mother broken on the ground beside the mangled body of Dane, Bastian bleeding and dying, and Macy. Macy pale and lifeless, covered in her own blood. He saw the Shadow Realm, the prisoners, the agony of life in the Dark. He saw the earth as it would be once the Dark had control.

I am Darsapean, ruler of the Shadow Realm, most high servant of the Dark. Bow to me Chosen one, or watch your love die…

The image of Macy dead reappeared in front of his eyes.

It was so real, so very real, almost as if he could reach out and touch her lifeless face.

His stomach turned. *In the name of Light please make it stop* . "No! Not Macy! Stop! Stop!"

Bow to me!

The tree holding Tolen suddenly burst into a million pieces and he was falling, falling into the misty black tentacles of the Shadows.

FIRE AND LIGHT

MACY'S LUNGS BURNED AS SHE MOVED THROUGH THE FOREST—NOT only from the effort to keep up her speed, but also from the strength of the Kuna building inside her.

The farther she passed beyond Jonas's shield the heavier the dread in her heart became. She was running toward a growing evil. Something was very, very wrong. Why was Nova taking him right toward the evil? What was she trying to do? Hand him over to the Dark? She caught a whiff of eucalyptus and roses at the thought and paused briefly to focus. She was using too much strength to run and aid her eyes in the dark; she needed to save her strength so she could call on her gift if she had to. If Nova really was trying to get him killed, she was going to have to go through Macy first—if she could get there in time!

She twisted the cap off her canteen and lifted it to her lips for a quick swallow. Suddenly, something strong and horribly familiar shifted the Balance. Cold fear washed over her and she dropped the canteen—the water gurgled out into the dirt.

She ran to the nearest tree, pushed her back into the bark, and looked around. "*To' konsh'la.*" Every tiny noise in the forest intensified.

A woman's scream carried from somewhere far in the distance—Macy edged around the tree and looked toward the sound. A blue light flickered faintly through a thick copse of trees.

Another scream, this one louder, more drawn out. Nova?

Another sound, this one filled with so much pain it made her knees buckle—it was the same moan of the dying she'd heard as she'd been carried from her home by Bastian. But this time it wasn't her parents being tortured by the Shadows.

It was Tolen.

"No! Not Macy—!" A huge explosion cut off Tolen's scream.

Macy's heart slammed in her chest.

A faint rustle nearby—three Raksasha jumped from behind the trees, their screeches deafening to her enhanced hearing.

A thousand emotions ripped through her.

I can't let him die! I WON'T!

She pulled three stones from her belt and threw them one by one toward the Raksasha. "*Mig'nata!*"

The stones hit their mark, one right after the other. All three Raksasha fell, dead before they hit the ground, their skulls shattered.

Macy ran forward, pushing her strength to her legs, feeling more Raksasha trailing her. She rubbed her palms together as she broke through the trees and stumbled over something on the ground.

Nova. Dead.

The Shadows' mist curled along the ground, over Nova's body and toward Macy.

Suddenly everything turned black, the darkness too thick to see through even with enhanced sight. The blackness licked at her conscious and tugged at her heart, she could feel herself falling under the power of the Wraiths.

"Tolen!" She fell to her knees and scrambled along the ground through the black. Sharp sticks and thick chunks of what felt like bark cut her hands as she crawled. Finally, her hand met flesh, it was cold and trembling, but she knew it was him.

"Tolen." She felt something warm and sticky on his face and arms.

Her breathing hitched as she felt his chest. It was moving.

Barely.

"Tolen! Don't you die on me! Don't you dare let them take you!"

She could just make out his eyes through the fog as they opened and locked on her face—but the look was dazed, almost deranged, his face covered in bloody scratches. "Tolen! Tolen, hang on! I'm going to get you out of here." She had no idea how badly he was injured, if it was even safe to try and move him, but they couldn't stay here or they would both die.

The heavy blackness curled over them, choking the air from her lungs. The tortured cries of stolen souls burned in her ears. She fell forward across Tolen's chest. His eyes rolled back in his head, his breath rattled once and stopped. Black tentacles wrapped around his body.

"NO!" Macy gripped his arms and laid across his chest trying to hold on to him, but she was too weak, the Dark was going to take him.

Pain ripped through her, not pain caused by the Shadows, but the crippling, heart-breaking pain of loss.

Dead or alive the Dark could not have him.

Scalding heat coursed through her veins and her chest burned as if someone shoved a branding iron through her heart.

The Kuna within her built stronger and stronger. She let it grow hotter and hotter until it felt as if she were trying to hold back burning lava with her bare hands.

"HE. IS. *MINE!*" Heat scorched her throat as she screamed. "*MI'NOHA!*"

The energy that shot from her palms went off like a nuclear explosion. The forest glowed brighter than daylight. Unnatural screams howled through the air as the fire ripped through the Shadow mist and ignited everything in view.

Trees broke in half from the impact. Rocks exploded and melted. Thick bushes and patches of grass blackened to ash instantly. The skeletal bodies of Raksasha burst into flames, their dusty remains carried away on the fierce wind.

She held tightly to Tolen's body waiting for them to burn—at least they would die together. As the fire around them grew, she could see some sort of transparent bubble had formed around them, protecting their bodies from the destruction taking place. Flame licked at the edges of their cocoon as everything burned.

It seemed to rage on forever before the bubble burst and the dying heat washed across Macy's face. She held Tolen on a raised piece of undamaged ground surrounded by a barren cavity of burning stubble at least a half mile wide.

Not a single form of life aside from them remained. Ash and dust rained down from the sky. Behind the cloud of ash, pink light grazed the horizon.

Tolen took a shuddering breath, but his eyes remained closed.

Macy took a deep breath of her own and looked around.

They were alone.

CHAPTER 16

WAKING UP

"I'm trying Areen. By the Light, I swear I am trying!" He tucked the picture back in his pocket and lifted his pack higher on his shoulder. Peering from his vantage point within the trees, he waited.

He didn't have to wait long.

He'd staked the area out for nearly a week. An almost imperceptible tremor in the Balance here meant he had to be close…so close…

The earth shifted slightly and a crack in the rock face before him glowed gold. He rushed forward and ran his hand along the rock. It opened slowly, painfully slow. He caught a glimpse of the Mountains of Promise and the first rising pillar of the citadel. His heart pounded. He was almost there.

The link began to close with an angry hiss.

"No!" Daedal rushed forward.

"You are no longer worthy to come through, Daedal Téloran." The joined voices of the Guardians spoke in unison. "You have forsaken that right."

"Wait! Wait, you have to listen to me, please!" The link was closing faster, the light fading. "PLEASE!" Daedal shoved his hand through the link and felt the flesh burning from his fingers. "Ahh!" He pulled his bloody hand from the crack just before the link sealed itself.

Wrinkles lined Daedal's eyes and mouth. The photograph he held in his scarred hand was rumpled and faded.

"I'm still trying." He buried his face in his hands, "and I'm still failing."

His son's shard burned against his flesh and he pulled it from beneath his shirt. White light burst from the crystal and it split in two. Daedal stared in shock as the second shard disappeared in a trail of light—

The second shard flew through the air toward a house, a small, pale yellow house with white shutters and a cozy wrap-around porch. An old tire swing hanging from a tall oak in the back yard twirled and clanked in the rain and wind. Children's toys lay scattered across the soggy yard. The gale pushed against the shard but it wasn't thwarted from its goal. It burst through a thin pane of glass in the back door, twisted and turned through the house, rushing straight into the outstretched hand of a tiny blonde little girl.

Thick black mist swallowed the house. Tortured screams filled the air. A huge white-haired man, with a machete strapped to his back, ran from the house carrying the girl in his arms. His eyes flashed bright blue in the glow of the streetlight as he lowered her into his car—

Daedal's hair was streaked with gray that fell in straggly waves past his shoulders. His thick beard was mottled with white. His determined eyes stared across the vast ocean before him. Thick black billowing clouds covered the sky. Lightning flashed and thunder boomed.

This was no ordinary storm.

Life in the empty void of relentless pursuit had taken its toll. Sixteen years he'd traveled the world watching, waiting, seeking, searching for a way to change his son's destiny—but his efforts had yielded nothing.

He'd failed them.

Tolen's shard drew in darkness wherever Daedal went. His own strength weakened as the crystal's power continued to grow. The effort to prevent it from pursuing its destiny was draining him of nearly all the power he had.

Daedal closed his eyes and wrapped his fist around his son's shard.

"I do not agree with your decision." He spoke aloud to the sky. "I did not want this fate for my son." His body trembled. "But I realize now that had I allowed it to take its course, I could have helped him, lessened his burden. I fear I have only made things worse for him. I have not been able to feel them, which

tells me Areen is still shielding them both and maintaining her promise to me. Tolen likely knows nothing of who he really is." He fell to his knees on the rocky shore.

"He is the Ninth Chosen. His shard revealed this truth to me, yet I let my pride, my fear, and my anger toward the Guardians blind me from what was best. The Ninth is needed. I see it every day. I see the need for him, for my son. I did not want to sacrifice him, to hand him over to the Guardians when I had yet to even know him." He lowered his head.

"I have spent so much of his life on the path to try to keep him, and in doing so lost him completely. I do not know my own son—" his voice caught. "I cannot know if forgiveness would have come to Areen and I had we turned Tolen over to them for the sake of the greater good. I see now that as much as I love the son I do not know, that is how much the Light loves all of its creations.

"I should have trusted in the Light. I should have known that all things would be made right. The Balance chose my son for a reason and I no longer believe that reason was a punishment, but rather because my son was exactly what this world would need and he had the parents who could show him the path."

Daedal collapsed and tears leaked from his closed eyes. "Please, please forgive me. Forgive us. Areen, I'm so very sorry." He pulled Tolen's shard from around his neck, untied the cord, and held it in the palm of his hand. He dropped his shield and waited.

Thunder boomed.

"Go ahead. Come for me." He clenched his teeth and opened his hand. "You'll never find him."

With a crack of thunder and a burst of light, the shard was gone and the Shadows held Daedal in their black mist.

Tolen mumbled in his sleep and his face contorted in pain.

Macy had been cradling his head in her lap for the last several hours, singing as much as she could remember from the healing songs of the Hidden off and on, trying all the methods she could think of that Bastian had taught her to help Tolen come back, but he wasn't.

She moved carefully, trying not to jostle him, so she could soak the piece of material she'd ripped off her pack in more Lucid, and put it back on his forehead. His fever had spiked again, even with the herbs.

Sunlight poured into the cave through the tangled web of branches she'd quickly fashioned to cover the entrance. Tolen's beat up watch told her it was close to noon, she couldn't see her own as it was on the arm buried beneath his head.

She fought against growing panic. Jonas should have found them by now. Something must have gone wrong. She could feel the Dark's vibes nearby, too close, and as soon as night was upon them they would come. They needed help. Her shield was in place, but the Dark knew where they were, she was sure of it. The amount of power she'd displayed would have caused a huge ripple in the Balance—one more reason Jonas should have found them. Something had to be horribly wrong back at the camp.

She moved her hand back to Tolen's chest, her opposite hand still cradling his head. The shallow rise and fall of his chest, and the occasional moan, the only indication he was still here in some form. She could barely feel his life force vibrations despite the fact that he was too weak to shield. The reason for this scared her more than any Dark creature ever had—he was hovering so close to death that his life force was too weak to affect the Balance. She tried to shake off the morbid thought, but she wasn't sure how long he would hold on, which made the idea of just sitting and waiting for someone to rescue them seem stupid. But she knew she'd never be able to carry him all the way back to camp before nightfall—and would the camp even be there if she tried? Not to mention she had no idea just how many broken bones he had and moving him could just kill him faster. She already feared she'd added to his injuries by dragging him the short distance to this cave. A wave of nausea followed the thought.

Bastian, what do I do?

Do not give up, LaUnahi.

"Tolen, please wake up, please, please!" She dipped her finger in Lucid and ran it across his cracked lips.

"M-Macy ?" His lips trembled beneath her fingers.

"Oh my hill," she jumped and then felt guilty when he grimaced.

"Sorry! Come on, wake up, please!"

His eyelids fluttered, "Macy?"

"Tolen? Tolen, are you okay?"

Tolen started to reach up to touch his head, but dropped his hand back to his side, curled it into a fist, and gave a slow nod.

"Good. It's about time you woke up." Fear and relief pounded through her so powerfully she felt light headed.

He chuckled and then groaned.

She took his clenched fist and started to sing again softly. She was sure she wasn't getting all the words right, but the crease between Tolen's eyebrows smoothed out and his fist relaxed.

"Thank you," he whispered, his voice barely audible, his eyes closed.

Keep him talking. Keep him awake… Bastian warned.

She adjusted the rag on his forehead. "Hey, you're in pretty bad shape. Do you think you can heal yourself?"

His breathing slowed and for a moment she feared he'd passed back out. She was about to nudge him gently when he barely shook his head. "I can't— I don't f-feel any warmth." The effort to say that much seemed to drain him.

Macy's heart fluttered painfully. "It's okay. I'm sure Jonas will find us soon."

"Liar."

She looked down to see him studying her face.

Macy ran her fingers through her tangled hair and met his eyes, knowing it would do no good to hide the truth of their circumstances from him, but not wanting to cause him worry that would further weaken him either. She took a deep breath. "They should have found us by now. I left a trail when I came after you so they could. Something must have happened at camp that's stopping them. I would have tried to get you back on my own, but you're in *really* bad shape…"

She fumbled with the rag and spoke quickly. "You've got at least three broken ribs, I tried to wrap them, but I'm not sure I did a very good job. You've got a nasty cut on the back of your head. I taped it shut best I could. You kept thrashing in your sleep, that's why your head is in my lap, because if you move very much it starts bleeding again. I think your right arm might be broken. You've got a bunch of small cuts all over that I cleaned as well as I could, and I'm sure you're covered in deep bruises…" She trailed off, not thrilled with reliving how bad he'd looked as she'd sat here in the growing daylight and tried to patch him up.

"And?" he whispered.

Her eyes snapped to his. "It's the wounds I can't see, the ones inflicted by the Shadows that worry me the most. They take the longest to heal. Bastian always said the wounds caused by emotional weapons do damage that can't be healed with herbs and medicine. Harm to the life force is a lot worse than harm to the mortal body. That's why the Shadows are so terrible. I think that's also why you can't access your gifts yet. Once we get you back to Jonas, he can help you better than I can."

She could still see a glimmer of the Shadows' pain in Tolen's eyes.

"I never truly appreciated your fear of the Shadows before now." He took a slow breath. "I felt them in California, but this was so much different, so…" He swallowed and squeezed his eyes shut.

"I know." She dipped the rag in the mixture again and put it back on his forehead.

"Thanks." Tolen tried to roll over and she held him down as the color drained from his face .

"Whoa, I wouldn't do that if I were you. Here, drink." She dripped more Lucid in his mouth.

He swallowed and took a few shallow breaths. "Nova. She's gone isn't she?" He paused, and closed his eyes again. "How did you…? How did you get us out of there?"

Tears leaked out the corners of her eyes and she scrubbed them away with her fists before Tolen opened his eyes again, his expression full of dread and yet pleading for answers.

She bit her lip. "Yes. She's dead. I'm so sorry Tolen. I was too late. I followed you and Nova when I felt you take off your shard. When I finally caught up to you…I-I heard you being tortured by the Shadows. Nova was on the ground, already dead. The Shadows were everywhere. Raksasha surrounded us. I had no idea how many other Dark creatures were coming. You were dying. I…I don't know what happened. My Kuna just exploded out of me. I leveled everything. Nothing survived except us. When it was over, Nova's body was gone…" She trailed off in a whisper, her chest tight.

"Macy?" She felt his head turn up toward her, but she couldn't bring herself to look at him.

"This whole mess is my fault—Nova warned me the Dark was coming to attack the camp to get to me. She said Jonas knew they were around, but it was kept from me. I hoped that if I left the Dark would follow me and leave the camp alone. I even dropped my shield so they would know I'd left, but…it was a trap." His breathing increased. "Nova had it planned the whole time—she'd made a deal with the Dark to hand me over. She tricked me. I'm sure the attack on the camp was planned as well. She'd told the Dark the Dominants were there…"

Heat flooded Macy's chest. "Tolen, it's not your fault. No one is to blame but Nova for her death. I never trusted her from the beginning." She looked down to see him staring at the roof of the cave.

He shook his head. "There's so much more to it than that. She wasn't evil."

Macy scoffed.

"It's true. Her reasons for her treachery were grounded in love and loss. It was her plans to get what she wanted that were messed up."

Macy's eyes narrowed.

Tolen took a deep breath and started to explain. He told of Nova's past, the Lafar battle, the loss of her parents, the pact with the Dark to try and get them back, "…by the time she realized her mistake she was in too deep. She tried to save me in the end—told me to run." He closed his eyes and licked his lips.

A thousand emotions were circulating through Macy's body. Hatred, fury, pain, guilt, and something else she didn't want to feel—pity. Tolen's next sentence pulled her from her thoughts.

"I can't believe after everything I said to you, after what you *think* you saw happen…I can't believe you still came after me. I don't know how to thank you. I owe you my life."

Her mouth lifted a tiny bit. "You saved me in the Lava Beds."

His eyes got the tiniest sparkle. "So we're even?"

"No way. You're not that cool yet, buddy." They chuckled softly, but it was short lived. Their situation was too dire, the experience too heart-breaking to really laugh.

"Macy, about what you saw—"

Macy held up her hand. "It's okay, Tolen. I know you didn't kiss her back."

A crease formed between his eyes. "You could tell?"

She nodded.

He sighed. "I'm sorry for telling you to leave, for saying I didn't need you." He waved a trembling hand over his body. "Obviously I do."

She shrugged. "I'm sorry for saying I hated you." *Because I don't, not even a little bit.*

The corner of his mouth lifted in a tiny smile.

CHAPTER 17

DESTINY

They were silent for a time and Tolen had to fight the desire to sleep. He could feel it, deep within his aching body, that sleep was a bad idea. His mind ran through all that had happened. Despite the fact that he'd moved away from the camp, he'd still left them in danger. He hated to think what could be happening back there while he lay here unable to help.

"Can I ask," Macy's nervous tone pulled him back into the conversation. "Why…?" she cleared her throat. "Why *were* you with Nova last night?"

Tolen reached back to take her hand—ignoring the stabbing pain shooting through his side—and thankfully she let him. She had no idea how much her presence, her one hand under his head, the other gently squeezing his fingers, comforted him, distracted him from the pain, not even the incredible pain medicine—the Soreah—they'd given him back in the Binithan could compare.

"I had the nightmare of my father again last night. I couldn't go back to sleep. I'd decided I was going to ask Jonas today to help me go after him, and if he refused, I was going to beg you to help." He swallowed the pain that came with this thought. The condition he was in now…how long before he'd even be in shape to go after his father, and what about the Radia Warriors, what was happening to them, all those people—families—back at the camp?

Macy squeezed his hand softly. "I would have."

He shook his head. The movement sent lights popping before his eyes. "It doesn't matter now." He sighed. "When I got to the river Nova was already there. I never planned to meet her. I was frustrated she was there, but she has a way of being so, I dunno, *kind*, if not a little annoying." The corner of his mouth lifted in a sad smile as he peeked up into Macy's face. "She offered to show me the door to the Shadow Realm…She had such a difficult life…It might be wrong to say, but I think in a way her death is a mercy."

Macy's eyebrows rose but she nodded. "I guess that's true. She's saved from a life of servitude for the Dark, or a death sentence here for her crimes. Wherever she is now, I'm sure she sees that."

Tolen nodded. "Thank you again, Macy, for facing the Shadows and saving my life. I can't imagine what it must have been like for you. I'm so sorry you had to go through that. I've made so many mistakes, I have so many lives on my head, I don't know how I'm ever going to make up for it."

Macy touched his chin and fire shot through his chest, warm, healing, fire. "It's the Dark who's to blame Tolen, not you. They are the cause of all this." She waved her hand in the air. "Forget the past. You can't change what happened—you said that to me remember? Become the Ninth. Show the Dark what you are capable of. Stop them."

A heavy weight settled in his stomach. "I won't be doing anything for awhile—and if we're not rescued by nightfall—"

"They'll come."

Tolen sensed the lie again, but didn't reply. It was a hope they both needed. "Why did you come after me?"

She broke his gaze and warmth crept into her cheeks. She started tracing her finger in the dirt. "I wasn't going to. I was really, really angry and then…I felt you take off your shard." She touched it where it hung around his neck.

He fingered it with surprise.

"I was ready to leave you to whatever you and Nova were up to, then I heard Bastian's voice…" She paused and he wondered what she wasn't saying, but her thoughts weren't focused on what she didn't want him to know. "I made myself stop and think about the reason why Bastian and I were picked to find you. The Balance never does anything without a purpose."

Her next words tumbled out in a rush. "I should have been fair to you and looked deeper, but I was too stubborn. I've been a total schmuck—pretty much since the day we met. I was selfish and scared. The idea of the Ninth terrified me, but I was more afraid of the way you made me feel, of being drawn to you when I didn't want to be close to anyone…" Her blush deepened and she turned her head away from him.

"Macy, please, look at me." He squeezed her hand and waited until she glanced his way. His heart started a painful rhythm in his chest. It was time to tell her, get her to see, and hope this time she'd really listen. "There's something we really need to talk about. I've wanted to talk to you about it for awhile, I tried that night by the river, and I thought I'd lost my chance—"

She shook her head. "No, Tolen. I know what drew me to you. I was right, I'm drawn to you because of our Chosen duty, and when I remembered the prophecy it proved it."

Tolen's fingers twitched. "What are you talking about?"

She looked down at him. "What are *you* talking about?"

His mouth opened and closed. "Something totally different, I think, but we'll get to that in a minute. What do you mean about the prophecy? How does it prove we're only drawn to each other because of duty?"

She took a deep breath. "*Eight there are and the Ninth shall lead them with Light's Aid beside…*"

His mouth turned down in confusion. "O…kay. I've heard the first part. *Eight there are and the Ninth shall lead them*—what does it have to do with us?"

"My name means 'helper of light' in some ancient language." She looked him in the eye. "I *am* Light's Aid. I'm meant to help you in the Final Battle. We're drawn to each other so strongly, not because we're Chosen, but because we're both part of the prophecy. That's why your shard went to my Watcher and not the Guardians or anyone else. The Balance was making sure we'd meet even though your parents had messed with your destiny."

Tolen's stomach clenched and he tightened his fingers over hers. "You're meant to fight with me?"

Macy leaned back. "You don't look very happy about that fact."

"Actually I'm very happy that the Balance brought us together, but I'm supposed to like the idea that you're meant to be in the middle of the Final Battle?" He chuckled once. "Sorry."

"Oh don't go all chauvinistic on me. You know dang well I can handle my own."

"I can't help it. I want to protect you." It sounded stupid, but it was true.

A smile lit her eyes even though she tried to glare. "Whatever. Together or not I'd still be in the Final Battle. Your turn. What did you want to talk about?"

He started to lift himself up, she protested, and he held up a finger. "Please?" She raised an eyebrow as sweat broke out on his forehead. "I might need…a little help, maybe?"

She shook her head, but gently pushed her hands under his shoulders and pushed him up. He had to hold back a moan as the pain shot through his body. Stars winked behind his lids as she helped situate him against the cave wall. It took a few moments for his surroundings to stop spinning and he had to really concentrate to keep from passing out. He'd never felt so weak and helpless in his life. What had the Shadows done to him? He was beginning to understand what Ardia had said about how they took all that you were until nothing was left, and you became a wraith like them. He felt thin and wispy, like a gust of wind could finish him off.

"That really wasn't a good idea." She held the cup of Lucid to his lips and helped him sip. He sat there with his eyes closed as she wiped the sheen of sweat off his face.

"I was sick of looking at you upside down."

"And people say *I'm* stubborn," she mumbled.

He gave a tiny shrug and fiddled with his bloodstained shirt, suddenly nervous. "So, we're both part of this mysterious prophecy?"

She nodded.

"Do you know all of it?" He looked up and met her eyes briefly.

"Not word for word," she shook her head. "Just bits and pieces. I was never very good at paying attention to Bastian's history lessons. Only that one line stuck. I guess we know why."

He nodded absently. "Can I ask you something?"

"Sure."

"Have you ever met any other Chosen?"

"Yeah, a few."

"And did you feel drawn to them the way you do me?"

Macy took a deep breath, he could see she wasn't sure where he was going. "No. With them it was just a feeling of familiarity. Like they were long lost friends or relatives. Something like that. It doesn't matter though. Of course it's not the same with them. The prophecy is why it's different for us."

"I get why you think that. But there's more to it…" He ran a hand over his eyes. How could he explain so she would understand? "I told you how when I sense your thoughts it's different than when I sense other people's. Your thoughts are pushed into my mind as if *you* put them there. I don't seek them out." He took a shaky breath that felt like shards of glass pushing through his side. "That makes sense now that we are meant to be a team. It will help us work together more flawlessly. But there's more, something apart from that. Something that has nothing to do with being Chosen or the Prophecy.

"When we talked by the river I tried to explain the other thing I felt growing between us, but you were convinced it was just hormones confusing duty with attraction—and I can see you still believe that—but I've felt for awhile now that there was something bigger between us, no matter what you said. Yes, the way I'm drawn to you so powerfully does fit with the prophecy. But it's not the strongest pull I feel…" he trailed off.

Macy bit her lip. "Don't you see though? It doesn't matter. The other pull, even if you think it's stronger, it can't happen." He could feel the hope in her fighting with the argument she was trying to give. Her hope fed his hope that if he could explain it right, she would see.

"Macy, how can this not be right?" He took her hand again, but this time he flipped it over, and traced the lines of her palm, along her wrist, and up her arm. Warmth zinged straight to his heart and he felt the Kuna heat up in her skin under his fingers. Her breathing increased in time with his as he raised his fingers to trace the side of her face stopping just beside her lips. "I'm new to the Hidden world, and you're right, I don't understand the Balance as you do. I've spent my life trying to ignore the Hidden side of myself, always seeking to connect to a human side that never really existed. But that life-long practice made it easier for me to separate the strong pull of my gifts, my duties, and my destiny, from the quieter pull of my heart.

"*This* feeling is all me. It's the clearest, most powerful feeling I've ever had, stronger than all my gifts combined. I *know* it's not because of a prophecy, it's not a duty. It's me. It's what *I* want. To be with you this way is *my* choice." He paused to look in her eyes. His blue eye started dilating like crazy, rushes of images flashed across his vision and he felt a flare of his gifts starting to return. "And I know with every part of my soul, life force, or whatever you want to call it, that it *is* right."

He pulled his hand back to cup her cheek. "I know you've guarded your heart for a long time so I don't expect you to completely understand, but in your thoughts I sensed you have the same feelings for me that I do for you, but they scare you so you fight them. I'm prepared to wait for you, until you're ready, until you're no longer afraid." He lowered his hand and wrapped her fingers in his. "We may be a prophesied *team*, but that's not the reason *I* want to be with you."

His heart pounded in rhythm with her thoughts as they filled his mind. She sensed the truth in his words, at least the truth the way he saw it, but worried whether it could really work between them. They were different. Human and Hidden. Did she even want to try? Everyone she'd given a piece of her heart to she'd lost. Could she stand to give her heart to him, really let him in, even deeper than she'd been starting to, just to lose him as they pursued their destinies? Was it really the right thing to do, no matter what she felt?

She looked back into his eyes and fire heated his chest. His Kuna had returned.

"I-I don't know what to say." She looked down at their hands.

"Just say you'll give me a chance. Let me try to deserve you."

Her next thoughts made his heart soar and something settled in his chest—another gift had returned, but he was too focused on her thoughts to know which one. *He's got it all backwards. I don't deserve him.* Her thoughts shifted to what she'd shouted at the Shadows as they'd nearly taken him from her. *He. Is. MINE!* Whether she felt comfortable admitting it or not, she had staked her claim in that moment as she faced losing him forever. She didn't want to share him with anyone else.

He couldn't hold back a tiny smile. "Macy, you don't have to stake a claim on what is already yours." Pink stained her cheeks as she realized he'd heard her thoughts.

○○○

Tolen leaned forward, but this time she was the one to close the gap, unable to stop the need, her heart pulling her toward a dream she never imagined was possible, a hope she'd never dared hope for, and a fierce wish that it could be all they ever wanted.

The smell of eucalyptus, roses, cloves, and earth, swirled around their heads. As their lips met, the most blissful, beautiful, warmth rushed from her heart throughout her entire body. It was the exact opposite of the painful burn she felt when her Kuna demanded release. It burned softly and yet somehow more powerfully. It was the sweetest, most intense feeling she'd ever felt. She twisted her fingers in his hair and pulled him closer, trying not to disturb his wound, but barely conscious of what she was doing. Somehow, the needs of her heart, a deep place she had ignored for so long, had taken over.

Tolen responded as if only waiting for her permission.

It was pure *fire*.

Macy's eyes flew open and she jumped back, breathless and embarrassed.

Tolen patted his smoking hair with one hand, and with the other patted her shoulder, the smell of burning cotton filling the small space.

Macy tugged her shirt around until she could just see a single brown hand print, singed into the material, still smoldering slightly. She chuckled. "Huh. Funny."

Tolen laughed so hard she worried about his cracked ribs, but couldn't stop herself from joining in.

She looked up at him and the wonderful warmth tingled through her again. She couldn't stop the desire to move back into his embrace and he leaned forward barely touching his lips to hers. Before they lit each other on fire again, he pulled back slightly. "We just need more practice," he breathed against her mouth.

She smiled, liking the idea more than she knew she should.

Tolen cleared his throat and leaned further back. "Maybe you should try to get some sleep. If Jonas doesn't find us before dark, we could be in for a really long night."

"I probably should regenerate just in case I have to fight." She could tell he didn't like the truth of this statement, but if his gifts didn't come back in time, he'd have to rely on hers. It was just a fact. She bit her lip and looked him over, her cheeks still warm. "Are you sure you'll be okay if I sleep?"

"I don't feel as tired as I did a while ago. I should be good for a couple hours." He opened his arms, but she reached back to grab the Lucid and a small bag of sugar tack.

"Try to eat something while I sleep." She scooted closer to lean gently against his chest. It felt awkward but nice at the same time. "Are you sure this is okay? I don't want to hurt your ribs."

He ran his hand down the length of her hair, along her arm to her elbow until she relaxed against him, her thoughts content, despite the fire still smoldering between them. "I feel great. Get some sleep."

It took a while before she finally felt calm enough to drift off—lost for once in a world full of light and joy, instead of darkness, fighting, and death.

CHAPTER 18

HEALING TRUTHS

Tolen twisted his shard between his fingers as Macy dozed. The pull from it toward her was stronger than ever. It seemed to be literally soaring with the same euphoria he felt in his heart. He felt its forgiveness right after he kissed her—to him just one more proof that their feelings were right.

He gently brushed the hair from her face. He'd always thought she was pretty—much more so than any girl he'd ever seen—but it amazed him how the more he got to know her, the more he saw into her heart, the more beautiful and irresistible she became to him.

It had come on slowly, in tiny moments from the first day they'd met, the knowledge that *he* was falling for her, not just drawn to her because of some weird outside connection because they were both Chosen. As they sat here and he held her, he knew beyond anything that what he'd told her was true, she was what his heart wanted. He knew it was right, and he hoped she'd give him the chance to prove it.

So much had happened, it made the last few weeks seem like years. The gnawing guilt that had been growing in him since he'd lost his mother and best friend back in Nine Mile canyon had left somewhat in the wake of the vision of his father. Daedal believed in Tolen without even knowing him. He'd felt the depth of his father's love for him. He shouldered the responsibility for Tolen's lack of knowledge and had paid the price so painfully for his choices that Tolen couldn't be angry with him. His father, although not present, had helped him to fully understand and accept that while he couldn't change the past, he had control over his decisions and how they would affect his future.

He wasn't the same boy who'd left a tiny unknown town in Utah scared and angry. The magnitude of his puzzling destiny as the Ninth Chosen still frightened him, but somehow knowing Macy was a part of it kept the fear from being incapacitating, and balanced the need to know everything right now. With *Light's Aid* by his side, he felt like he could go forward into the dark quiet of the unknown and be strong enough for whatever lay ahead. The biggest issue moving forward was the danger this put her in. Destined team mates or not.

He shifted slightly against the wall. Nova's death was a tragedy, as was Macy's stolen childhood and his parents crushed dreams. The way the Dark destroyed lives was unforgivable. As heart wrenching as the last few weeks had been, could he say he wished he'd never learned who he was, his destiny—a destiny he felt he was finally ready to accept?

No, he couldn't. He let his breath out in a long, slow sigh.

He was not going to sit back and let the Dark destroy innocent lives any more. Not if he could do something about it. He'd learned some things while under the Shadows' veil and he knew what he needed to do next.

He still felt exhausted, but there were things to do. He wasn't going to sit here and let the Dark find them. He wouldn't let them hurt Macy. As they'd kissed, he felt the connection to his trigger solidify, and he finally understood what made *Macy* his trigger. It was because they were two halves of one whole. He may be the Ninth Chosen, but without Light's Aid beside him, he was like a car without a motor, a body without a heart. He had all this power, but without a guide, a central force to keep him balanced, the power of the Ninth would not, *could not*, work. His gifts had manifested before he'd ever met her, but they hadn't been fully a part of him until the missing piece was added. It also explained why Macy had been able to use her powers in a way she never had before—once she claimed Tolen as hers. He was likely her trigger too. She just didn't recognize it yet, or the power that came with accepting it.

He hadn't shared this new knowledge with her for fear she would see it as another excuse for their feelings—making them a stronger team. But falling for her was just a blessed perk to an already huge destiny. A choice brought on by circumstance and rightness. Someday she'd see that. He had to believe she would.

He took a deep breath and turned his focus to the growing warmth fighting to come back into his body. He felt the colder pull of the Shadows on his gifts, and it scared him a little. The darkness of the Shadows, the pain inflicted by the images Darsapean had shoved into his mind, kept fighting for place in his thoughts, only Macy's warmth seemed to be holding them back. He somehow knew once he consciously tried to grab hold of his gifts—the light within himself—that the poisoned darkness left by the Shadows would fight back.

"*Lon'adras,*" he whispered, and the effect was instantaneous. Pain, nearly as incapacitating as when he'd been within the Shadow's clutches, coursed through his body. It took all his effort to hold still and not arch his back against the feel of cold flame licking over his skin. His fists clenched by his side, his eyes went dark, and for a moment he feared they had him, that he would be lost in this dark, pain-riddled prison for all eternity— And then he saw it, a light in the darkness beckoning him to return, and a voice, a gentle voice calling his name.

The warmth was slow to come, a trickle not a flow, but powerful as it pushed at the heavy darkness, shoving it from his limbs. He could feel the evil fighting back, desperate to hold on to him, it did not want to leave his body, but it was no match for the light. His shield descended over him as the darkness fled and his gifts began to fully return. Layer by layer he felt his shield strengthening, expanding so easily, so incredibly strong—he felt it move beyond him and over the girl lying against him. His Sphere gift manifested stronger than ever and he instantly knew why. He was calling up the shield and the ability to heal, not for himself, but for someone he was falling in love with. To be a true Sphere one had to be selfless—he could see that now and he knew he couldn't protect her wounded and weak. He needed to be whole, so they could be whole. The reality of this truth felt so amazing—he *couldn't* be whole without her. They balanced each other. Her strengths strengthened his weaknesses. Being with her made him want to be better, stronger, try harder.

With the darkness gone, the warmth could now fill his whole body, flooding his limbs with strength and energy. His ribs shifted back into place, the wounds on his head and arms knitted back together, and a tiny fissure in his right arm fused, but the pain stayed bearable with Macy's warmth against him.

He finally opened his eyes and looked at Macy cradled in his arms, her mouth slightly open, breathing softly. He trailed his fingers lightly over the scratches he could see on her face and arms, somehow knowing how to take the pain into his own body so she wouldn't feel anything—the way his mother had always healed him. He knew he was successful by the way her breathing stayed even, her expression peaceful. He held his hand barely above her heart seeking out injuries he couldn't see, coaxing her cells to realign, heal, strengthen, and push nutrients to her muscles.

It was almost too easy.

When he finished he brushed her cheek gently with his fingers. As the warmth slowly faded, he wanted badly to kiss her again, but he held back. He knew what *he* wanted, but he needed to give her time to consciously accept what he could feel in her thoughts. That she wanted to be with him too.

He glanced out the cave entrance; the light had shifted. It was past midday and time to wake her up.

He looked back down at her—her head on his chest, her hair falling in tangled waves to her waist—and was tempted to ignore the plan taking shape in his head. What he was about to do wasn't safe and he wanted her back in Jonas' care before he made his next move, but he knew she'd never agree.

He took a deep breath and trailed his finger across her lips.

∘∘∘

The dream faded slowly. She clung to it and tried to stay in the warm, safe haven her subconscious had created. She was free to love there, no complicated destinies, duties, or restrictions. But as the dream slipped away and reality settled back into motion like the winding of a clock, she jumped awake and her eyes widened. *Tolen…*

"Tolen!" She patted her hair self-consciously and leaned out of his arms. She cursed her cheeks for giving away her embarrassment again. "How long was I out?"

He touched her chin until she looked back at him. "A couple hours." She could see the warmth in his eyes, the same warmth that had made it impossible not to bridge the gap between them and kiss him earlier. "You're healed." She touched his cheek below his eye to distract him from her thoughts—or maybe to distract herself.

He nodded, and her fingers heated up—not the *I'm-setting-something-on-fire* burn, but the pleasant burn she'd felt when they kissed that filled her whole body with tingling warmth.

She pulled her hand away and he grasped it between his own. There was something else in his eyes, a powerful confidence that sent shivers along her spine. She glanced at her arms as her heart sped up, seeking a diversion. "You healed me too?"

He nodded and her eyes unintentionally flicked to his lips. He leaned forward. The thought came to pull back but she ignored it—he placed a single gentle kiss on her lips, and her resolve snapped. She wrapped her arms around him and buried her face in his neck. He pulled her close, kissed the top of her head, and tears filled her eyes.

"Macy?" He tried to pull her away to look at her but she held tighter. "What's wrong?"

This is so unfair! She cared for him, and she was terrified to lose him. Was it stupid to try to live a lie, to enjoy his kisses, his presence now, only to lose him later to a destiny neither one of them could control?

He brushed her hair off her neck and leaned his face against her cheek so he could whisper in her ear. "McLacy Allicandra Burdow." She sucked in a breath. How did he know her full name? "Bastian told me in the Binithan that no matter what destiny I have in store, I still have a choice. Yes, you are human and I am Hidden-kind, but just because it hasn't been done before doesn't mean we can't choose to try to make it work."

"You don't understand." She kept her face in his neck, not wanting to tell him, but knowing she must. "It has been done before, and bad things happened. It's not allowed. We'd be breaking a Hidden law set from the beginning—look what happened to your parents when they broke a sacred law, look how much their disobedience has hurt your future!"

His hand paused on her hair. "This is right Macy, I know it as much as I know the sun hangs in the sky outside. We'll figure out the details together, I promise."

"How?"

He sighed. "Together."

"Tolen, our destiny—"

"Macy, I *am* the Ninth Chosen and you *are* Light's Aid. Jonas kept referencing puzzle pieces when he talked about us. I thought he was just kinda crazy, but I think I understand what he meant." He paused and her palms tingled as she waited for him to go on. "The prophecy defines a duty we both must fulfill if we want to stop the Dark. But that is just one piece of our lives, not the whole picture. Yes, our choices, all our choices, need to reflect our ultimate destiny to help us reach it, but I don't believe the prophecy says that duty trumps love. Loving you is just another piece of the puzzle that makes up Tolen Parks Téloran, and I honestly believe it only adds beauty to the crazy puzzle of my life."

Her heart stuttered and sped.

"Maybe it doesn't make sense, Macy, but that doesn't make it wrong."

"It doesn't?"

"No."

"But what if—?" She couldn't finish the thought, but he went on and she knew he understood.

"What ifs aren't a reason to not be together Mace. Yes, our roles in the prophecy could end up killing us both." His voice cracked, but his hands didn't pause in stroking her hair. "But I know the way I feel about you won't leave with death, just as your parents still love you, and Bastian still loves you, that will never change. Love is eternal, it bridges death. It can't be stopped. And as scary as it might be to risk it, love is the one thing worth fighting for, worth dying for, worth questioning a Hidden law and things we don't yet understand. Macy I promise you, I will fight for what is right, and being with you is *right*." He squeezed her tighter to him. "I will do all I can to fulfill my destiny as the Ninth, defeat the Dark, and make a world without fear."

Macy wiped her eyes. "That was a good speech."

She felt him shrug and she forced a laugh. He let her keep her face hidden, running his fingers through her hair. She mulled over what he'd said wondering, barely daring to hope, that they really could be together somehow. Could she really stay away from him, even if it was wrong? The way she felt here in his arms, when he kissed her, or touched her in any way, felt like a need as important as breathing. She didn't want to stay away. She wanted him to be part of the puzzle that made up Macy Burdow.

She took a deep breath and he continued to untangle her hair with his fingers as she spoke, her cheek against his collar bone. "The first time I realized you could sense my thoughts I hated it. It was only when I was thinking something about you. It made me feel exposed, almost violated. Now…" she reached her hand up to stroke his cheek, the movement awkward, a surrender. She'd held back her heart for so long she felt self-conscious being bold in this way, terrified, but also *free*. He reached up to hold her hand against his cheek.

"Now?" he prompted.

She looked up into his odd, yet beautiful eyes. "I realize that deep down I've always wanted you to know my thoughts, how I feel about you. Maybe it was subconscious before, but now I choose to share it all with you. I've spent my life thinking I didn't need protection or security from anyone. I never let Bastian coddle me. But with you, I feel safe, *protected*, and I like it." She shook her head. "It's weird, but sort of a relief too." She took a deep breath. "I don't want to fight the way I feel, Tolen. I want to be with you too—even if it isn't right, or until we make it right," she amended at the tightness in his eyes. "If only Bastian could see me now…" She trailed off and he lowered their clasped hands.

"He knows Macy. Bastian knew you loved him, and he loved you so much."

I love you Macy. I always have and I always will. Bastian's voice echoed through her mind clear and strong.

"He's telling you now, isn't he?"

"You can hear him? I thought I was just having grief induced hallucinations."

"No, they're not hallucinations. I hear him, too…sometimes. But it's not the same way you do—the two of you have a special connection. He was like a father to you. I'm sure that created a bond that goes deeper than just Watcher and Chosen ward."

He took a deep breath and glanced out the entrance again. She wished they could stay like this forever, but they were running out of time.

"Time to go?" she asked trying to hide her disappointment.

He nodded but didn't look at her. A feeling of dread pushed against the warm moment.

"What's wrong?"

"Nothing." He glanced down, touched the corner of her mouth and pushed it up. It didn't work. Her frown turned into a full-out glare and she pulled away from him to look directly in his eyes.

"Bull. I've had ten years to learn the art of deception. I know when someone is hiding something, so spit it out." She crossed her arms and waited, fighting the concern rising in her chest.

Tolen sighed. "One day you're going to have to get used to not always getting your way."

She lifted her eyebrow. "That day isn't today. You're still not that cool." She bit back a smile and he chuckled.

"Okay, I'll tell you, but there's something I need to ask first."

She tilted her head. "O…kay?"

He held out his arms and smiled. Despite wanting to watch his face to make sure he didn't try to hide anything she leaned back against his chest. Warmth surged through her again. He rested his chin on her shoulder. "The house you grew up in, was it yellow?"

She tilted her head to look at him. "Yeah, how'd you know that?"

"Did you have a tire swing in your back yard?"

"Yeah—"

"The day you were chosen. Was it really bad weather?"

She pulled away from him, confused. *How?*

"Macy—did your Radia shard come flying into your kitchen and you caught it?"

Her voice shook. "Tolen, how do you know that?"

"I saw it—I'll try to explain in a minute. First, can I see yours and Bastian's shards?"

She gave him one last quizzical look before lifting the necklaces out of her shirt.

His fingers trembled as he pulled his shard closer to her two. The nearer the three shards got to each other the brighter they glowed.

"They did that when I put yours over my neck back in the woods. What does it mean?"

With his arms around her, Tolen first slid his and her shards together. They fit perfectly like two pieces of a broken vase. White-hot light burst from them, illuminating the tiny cave.

"It means we each have a piece of the same shard." Tolen's voice shook. "We each *were* Bastian's wards. He was my Watcher too. The Light had our coming together planned from the very beginning—" he connected all three shards. Bastian's larger shard slid right into place over the other two. The light became so bright they couldn't look straight at the joined shards. "So we could grow up together, train together, and know each other so well that we could fight in perfect harmony with one another, our gifts heightened by our sibling-like relationship, our combined destiny."

Her heart sank. "But then—"

Tolen put a finger to her lips. "Our destiny is to fight together as a team Macy, falling for you may not have been part of the plan, but someday I think we'll see that's exactly why it's right."

This didn't make any sense, but she didn't want to argue. There had to be a way! He pulled the shards apart and the cave that had seemed bright before the light from the crystals, now seemed dark as evening.

He tucked his beneath his shirt. "There's something else besides the shards. I also saw my father."

"What?"

Tolen told her about the vision he had while unconscious in the cave. He saw his father looking for the links to the citadel, trying to find a way to give the shard back and then years later finally admitting he'd made a mistake. "I saw the location for two permanent doors, or links, whatever they're called; one to the citadel, the other to the Shadow Realm."

She shook her head. "But the doors aren't supposed to be permanent. They always open somewhere unknown and only from their side."

"Well, these are permanent and extremely well hidden. It took years, but my father found them. When he'd given up, accepted that he'd failed, he went to the door to the Shadow Realm, released my shard, and let the Shadows take him. He felt he deserved it."

"I'm so sorry Tolen." She wrapped her arms around his waist and squeezed.

"Macy," he grabbed her hand. "I saw where he was. I know where the door to the Shadow Realm is. I know how to get there. I may not know enough about my gifts, and I know Jonas wanted me to wait, but I can feel it. Nova was leading me into a trap, but I know what I felt before about going was right, just the timing was off. I needed to understand…" he ran a hand through his hair. "It's hard to explain, but I know I'm supposed to try *now* to save my father, and maybe my mother—or at least find out what happened to her."

Her heart sped up and she bit her lip. "Then what are we waiting for?"

"Macy, I *am* going after him but you can't come with me."

"Bull crap."

"Listen—"

She squeezed his fingers so hard her own started to throb. "No, you listen buddy, and you listen good. I didn't just risk my life to save your— you-know-what—to see you go off and try to get yourself killed again. You might feel all tough now that you know about you're gifts and accepted your *destiny*, but I'm part of that destiny too. I'm going to fight beside you from here on out, you're just going to have to get used to it." She gave him a glare that dared him to argue.

"I can't stand the thought of you getting hurt because of me."

"That's sweet and all, and I'm sorry if this sounds rude, but you don't know crap about what's waiting for you in the Shadow Realm. Have you thought that maybe the reason you know now is the time to go is because I'm *with* you, in every way this time?" She shook his arm. "Admit it; you won't last ten minutes without me."

"Macy—"

She put her hand over his mouth. "Listen Tolen. Don't you see? I *won't* let you go in there alone. Not when I *know* I can help you. I'm *meant* to help you. Deal with it."

CHAPTER 19

CRAZY PLANS

TOLEN SHOOK HIS HEAD, BUT COULD TELL THIS WAS AN ARGUMENT HE wouldn't win. If there was one thing he'd learned about Macy in the last few weeks, it was that she generally got her way. "What are we going to do about Jonas? If the camp is in trouble can we really just leave?"

Macy tapped her finger next to his blue eye. "Well, Mr. Ninth Chosen, I think it's time you used some of those nifty gifts." Her dimple winked beside her lip.

His eyebrows pulled together and she smiled.

"Your Second Sight? See if you can find out what's going on back at camp." She leaned forward out of his arms and met his eyes with a calculating expression. "I've been thinking about your nightmares too. Bastian told me once that his visions of my future sometimes came as dreams, but he couldn't flesh them out until he was in my thoughts, sensing my next choices. Maybe now that you understand your gifts a bit better, you could try and find your dad's thoughts. He may not be in this realm, but you're still meant to *watch* for him, so it could work. I'm not saying it will, but it could. It might give us a clearer picture of where he's at in the prison, who's guarding him, stuff like that. We need all the insights you can give us."

Tolen stared at her in shock for several seconds. He hadn't even thought about trying to use his Sight to guide him. But of course it made sense. He really did need Macy's knowledge if he was going to succeed. This thought sent waves of guilt crashing over him. Going into the Shadow Realm to try to save his parents was the right thing to do, and taking Macy was seeming more and more of a necessity, but he didn't have to like it.

She watched him expectantly. He squeezed his eyes shut, concentrating on the warmth of her body next to his and tried to focus.

"Iy'hika don Jonas, Incrah…" He began naming off everyone he could remember at camp; as their faces became clear, other names and faces followed, until he'd named as many as he could think of. His Watcher's eye went wild behind his closed lid and the pictures began to flash so fast it took all his concentration to sort it out. He wasn't sure how long he was lost in a vision that flickered between past, present, and future, but when he opened his eyes to see Macy staring anxiously at him, he noticed the light coming through the doorway was significantly dimmer than before.

He rubbed his temples, still trying to sort out everything he saw. "Jonas is really sick. The Kornikye aren't supposed to be picked at night—Nova poisoned him to keep him from noticing I was gone." He ran a hand over his eyes, trying to rid his mind of the image of screaming children, the depth of their fear too heart wrenching. "It was…bad. The Dark attacked about the same time the Shadows tried to take me. The Radia Warriors and trainees fought all night. Jonas's shield keeps flickering. They've been evacuating the families all day, and preparing for the Dark to attack again tonight. Why did I leave?" He grabbed handfuls of his hair. All those innocent people, hurt, because he hadn't been strong enough, because he drew in the Dark wherever he went.

"Tolen, stop it!" Macy shook his shoulders until he opened his eyes and looked at her. He clung to her words like a life vest as the guilt threatened to drown him. "This is Nova's fault not yours." He tried to look down but she grabbed his chin. "Listen to me! Those people would have stayed protected if she hadn't betrayed them. There's no time for 'if onlys'. Bastian always said we can't change the past so there's no point in wallowing over it. Get up and get back to work. Now concentrate! What happened to the Dominants?"

He squeezed his eyes shut. *I can't fix the past…Focus.* "They're being sheltered in an underground cave beneath the Eighth arena; their

Protectors are above them, and warriors surrounding the area." His voice sounded hollow, an echo, the guilt he was trying to push away fighting hard to return to the place he'd kept it for so long.

"And your dad?"

Tolen pinched the bridge of his nose. He didn't want to *see* any more pain, or worse, feel responsible for it. He spoke through clenched teeth, "*Iy'hika*, Daedal." And suddenly he was there, his mind linked to his father's mind, his father's pain becoming *his* pain.

"Tell me! Tell me now!"

Daedal twitched on the floor, flowing orange hair from a tall gray-skinned woman swirled across his face. He clenched his fists and gritted his teeth. "Never…" he rasped.

"Again!" A cold deep voice shouted.

The woman opened her black eyes and her huge mouth filled with gray mossy teeth, and let out a blood-curdling wail.

Pain shot through Daedal's broken body as if he were being burned alive.

"I will kill her." The cold voice spoke into Daedal's ear. "I will kill your precious wife if you do not tell me what you know. How do I get in? How do I destroy the citadel?"

Daedal spit blood on the black boots of his captor. The woman shrieked again.

He pulled his thoughts from his father's mind and focused on trying to find his mother. They'd threatened to kill her, that must mean they held her prisoner as well. "*Iy'hika*, Areen." His heart sank with what he discovered. He opened his eyes and swallowed hard. His voice came out thick with emotion. "My father's fading. His life force is so weak. They were torturing him—they want him to tell them where the door to the citadel is. A tall woman with gray skin, empty black eyes, and floor length orange hair, she-she opened her mouth and screamed—the worst pain I've ever felt."

"Tormentors," Macy whispered with disgust. "It's how they extract information. No one can withstand the pain."

He pushed his hands over his eyes and tried to block out the images of his father screaming and writhing in pain.

"We should go to him first. The camp has enough protection without us. Did you find your mom?"

His voice broke and she grabbed his hand. "They have her." The words tumbled from his mouth. "They threatened to kill her if—if my father didn't give them the information they wanted. I found her. Her cell is warmer and lighter, she doesn't seem to be injured, but something's really wrong with her. Her thoughts were all cluttered; they didn't make any sense at all. Not like she was sleeping. I dunno. Drugged maybe?" He pushed his thumbs against his closed lids, joy that his mother was still alive mingling with horror over her situation.

Macy's breath whooshed across his face. "Tolen I'm so sorry."

"Going into thoughts…" Tolen glanced up, his stomach turning. "It's horrible."

Macy squeezed his fingers, her eyes filled with sympathy, yet determined. "Do you think they could have Dane too?"

He tried to swallow the sick knot in his throat. "I don't know."

She put her other hand on top of their clasped fingers. "Try."

He nodded resolutely and closed his eyes. He wanted to know, but he was afraid. Afraid of what he might find and what he might feel again. He concentrated on the warmth Macy brought as he focused again with his Second Sight, but he couldn't find Dane anywhere.

"Dane really is gone. The Doogar were right." He looked out the cave entrance, lost in turmoil. "I keep hearing what Jonas said to me when I asked him to help me save my father. He told me I wasn't ready to face the darkness of the Shadow Prison…he said if my gifts were too erratic it would be a mission doomed to fail, no matter how many warriors came with me." Panic threatened to overwhelm him. "We *are* doing the right thing, aren't we?"

Macy grabbed his face in her hands, forcing him to look at her, and leaned her forehead against his. "I know it's hard Tolen, but you're fulfilling a piece of your destiny. Bastian believed you were meant to do this. So did Jonas. If you feel like you are supposed to go now, then I trust that feeling. So should you." She barely brushed his lips with hers and a burst of warmth entered Tolen's body, pushing most of the despair away. She leaned back and let go of his face. "Send word to Incrah through the trees. Let him know what we're doing and that we're okay. If the warriors can afford to send help, they will."

Tolen guessed her brisk attitude had come from years of training. He could wallow in the moment or get up and get back to work as she said. He took a deep breath, fought against the emotions plaguing him and tried to focus on what she was directing him to do. He grabbed her hands. "Okay…we're going to do this, but if something happens to you—"

She pulled her hand free to slug his arm. "Look. I appreciate the 'protect me' stuff. I really do. It's kinda nice, but if you don't reign it in, I'm going to punch you hard enough to knock some sense into you. I've hunted and killed more Dark creatures than I can count. I know what I'm getting myself into. If either of us should feel guilty about heading in there, it's me. I *know* what we're going to face. I know what to expect, at least more than you do, and I'm prepared to lead a barely trained Chosen in there." She closed her eyes, licked her lips, and he knew she was just as worried about him as he was about her, but she would move forward, despite her fears.

She leaned over and began rummaging in her pack. "We need a plan, and I don't mean something like, 'let's go down to the Shadow link and announce the arrival of the Ninth' kind of plan." She started unloading a myriad of stuff—food, weapons, herbs. "Put us together something to eat. We need to find a safer place to hide for the night, where I can work. And I know it's not going to be fun, but I'm going to need you to concentrate on your visions and describe, in as much detail as you can remember, everything you saw in the Shadow Realm."

∘∘∘

It took a little less than two hours for Macy to lead them a mile away from the cave, disguising their footprints and dropping herbs to cover their scent, and find a new hideout—an outcropping where the river had carved out a space hidden from above, too small to draw attention from any Dark servants that might travel on the river in search of them—but still she worried they hadn't moved fast enough, or had left a trace somewhere that would lead the Dark straight to them.

It had been a wet crawl to get inside and they had to carve out more of the dirt to make it high enough for Tolen to sit up. It wasn't great, but as long as they maintained their shields, the thick mud should block their scent from any patrolling Raksasha.

While they sat in the glow of a small flashlight, she filled Tolen in on the technicalities of the Shadow Realm. He sat quietly and listened, occasionally rubbing the back of her hand with his thumb, whether to get comfort or to give it she wasn't sure, but it was nice all the same. She tried to keep some of her thoughts subdued and out of Tolen's mind. They were going to have to face the consequences of their decision to be together at some point and she really didn't want to worry about it right now, but a part of her, the part that really wanted it to work, wouldn't shut up. She wasn't as worried about going into the Shadow Realm as Tolen was, yes it was likely going to be far worse than fighting the Dark from this realm, but if her plan worked, they wouldn't be fighting anyone—just sneak in and sneak out. She'd done enough sneaking up on the Dark in the last ten years that she knew what she had to do to stay unnoticed. The scary part was if they *were* noticed. She wouldn't think about what could happen if they were caught.

"So you've been there?" He asked after she described the quality of light and air in the realm of the Dark—gray, sulfurous, acrid.

"No, but I've heard the legends. You don't forget those kinds of stories in a hurry. Let's hope reality is a little less elaborate." She filled a small pouch with eight rolled Glockshaw. "We'll focus on your Nature Speak and your Kuna since that's where you're the strongest. You may know the language and the theory behind how your gifts work, but it'll be a lot harder to call on something you haven't practiced a lot if we're ambushed. How confident do you feel with your throwing?"

Tolen looked at the pouch with apprehension. "About as confident as I feel with the rest of my gifts."

Macy lifted an eyebrow.

He swallowed and met her eyes. "I'll be fine."

"You make me crazy." He grinned and she slugged his shoulder.

Tolen rubbed his arm dramatically. "What's with you and all the slugging?"

She shrugged. "Gets the point across."

He touched her chin. "There are other ways you know."

Her eyebrows rose again and he leaned across the small space to kiss the end of her nose. "See."

She cleared her throat. "I don't imagine kissing you would show my annoyance as good as a well-placed punch." She grinned. "Should we get back to business?"

A smirk touched his lips and he motioned for her to continue.

She had to look away from his eyes to remember what she was talking about. "I've never been through a door, but Bastian taught me about them. Someone on their side has to open it and let us in. This poses a slight problem. So here's my theory. We'll stake out the area you saw your father taken from, wait for a Dark creature to access it, and follow them in."

"Sounds easy enough."

She snorted. "It won't be, I promise. We could be stuck for days waiting for servants to show up. Or worse we could be discovered before we even get an attempt to try to get in—"

"Destiny or not this is completely nuts." Doubt and fear clouded Tolen's eyes. "I may be the Ninth, but I barely know how to use my gifts, I don't know a thing about the real situation out there and yet I'm ready to risk both our lives to save a man I don't even know."

Macy put her hand on his shoulder and bit her lip. "I'm not very good at the mushy pep talks; it's a skill I never bothered to master. But you *are* nuts, buddy."

"Thanks a lot."

"Wait! Wait. Listen." She tucked a strand of hair behind her ear. "You're nuts, but not stupid. Is this really the best idea? Probably not. Is there a chance we could both die? Yeah, sure. But guess what, Tolen? This is the life of a Chosen. Every day is crazy, and risky. If saving your dad is something you are destined to do, then it's all part of the job. Our destinies as Chosen were not meant to be easy, just worth everything we go through in the end."

He took her hand off his shoulder and squeezed it. "Thanks. I like your way about things. It might not feel the best, but at least you're not trying to give me a false sense of reality."

She pulled her hand free and tied the pouch of Glockshaw along with three other filled pouches onto the belt she'd fashioned from the material of Tolen's pack. "Here." She held it out.

He tentatively took it and tied it around his waist. A curved Doogar dagger rested at his hip. His discomfort was obvious.

Reaching over she lightly bumped his chin with her knuckles before moving her fingers to the largest pouch. "Save the Glockshaw for last and only if you absolutely need them." She pointed out the second pouch. "Sleep Dust—I gave you most of what's left so make sure you don't use it too soon. Save it for the sentries outside the prison cells."

She pointed out the third and fourth pouches. "Camouflage and Heat. Sprinkle the Camouflage over your father before you pull him from the cell. It blocks body heat and the scent of blood."

"The stuff you put on us as we ran to the Binithan?"

"Yeah. I used up most of my supply when I dragged you into the cave, and to cover our tracks here, but we've got just enough to get us through the door and cover your dad. With all your dad's been through, I doubt his life force is strong enough to shift the Balance, but the Raksasha will still be able to track him by his scent, and I'd rather be safe than sorry. Remember, the herbs only last a few hours, so we'll have to be quick."

"Okay, and the Heat?" Tolen lifted the last pouch; the one that would be warm to the touch.

"Sprinkle it in his cell. The sentries don't check on the prisoners very often, they just sense their body heat. The Heat, hopefully, will keep them from discovering anything's off after they wake up, giving us time to escape."

Tolen nodded. "How are we going to sneak past a realm of Dark creatures and get into the prison without getting caught?"

Macy shrugged. "I'm still working on that. I've got a few ideas but we might just have to take it as it comes."

CHAPTER 20

TORMENT AND TEARS

Tolen trusted Macy completely. He believed her when she said their hideout was safe and they were shielding themselves well enough, but as the last shimmer of light disappeared off the water and the first shriek of the Raksasha rang out, he'd never been more scared. He held onto Macy not daring to speak, wondering if she was as terrified as he was. His arms started to tremble as the shrieking increased, followed by menacing growls and other unearthly sounds he couldn't put a name to.

His breathing increased. Macy touched his face and squeezed his fingers, signaling him to calm down.

It was nearly impossible. Macy's presence was the only thing that kept him under control. They were trapped in here like sitting ducks. If they were discovered, there would be no escape. He couldn't let them get her, somehow if they were discovered, he had to make sure she got away…

Just before sunrise, the ground above them shook with the unified frustrated howls of who knew how many creatures. Macy's fingernails dug into his arms.

Neither of them moved until the first ray of sunlight flickered into the cave off the water.

"That was interesting," Macy whispered hoarsely. "I've never felt a patrol that large before. There had to be at least a hundred Raksasha and dozens of other creatures I didn't recognize up there. They knew we were here somewhere. We're going to have to be careful even when we pass shady areas as we make our way. They could be hiding anywhere."

"Where are we heading?" His voice came out shaky and he cleared his throat.

"Klamath Falls is the closest city."

Tolen nodded and ran his fingers through his tangled hair. "Were you scared at all?"

"Are you kidding? I thought I was going to pee my pants half the night. It was taking all I had to not start screaming and give us away. Thank goodness they didn't have Shadows with them."

He nodded, kissed her cheek and leaned his forehead against hers. "That was the longest night of my life. If you hadn't been here keeping me calm…well, I do need you with me."

Macy smirked. "Told ya so." She slugged him before wrapping her arms around him. He rubbed her back and she sighed. He pulled her barely away and touched her cheek. "Do you have any clue how incredibly beautiful you are?"

Her cheeks turned pink and she ducked her head. Her thoughts were quiet, but she felt the the same need he did. He grabbed her chin, pulling her face up so he could kiss her. The feelings that surged through him when their lips met were both thrilling and terrifying. Was love always like this—so intense that it was almost unbearable?

He pulled away and took a deep breath. "See what I meant about practice?" He pointed to their hands. "No fire." He forced a smile. "What's our next move?"

Her face still slightly pink, she reached into her bag, took out some Sugar Tack and a sweetened meat cake, and tossed them into Tolen's lap. His nose wrinkled.

Macy chuckled. "I know the cakes are disgusting, but we're going to need our strength. Let's eat then try to sleep for a couple of hours. We need to give the sun a chance to fully rise."

She tucked a piece of hair behind her ear. "It's a little bit of a hike to town, but hopefully we can snag a car to get us up to the coast. You are sure it's in Oregon, not Washington or California?"

"My mom had a book of pictures of the Oregon coast." Tolen nodded, certain. "I know the spot where he was standing—I've seen the rock formation a dozen times. I'm just not positive where it is, exactly, along the beach."

"That's okay. I'm sure gas stations will have tourist maps. We'll just keep driving until we find it. It should only take us a few hours to get to the coast once we hit the freeway."

"That's encouraging." Tolen shifted his legs out from under him. "Does Bastian have another car stored in Oregon?"

Macy sighed. "Not where we're headed. We're going to have to borrow one."

"You mean steal one?" His eyebrow lifted.

"No, we're going to borrow it. Just without the owner's, um…permission. I'll give it back with money in the glove box." Macy glanced at him, likely saw the skepticism on his face and quickly added, "I risk my life every day for the human race, they can loan me a car now and again."

He couldn't argue with that.

She lay down and folded her arms behind her head. Tolen folded in beside her as best he could in the cramped space, put his arm under her head, and fell asleep surprisingly fast.

"Wake up, sleepy head." Macy was shaking him awake after what only felt like minutes later.

The light reflecting off the water filled their tiny hideout as he sat up and she passed him his pack.

She pulled hers over her shoulders. "Stay beside me and remember to be careful near any shade or dark places where something might be hiding." She turned away and he touched her shoulder.

"Thank you, Mace. For everything." In spite of the night they'd had, and the journey awaiting them, he couldn't help but feel a slight sense of anticipation. He was actually doing it. He was going to save his parents. Well, *try* to anyway.

Macy smiled her dimpled smile and, after a moment's hesitation, crawled outside.

Tolen slowly warmed up as they made their way along the stream to a country road. Nothing jumped out at them. The sun poured down and birds chirped as they hiked the miles into the nearest town. It might have been just another beautiful summer day.

It was late afternoon before they finally reached the city of Klamath Falls. They walked past a park, chewing on the horrible meat-cakes and guzzling canteens of warm water. Tolen watched in envy as a little family sitting at a table pulled hamburgers and steaming french-fries out of a fast food bag. The parents kept sending nervous glances in their direction.

Tolen looked down at his torn and dirty shirt and blood-spattered jeans. They did look pretty bad. Probably like a couple homeless runaways. They hurried off before the parents decided to call the police.

Macy led them to a narrow alley where he stood sweating nervously while she hot-wired a rusty Ford Mustang.

He kept expecting to hear sirens all the way out of town, but nothing chased them.

Nothing.

The darkness was out there, he could feel it, but just as Macy had told him, he could tell where it was and as of right now, it didn't know where they were.

He sent out a simple hope that it would last as they drove westward along the twisting mountain roads that would take them to the coast.

"Is that it?" Macy pointed to a huge rock jutting out into the sea not far ahead. Tolen shifted in his seat to look out her window.

"I think so. But what if I'm wrong?" Tolen tapped the windowsill with his fingers.

She shook her head. "I don't think you're wrong. Can't you feel that? It's subtle, but it's there."

He could feel something when he really focused, almost like they were trying to sneak past a giant sleeping attack dog.

Macy pulled off onto the gravel shoulder. They both stared out the windshield at the foreboding sight. Light gray mist encircled the rocks out to sea. Monstrous waves crashed and broke across the surface, the bleak sight eerily accentuated by black billowing clouds.

"I thought you blasted the Shadows?"

Macy swallowed loudly and ducked down to look at the sky through the window. "I wish. The Shadows can't be killed. They can be broken, but just like when you wave a hand through smoke they're still there. They just have to regroup." She continued to look up at the sky. "The Shadows aren't in that storm, yet. We'd know it if they were." She sighed and turned in her seat to look at Tolen. "Let's circle around and park. We'll hike in and see what we feel when we get closer."

He nodded and she flipped a U-turn, driving until she found a barely used tourist trail. She parked a half mile from its head, placed a thousand dollars from Bastian's "emergency stash" in the glove box with a note that said "Thanks for the ride," put the keys under the driver's seat and locked the doors. "There. This car'll be back to its owner by tomorrow and they'll have a grand to help'em fix it up."

"Not to mention a better running motor." Just outside of town she'd spent a precious half hour with a set of tools from the trunk while Tolen paced.

She shrugged modestly.

Tolen's palms were sweaty and his stomach twisted. Macy seemed to sense his anxiety and grabbed both his hands in her tiny ones. Her bright green eyes were filled with determination and a calm he wished he could feel.

"Everything is going to work out, Tolen. I've completed dozens of missions and snuck up on the Dark a million times. We just have to stay focused. We can do this." A sliver of light broke through the clouds, catching the golden highlights in her hair. Tolen pulled one of his hands free to tuck a stubborn lock back behind her ear. He leaned down and she stood up on her toes to kiss him. It was a quick kiss but it still sent warmth pulsing through his body.

Yes, he could do this—Macy would keep him grounded. She knew what she was doing. He just hoped he could keep his head straight if her life was threatened. He shook off the thought and tried for a reassuring smile—it must have looked more like a grimace because she shook her head and rolled her eyes.

"Have a little faith, Tolen." She tugged on his hand and he moved into step beside her.

"If this really is a door," she started walking faster, "you can be sure there will be all sorts of creatures guarding it. They won't be out in the daylight, but there'll be crows patrolling the area. And if we don't get in position before that storm covers us in darkness, the Raksasha will definitely find us."

"If you're trying to give me confidence, it isn't working."

Macy took a deep breath. "I'm just stating fact. As long as we can find a decent vantage point where we can hide, we should be fine."

He still didn't feel better.

She led the way to a small clump of dry grass. "Let's take a minute and have you check on your parents. Make sure nothing has changed."

Tolen nodded, understanding why she wanted him to do it, but not really wanting to venture back into his father's pain or his mother's strange thoughts. "*Iy'hika*, Daedal, Areen." His eye went nuts beneath the lid. Pictures and thoughts raced by, and he searched through them for the three life forces he wanted to see the most.

He could feel Macy, bright and warm beside him, her thoughts swirling with concern as he found his father—weak, incoherent, filled with pain. He quickly skipped away from him. His mother was still lost in her strange world.

Tolen let his breath out slowly and opened his eyes. Macy rubbed his arm. "They're both still the same." He shuddered. "I can see both cells that hold my parents but I can't tell exactly where they're located."

"That's okay. Once we're inside, you should be drawn to them." She looked up at the sky. "Ready to move?"

Tolen nodded and stood up, pulling Macy with him. "As ready as I'll ever be."

CHAPTER 21

NO TURNING BACK

Tolen rolled to his side and propped his head in his hand. They'd been lying in the tall grass for the better part of the afternoon and the moist evening air made his clothes stick to his skin. "Mace, can I ask you something?"

She rolled over to mimic his pose, her eyes curious. "Sure."

"When I saw into Nova's memories I saw this creature. I'd seen him in dreams before, and he seemed really familiar. I'm sure it was his voice I heard when the Tormentors were torturing my father. I think he's important to the Dark."

Macy's eyes narrowed. "Can you describe what he looked like?"

Tolen took a deep breath and described the demon in his nightmares, the horrible reptilian red skin, poisonous yellow eyes, and thick rippled black horns.

She shuddered, sat up, and hugged her knees. She was so tiny her head wasn't any higher than Tolen's. "It sounds like Daemon, the Demon Master. It would make sense. He's the highest captain of the Dark, second only to Darsapean himself."

"Darsapean…" Tolen felt sick. "Leader of the Dark. Epitome of evil." He would never forget what Darsapean had shown him while under the Shadows power. It would haunt him forever.

Macy's eyes narrowed, but he didn't tell her what he'd seen. Voicing it would just make him see it again. She watched his face as she continued.

"Darsapean is stuck in Misery, a prison built by the Guardians, and the world better hope he stays there."

He looked away from her gaze. "If this Daemon is in the Shadow Prison torturing my parents, and he's as important and powerful as he sounds, how are we going to get past him, or beat him if we end up having to face him?"

He glanced back to see her calculating their options. "If we face him Tolen, I don't think either of us is powerful enough to defeat him, not yet." He reminded himself that he liked the fact that she was brutally honest as she went on. "But, like two fleas on a dog, we can find ways to distract him long enough to escape right under his nose."

She laid back down and they were silent as the sun fell lower and lower in the sky.

Finally, when they were cast in shadow Macy propped herself up again. "Something isn't right. The Dark is here, I know it is, but it's getting late, the sun is low enough in the sky and there's enoug h cloud cover that creatures should be moving, but I haven't even seen anything lurking in the shadows, and we've only seen one patrol of crows. It's giving me the willies."

"Maybe they stay inconspicuous so that the Light won't know the door is here?" He glanced around and focused his Watcher's eye on the sky. It shifted, pulling in a flock of birds a half-mile away—but nothing that shouldn't be there.

"Maybe." She bit her lip. "Something *is* moving toward this spot, but it's weak in strength. I'd bet anything it's a band of Kreydawn, which should be good news."

"Why? What are Kreydawn?"

"Mindless slaves. The only thoughts they have are whatever their masters plant in their heads. They follow direct orders to the end, even if it means walk 'til they die. The Dark uses them to carry out jobs they don't want to lose their valuable servants doing. They're not much fun to fight. If you get in their way, they just stand there and stare right through you. Way easy to pick off. If it is Kreydawn, we can kill their Suppressors, disguise ourselves, and walk right in with them." She chewed her lip and clenched and unclenched her hand against her leg.

He reached over and tried to smooth out her fingers. "You said *should* be good news. What's wrong?"

"It's too easy. It makes me nervous. It's almost like they're expecting something."

A tiny bird landed in the grass beside them and Tolen was struck with sudden inspiration. "*Ma'sha.*" He whispered.

Macy paused and glanced over at him.

The bird tilted its head looking at him.

Tolen held out his hand, and said softly. "*Ma'sha. Y'na to'Conchla Mindra. Y'na hai iy'vast to'Degani.*"

The bird hopped into his palm and Tolen stared into its eyes—it was hard to concentrate on the bird's wild thoughts. Several seconds later she jumped off his hand and took off into the darkening sky.

"What did you just do?" Macy watched the bird fly off.

"I told her who I am and that I'm here to fight the Dark. I *think* she's going to scout ahead for us."

"You think?"

"Thoughts are hard to read, people don't necessarily think in words, they think more in pictures, and animals—" He rubbed his temple. "It's so much different, more feelings than pictures, more instincts than focused decision…She was so concerned about her nest nearby she had a hard time focusing on what I was asking."

Macy looked from him back to the sky. "Interesting…So, now what do we do?"

The bird reappeared before he could answer, her thoughts fixated on a strange shimmer on the shallow part of the water between the shoreline and the rocks out to sea and the way she felt whenever she flew near the area—cold, scared.

This was definitely the place.

"The door is right off shore in front of the rocks. She didn't show me any guards or crows."

Macy nodded. "We'll just keep waiting for whatever's coming and hope it's the Kreydawn."

"What if you're right? What if the Dark is expecting us?"

"I don't know how they could be…"

o o o

Time passed slowly, ticking by in snail-like increments, making Macy's skin crawl in anticipation. Tolen's nerves were shot. She could feel it. She wished he'd had more time to train with the Dominants. He had so much power that he didn't know how to utilize to its fullest. She had faith in him, but he had very little in himself.

She'd covered them in Camouflage, but still she was nervous. She hadn't lied to Tolen exactly—she had completed dozens of missions, just never on her own before. Dusk loomed on the horizon and still there was no sign of Dark creatures or spies. It felt so *wrong*. Instinct told her it could be a trap, but she couldn't turn and run. Tolen was supposed to come here and she knew she was supposed to help him.

She watched him from the corner of her eye. He sat super still, staring out toward the door of the Shadow Realm, his eye dilating, with his hands curled into tight fists in his lap.

She reached over and placed her hand over his. Slowly his fingers relaxed. He took her hand in his and half-smiled. She loved his smile— except when it was full of doubt and put there just to try to reassure her. She resisted the urge to shake him. "Tolen, you have amazing power and unbelievable gifts. Trust in the Light, trust *yourself*. We're going to succeed. I promise."

He lowered his forehead to hers. "Thank you."

A low moan met her ears. It was far away and carried softly on the wind.

"Kreydawn! Get down." She grabbed his arm and dragged him to the ground until they were completely hidden by the tall grass.

Her heart pounded in anticipation—this was familiar, she could do this. She'd treat it like any other mission and deal with the rest as it came. "We'll wait for them to pass and come in from behind. That will give us the chance to see how many Suppressors they have controlling them."

The small and lanky Kreydawn slowly trudged into view. The weak light of dusk barely concealed their emaciated, chalk-colored features hidden beneath the cowls of their ash-colored cloaks. If it weren't for the stubby horns that ran five in a row across their forehead, they could be mistaken for deathly-ill humans. The creatures walked slowly, almost lazily—like a herd of cows. Some pushed carts while others lugged large packs laden with a strange variety of tools.

Macy's eyes narrowed and she whispered in Tolen's ear, "I would swear this is the same group Bastian and I tracked back in Nevada before we came to find you. I recognize the slave out front with the broken horn. They were digging through a small area in the desert. We never had the chance to find out what they were up to." She looked at the covered carts wondering what she'd missed. There had been no rhyme or reason to the collections of rocks in Nevada. What was in those carts?

"Where are the Suppressors?" Tolen whispered back.

She scanned the marching crowd and pointed. "They're the ones in the black cloaks; they stand about a head taller than the Kreydawn. It looks like there are three in front, and," she craned her neck to peek around the grass to the end of the procession. "Maybe three in the back, I can't tell for sure yet."

Tolen peeked through the grass at the looming hooded figures.

"What do they look like under the cloaks?"

"Tall and bone thin—gray skin and one large eye in the center of their face. No mouths, no nose."

Tolen's nose wrinkled. "Sounds repulsive."

"Very."

"What's the plan?"

"We need to stop them before they reach the link." She bit her lip. "I think I should go to the back and try to take care of the Suppressors there. Do you think you can you take out the three in the front?"

Tolen nodded.

"Great, give me twenty seconds on your watch and then go. We'll try to time it to attack at the same time." She looked into his eyes and squeezed his hand once. "Enhance your sight. Good luck." She slithered on her belly through the grass, leaving Tolen behind. She took a deep breath and moved forward without looking back.

○○○

Tolen stared at his watch. He could barely see the second hand, even with enhanced sight, through all the scratches. If they lived through this, he was going to need a new watch.

Ten…nine…It was amazing how fast twenty seconds went by when you were terrified.

Five, four, three…

He took a deep breath and closed his eyes, counting the last two seconds in his head. He pulled Macy's face to mind, the way it felt to hold her against him, the brush of her lips on his.

He snapped his eyes open and whispered, *"To'inreedo, Tin'ruhl, Nit'ahi."*

Eyesight enhanced, he watched as the earth beneath the feet of the lead Suppressor opened into a cavernous hole. The monster thrashed his arms trying to grab the edge but the gap only widened. Tolen almost pitied the creature's silent descent—he could not even call to his peers who were quickly scuttling back away from the hole, but the grasses beside their feet snaked around their ankles and dragged them into the deep.

Tolen twisted his hand in front of him and waves of dirt pitched and rolled until the hole sealed—the grasses furled back into place and the pathway appeared exactly as it had before it had swallowed three Suppressors.

The Kreydawn suddenly stopped, no longer under the control of their masters.

Seconds later, Macy ran back to his side with two of the Suppressors' cloaks draped over her shoulder. "There were four of those suckers in the back. I almost missed one." She looked around. "Where're your three?"

Tolen shrugged and pointed at the ground beneath his feet. "Taking a dirt nap."

Macy whistled. "Nice job for your first ambush."

He smiled, took the cloak she held out, and walked over to the band of Kreydawn. He waved a hand in front of their faces. They didn't move or even blink.

Their odd features reminded him of the mindless zombies in horror movies. There was no darkness about them, but there wasn't anything else about them either. The shift they caused in the Balance was more a wave of movement, no longer sinister now that their minds were not controlled by something evil.

Macy walked to one of the Kreydawn hauling a cart and lifted the flap up.

"Tolen, what do you make of this?"

He walked over and looked in the cart. It held what looked like shiny chunks of silvery stone, barely visible beneath piles of normal gray rocks. "I don't know. Can they tell us?" He motioned toward the band.

"No. Their only thoughts are the ones fed to them by their masters—as soon as they complete, or are thwarted from completing a task, their minds go blank." She pointed ahead. "Well, are you ready?"

He gritted his teeth and nodded.

Macy handed him Serenity Stones and he put them in his ears. She double-checked their pouches, and walked to the head of the line of Kreydawn.

"Okay freaks, I'm your new master. Now move." She pushed the back of the head of the first Kreydawn, but he didn't move an inch.

"Come on, forward."

A dismal thought crossed Tolen's mind. "Mace, let me try."

Macy stepped aside and motioned him ahead.

He walked to the front of the group and closed his eyes. He let the pull of his subconscious free, something he hadn't allowed since he'd learned he had the gift of the Dreamers.

His Sight showed him the Kreydawn as they were in the other world—almost like living robots, programmed to run a task, and when the task was complete they went to sleep until a Dreamer told them what to do next. Their natural functions, like breathing and eating, were the only constant programs in their minds.

"Move. Take us through the link." The voice that issued from Tolen's mouth scared him, but he was sure he could control it now, he could feel the truth of Bastian's words. His conscious mind was stronger; he just had to accept it. The dream-like power flowed through him and the Kreydawn marched forward. Completely linked to his thoughts they mimicked his every move, even lifting their hands to scratch their noses when he did.

Tolen grabbed Macy's hand and they followed behind the first three.

The head Kreydawn walked into the water and the waves slowed around it. Cold wind blew across their faces. When they reached the shimmering spot, the air in front of them seemed to open and instead of looking out to sea, they found themselves staring into thick darkness.

"Who seeks entrance?" An oily voice asked.

The first Kreydawn put his arm into the opening, grunted, and it widened farther.

"Enter. Take your findings to the factory. Suppressors report to the Master." The voice trailed off, sounding bored.

Tolen glanced at Macy and pulled out of the Dreamers state. The Kreydawn were now under the control of whatever voice had come from the link.

Macy squeezed his hand and they slowly followed the Kreydawn from the warmth of their dimension into the cold emptiness of the Shadow Realm.

CHAPTER 22

DUNGEONS AND DEMONS

M ACY STAGGERED AS SOON AS THEY WERE THROUGH THE LINK. T HE weight of the Dark's power was smothering, the air thicker, heavier, making it literally hard to breathe. The lack of light felt unnatural, as if the sun never rose and dusk was the only time of day in this place. She shuddered—maybe it was. Bastian's stories had in no way prepared her for the depth of their situation; the reality was not something she could have imagined.

Even with the help of the Serenity Stones they couldn't survive here for long, the darkness was too powerful. Already she felt the strain on her life force, on her shield, the pull of evil at her mind and heart. She gasped and stumbled forward. Tolen grabbed her elbow to steady her. She met his eyes and could see the same concerns on his face.

She looked up and pointed a shaking finger into the grim light above them. "Tolen, there it is."

Tall and terrifying—swathed in the curling, twisting mists of the Shadows—stood the Shadow Prison. Mismatched turrets built from roughly cut gray stone grew so high they disappeared into the sulfurous sky. Gaping black windows sheathed in thick iron bars pierced the stone every few feet, spewing out the painful wails of the occupants within. Numberless Raksasha wielding rusty spears, and giant hairy guards with long bows hanging from their furry backs, paced the parapets of never-ending balconies and tall stone walls.

Tolen's eyes widened and she knew he was remembering his nightmares. "It's even worse than I imagined. I can feel the Shadows, but it's not like before. Is it the Serenity Stones?"

Macy took a ragged breath. "No. I think it's because they don't know we're here. They're not focused on us."

The Kreydawn began to turn and Macy tugged Tolen behind a tall mound of black rock.

"How are we going to get past all those guards?" He yanked on his collar.

The cloak felt like it was getting heavier too. Like it knew she wasn't supposed to be here and was trying to squeeze the life from her. She pulled it off and dropped it to the ground where it seemed to sizzle and hiss.

Tolen did the same and she swore she could hear it laugh.

Macy pointed again, trying not to think about how drained she felt—like she'd been battling Dark creatures for hours already. "Over there. Those are Ookra, they're taking supplies into the prison using the same carts as the Kreydawn. If we can get inside a cart, we'll just let them haul us in."

They watched the tiny pale creatures, no taller than a Doogar, with their overlong fingers ending in sharp claws that scratched the sides of the carts they pushed. Black tufts of hair sprouted from their bat-like ears that jiggled when they walked. Their faces were drawn, wrinkled, and cruel looking.

Tolen looked away and took a deep breath. "Say when."

Macy grabbed his hand and leaned around the rock pile. She watched with nerves tingling until the right moment and then dragged him at a sprint across the dim rocky ground. She paused beside some sort of stockyard. Vicious growls and periodic scuffling came from various barred paddocks.

She shivered. They did *not* want to know what was behind the bars.

A group of Ookra walked between the cages, throwing in dark blobs of something; the smell that wafted toward them was of rotting meat. She resisted the urge to pinch her nose.

"Look, there's a row of carts." Macy tipped her chin toward two Ookra who were tossing filled burlap sacks into the carts. When they finished they turned back toward the building.

"Come on, now's our chance," she whispered.

Tolen let her lead him toward the cart, gave her a leg up, and then dove into the cart beside her. What she'd hoped were bags of flour held something else. Something moving.

"Maggots," she whispered, her nose wrinkled in disgust.

Two more bags of maggots landed on their heads and the low raspy voices of the Ookra met their ears.

"Is this all then?"

"Yes, Master has asked for three hundred bags. This cart holds the last fifty."

"Good. I'm exhausted. The harvest was more difficult this year. I think even the insects have sensed what is coming. They are becoming restless."

The Ookra tossed a grimy woven tarp over the cart, grunted, and the cart started to move. Tolen covered his nose with his shirt and Macy hoped the sound of her pounding heart couldn't be heard over the wheels of the cart and the hiss of the squirming maggots.

A small hole in the tarp showed them a sliver of what was above. When they passed beneath stone statues of hideous beasts and demon like figures, she decided she'd rather not look.

A loud growl stopped the Ookra in their tracks. Macy met Tolen's eyes and mouthed. "DéHool."

Tolen nodded. His legs twitched against hers.

"What is in the cart slave?" A deep unpleasant voice shook the cart.

They began silently shifting bags until they were covered by so many Macy could barely breathe.

"Only maggots for the dungeons, Vikro."

"Slackdron believes differently. Perhaps you are trying to steal something, eh?"

Another growl from the DéHool.

The Ookra snarled under his breath. "See for yourself."

Macy clenched her teeth, her heart thumped, and her stomach turned from the smell and fear. Was Tolen ready to use his gifts? They hadn't even made it into the prison yet. If they had to fight already, there was no chance he could save his parents. *Please, please don't let them see us.*

She held her breath as the tarp was whipped aside. She could feel Tolen's nervousness and she pushed her hand beneath a bag to give his knee a reassuring squeeze. He grabbed her hand and the seconds ticked by as she waited for the exclamation that would mean they'd been discovered.

"Hmm, tasty lot. I'll just take one of these bags and we'll forget all about this."

The creature smacked its lips. He was going to reach in here and grab a bag. He was going to see them. Tolen's hand twitched in hers.

"Sure—"

A bag shifted as if about to be lifted out.

"Only—"

The bag stopped.

"Only what?"

"Master Daemon asked for three-hundred bags. This cart holds the last we have and equals three hundred. If we go in and have less, he will want to know why. We will have to tell him. He will pull it from our brains. You know this."

There was an angry grunt and the bag settled back over Tolen's head. Macy released the breath she'd been holding. "Fine. Get out of here."

The cart started to move again. Macy slid a bag off her head and Tolen plucked a maggot from her hair. Her eyes met his and she shook her head slowly.

Darkness engulfed them and an eerie blue light filtered in through the hole.

They were inside. They'd actually made it inside.

"Stupid sentinels. I hate them," the Ookra muttered.

"As do we all. Is this load to be taken to the dungeons as well or straight to the Master?"

"The dungeons. Master Daemon wants them to have time to ferment for a while before he sends them on. Darsapean prefers them that way."

The cart rolled to a stop and the Ookra resumed their conversation.

"Let's get something to eat before we unload. We've been working all morning."

"Yes. I have a plate of Junga worms that have been calling to me."

The Ookra laughed and their footsteps slowly faded into nothingness.

"Did that little creep just say Darsapean?" Macy asked in a strained whisper, her heart ready to burst out of her chest.

"Yeah."

"Souvlaki!"

"What?"

"This is *so* not good. If he's locked up in Misery, how can they be sending him supplies?"

Tolen shook his head. "So he probably shouldn't be able to talk to people in the earth realm either then?"

Macy's eyes widened. "What?"

"He spoke to me when I was under the Shadows' influence." He closed his mouth quickly and she wondered what it was he didn't want to say.

"That's impossible. He's in Misery."

Tolen tilted his head. "Just like the DéHool were supposed to be locked up in Misery?"

Macy grabbed his leg. "Tolen, this is really, really bad. First the DéHool, now Darsapean? He couldn't have escaped yet, the Guardians would know. They would have to know. But what if he's found a weakness in Misery's defenses?"

She shoved the tarp off the cart and started to climb out. "We've gotta get our job done and get the message back to the Guardians. They need to know what's going on."

Tolen climbed out of the cart and helped Macy down. "What exactly is Misery?"

"It's the prison kept by the Guardians. It's not supposed to have any form of connection to our world."

"So it's a place, not a building like the Shadow Prison?"

Macy stared down the frigid passageway where the Ookra must have gone. They stood in some sort of storage room surrounded by more bags of maggots. The smell of rotting meat, decay, and mildew burned her eyes and nose.

"A world actually. They captured so many Dark creatures there wasn't room for them in a building, or even hundreds of buildings. They needed a world, far enough away that they could never come back." Macy bit her lip. "Well, there's nothing we can do about it now. Let's enhance our eyes and ears and use your Sight. Search for your parents again."

They both whispered the words for sight and sound, Tolen also muttering, "*Iy'hika* Areen, Daedal."

"My dad's unconscious, his torturers are gone. My mom's still lost in her strange jumbled thoughts. They are on opposite floors and sides of the prison. My mother seems to be in some sort of living quarters. It's less dim and dank there. There's normal food. My father is near us in one of the dungeons. There are two guards outside and one patrolling the halls. I can feel them but I can't feel their thoughts."

"That's because the Ninth is not meant to protect servants of the Dark, you'll probably only feel their life force," Macy said absently.

"What are we going to do?"

She took a deep breath and faced him, knowing he wasn't going to like her plan. "We split up. I'll go after your mom."

"No." Tolen grabbed the top of her arms. "Macy, don't be ridiculous. You're not going off on your own in this place."

She closed her eyes so she wouldn't have to see the concern on his face. "Tolen, listen. We don't have time to go together and I'm sure your parents aren't going to be strong enough to be drug all over the prison. We have to make a straight shot there and back. I'm better at sensing the Dark. I'll be able to get to your mom easier than you will. You go get your dad. Do what I said with the Sleep dust and the Heat and meet me back here in one hour."

"Then what? We're not going to get by all those guards with two escaped prisoners."

"We'll create a distraction if we need to, remember? We're the annoying fleas. Don't worry." She squeezed his arm. Hard. "We'll figure it out. I promise."

Tolen clenched his teeth. She knew he could see it. They had no other option now. They'd made it this far. He cupped her face in his hands. "You stay safe. Promise me you'll stay safe."

She wrapped her arms around his waist. "I promise." She wrenched out of his grasp, afraid he would sense her fear.

"Check your watch—it's 9:04. If either of us isn't back by ten, we don't wait. We get your parents out. *Then* we come back for each other." She took off down the hall without waiting for him to protest.

C HAPTER 23

UNINVITED

T OLEN STARED DOWN THE DARK HALL UNTIL THE SOUND OF M ACY'S light footsteps died away.

He took a deep breath and moved toward the dungeons, his heart hammering in his chest, his mind replaying Macy's words over and over, *I promise, I promise.* She would stay safe. She would. She was strong. He needed to be strong too. He had to stay focused, keep his head. Succeed.

I am the captain of my soul.

He took three steps down the dark hall leading to the dungeons, and his resolve was put to the test. He'd plunged right into his nightmare. The dark stone walls seeped what looked like black blood between the cracks, the heavy blue-flamed torches hung high on the walls, the thick, oily, darkness, even the smell of death and decay. It was all disgustingly familiar.

He kept his senses focused on Macy's life force, and his nerves tensed to react to any indication that she was in mortal danger. While his mind stayed with her, he let his body be guided toward his father.

A left turn and then a right.

He could feel Macy's anxiety. She was okay, just focused.

A soft scratching noise ahead—he pulled himself against the wall and waited, but nothing appeared—a rat or mouse maybe? He hated to think what might pass as a rat in the Shadow Realm.

Another right turn, then a left. He slowed down and pressed against the wall.

There at the end of the hall stood one of the hairy guards, thankfully facing away from him. Towering at least ten feet tall, the guard seemed man-like in shape but patches of curly black fur covered the muscled body that peeked beneath his rusted armor. His thick, night-dark hair twisted down his back in dirty ringlets.

Tolen lifted the Sleep Dust pouch from his belt, pinched a tiny bit between his fingers, tossed it into the air, and thought, *Vin'akra.*

A gentle breeze blew the dust forward and swirled it around the guard's head.

Tolen ran forward to catch the hairy guard before he crashed to the floor. His knees buckled from the weight and he had to call more strength to his arms and legs in order to lower the massive creature to the ground silently.

He lifted the thick ring of keys from the guard's belt and stepped around the corner.

His father's cell was the first down this hall. Two sentries stood outside. None of the other cells had guards. The sentries were bald, their pasty skin translucent—Tolen could see the veins pulsing beneath the surface—and where they should have had eyes the thin skin stretched tight and smooth down to over-large noses that sniffed the air.

Tolen took two steps forward and his toe scuffed against the floor.

The sniffing increased and the sentry's blood-red lips curled back over black fangs. Low growls gurgled from their throats.

Tolen stopped, hardly daring to breathe.

The growls stopped. They couldn't feel his heat or smell him, but they'd heard his movement. The herbs were working. Tolen stood still for several seconds until they resumed their sightless watch toward the opposite wall.

He tiptoed between them and peered through the tiny barred window set high in the door.

His father lay curled in the fetal position in the center of the floor, his chest rising and falling slowly.

Tolen blew Sleep Dust at the sentries and waited while they slid slowly down the wall and crumpled on the floor.

He lifted the set of heavy keys and fit the first one in the lock. It didn't fit—nor did the following three. The rusty metal lock was hard to maneuver, and the jangling keys echoed loudly in the stone corridor.

When there were only two keys left and Tolen's heart felt like it was going to explode, the lock finally clicked in his hand and the door creaked open.

Tolen stepped into a black cloud of despair. He took a deep shuddering breath and moved toward his father. The closer he got, the worse the feeling became. Dread, sorrow, anxiety, terror…the *Fear* of the Dark in its purest form.

He fell to his knees and sprinkled the Camouflage over his father with trembling hands. He checked the rocks in his ears and then stuffed some into Daedal's—not knowing if they'd even help since his father had been under this blanket of despair for so long. Slowly Daedal's breathing deepened.

He was as tall as Tolen—maybe even slightly taller—but when Tolen lifted him, it felt like carrying a child. Daedal's body had been tortured for so long Tolen feared that if he held him too tightly he might break something.

He sprinkled the Heat in the cell, cradled his father against his chest, and forced his feet to take him out the door, past the sentries, the hairy guard, and back down the hall.

He was almost to the storage room when he felt it. Some shift in the Balance that told him Macy was in trouble.

His heart rammed to his throat and he almost dropped his father as he began to run silently back toward the dungeons.

o o o

Macy pushed her back against the wall and waited. Something was following her, but every time she stopped to let it catch up, it stopped too. She wanted it to try and attack, come out for a fight, but it didn't.

The living quarters were just ahead, she could tell by the slight brightening of the light and the smell of rot and decay no longer burning her nose.

She pushed her back against the wall and shuffled forward slowly. The presence behind her moved too. She sped up and could feel it increase its pace as well. She stopped and it stopped.

"You wanna play games?" she whispered and pulled her knife from its sheath. She lifted out a handful of herbs from one of the pouches and blew on them. "*Mi'no…*"

The herbs burst into a cloud of smoke and something coughed. She ran as fast as she could towards the sound. The smoke did not affect her eyes—she could see the squat figure less than ten feet away. She jumped through the air onto the creature's back, wrapped her arms around its neck, and placed the blade of her knife against its throat.

"Who are you?"

The creature twisted trying to throw her off. For a small creature, it was surprisingly strong. She pushed the knife deeper into its neck. It gasped and stopped thrashing. "I is a friend," he wheezed.

This response surprised her so much she eased up on the knife. "What are you talking about?"

The creature coughed and spluttered. "Please, no kill me. I am wanting to help you. I promise. I am seeing you come past my Master's quarters, and I knows you not one of *them.*"

Macy let go of his neck, but kept the knifepoint at his throat as she circled around to look at his face. Her eyes widened in shock.

He was a Doogar, weary looking, but without the features of the Dark.

"Who are you?" she asked.

"I am Kelner. Goblins kidnapped me from my home four years ago. The Dark took my family. They force us to use our skills to help them in their plans. Already my ma has died from the torturous work. I isam fighting them and so am sentenced to clean bed-pans instead of working metals and stone with the others."

"Metals and stone? That stuff the Kreydawn are bringing in from the earth dimension?"

"Yes." Kelner grabbed her arm. "Please, you must go. I show you a way to escape. They knowing someone here who not 'posed to be. Take this," he shoved a piece of the strange shiny stone in her hand. "Give it to the Guardians. It will tell them all they need know." He tugged on her arm.

"Wait. I'm here for a woman. She's tiny with auburn hair and brown eyes. She's up here somewhere. Can you help me find her?"

The little man trembled. "I sorry, but too dangerous."

"You can either show me or I'll find her myself."

"You not understand. She is held by Daemon, she is his."

Cold chills ran down Macy's spine. "What do you mean?"

"She belongs to the Master of the Demons. She gave her life to him to stop him from finding another."

"Do you know who?"

The little man bowed his head. "Her son."

Macy narrowed her eyes. "Do you know who her son is?"

"Tolen Daedal Téloran." He looked up at her beneath his eyelashes. "The Ninth Chosen."

The breath whooshed out of Macy's lungs. "How do you know this?"

"She is drugged, she rambles in her sleep. Come Miss. I take you safe way."

Macy stood up and grabbed Kelner's shoulder. "No. Take me to her. I'm going to get her out of here."

Kelner glanced down the hallway and sighed. "This way. You will not succeed Miss. You do not understand."

Macy motioned him ahead.

The hallway grew lighter and lighter, the walls themselves glowed blue. Kelner stopped at a huge doorway, bearing ornately carved snakes with long fangs and howling DéHool, that reached from floor to ceiling.

"She in there, miss. Dark powers hold her there."

"Do you know how I can break through them to get her out?"

Kelner ran a hand over his eyes. "Yes."

Macy shook the man's shoulders. "Well?"

He walked through the door and ran his hands through a smoky gray film. The smoke dissipated enough for Macy to see Areen suspended in midair, wrapped in a thick black cloud that twisted and swirled around her body. Occasionally she twitched and moaned.

Kelner lifted a box from a table beside the door and opened it. The cloud gathered and flew straight into the box.

Macy ran forward to catch Areen before she fell.

"*Fear.*" Kelner whispered. The box rattled in his hands.

Macy's hands trembled as she ran them across Areen's forehead.

"Is she all right?"

Kelner shrugged sadly. "Only time will tell."

Surprisingly, she looked better than the last time Macy had seen her—physically at least. Her cheeks had filled out; her hair was shiny and full around her face. No longer having to shield Tolen had done a lot for her health.

Areen's eyes suddenly flew open and she started to scream.

Macy clapped a hand over her mouth.

Areen thrashed and tried to throw her off.

Macy pulled a pinch of Sleep Dust from her pouch and sprinkled it over the woman's nose. Her eyes rolled back and she drifted into a deep sleep.

"*Mig'nata.*" Strength rushed through Macy's arms and she lifted Areen over her shoulder. Tolen's mother was a little taller than she was. Hopefully it wouldn't take too much toll on her life force to carry her back down to the dungeons.

"You are a Chosen one?" Kelner whispered in awe.

"Yes."

He dipped his head once. "It is an honor." He set the box on the table where it rattled angrily. "Come, let's go."

"Wait, I need to go to the dungeons. Someone is meeting me there."

Kelner sighed and led the way back into the hall. He touched a crack in the wall and a door opened. He walked through and motioned Macy inside before closing the door behind them.

"This be the servant's stairs," he whispered. "It goes past the kitchens and down to the dungeons. We must be quiet."

Macy hefted Areen higher over her shoulder and followed Kelner down the dark stairs.

He paused halfway down the steps. "Stop. Wait here." He disappeared through another hidden doorway.

Macy glanced at her watch. Forty-five minutes had passed. If she didn't hurry, Tolen would think something had happened. She was about to try to find the door herself when Kelner appeared below her.

"It's safe. I sent the others away. Come." He walked quickly and opened yet another door. Macy knew they were in the right place just by the smell.

"Where is your friend?'

"He's supposed to meet me in the storage room with the maggot bags."

Kelner nodded and led the way down the passageway. They walked for a while longer when shuffling sounds met her ears. Kelner grunted and fell forward.

Macy propped Areen against the wall and scurried forward on her hands and knees. She rolled Kelner over to see a dagger protruding from his chest. She glanced up to see where it'd come from and saw an Ookra charging toward her, readying to throw another knife.

She ripped the dagger free of Kelner and snapped it toward the advancing creature.

The Ookra collapsed, the blade wedged between his eyes.

Kelner gurgled and Macy leaned over him. He pushed something into her palm. "Gateway…don't let them…you must stop them from…" His dark eyes closed and his body went limp beneath her.

Macy lowered him gently to the ground, shoved the stone in her hand into her pocket, crawled back, and lifted Areen over her shoulder, before taking off at a run to the end of the passage.

The storage room was empty.

She looked at her watch. Sixty-three minutes had passed since she'd left.

Chapter 24

THE PRICE OF SOULS

Macy lowered Areen behind a stack of maggots, ignoring the hiss of their tiny bodies sliding against each other inside the bags.

Quiet footsteps echoed softly nearby.

Two dead bodies lay in the hallway. If the footsteps didn't belong to Tolen, they were in big trouble.

Sweat beaded on her forehead and heat flooded her palms. She pulled her Kuna just barely to the surface. The smell of eucalyptus and roses swirled faintly around her head, masking the horrible stench of the dungeon, and steadying her nerves.

Her shard pulsed with energy. Familiar pleasant energy.

Tolen was coming.

She peeked around the bags and her heart rammed into her throat. "Tolen duck!"

Tolen dropped and his father rolled out of his arms. A long knife sliced through the empty air where he'd been standing.

Macy thrust her palm out. "*Mi'no ha!*" A small ball of fire shot from her hand and slammed into the Ookra. She pushed her Kuna until the heat of the fireball burned so hot the Ookra burst to ashes. She called the heat back to her, held her breath, and listened for anything else coming.

Tolen lifted his father again, holding him gently. "Are you all right?" he whispered as he walked toward her. "I felt something shift in your direction."

Macy looked down at Tolen's father. Daedal Téloran looked more dead than alive. His eyes were closed, his chest barely moving. Macy's stomach dropped. He didn't have much time. She swallowed. "It was just another Ookra, I killed it—" She stepped back behind the maggots to lift Areen again but she was gone. "Areen?""

"You found her?" Tolen looked at the floor by Macy's feet.

"I did, but—where'd she go?"

Tolen propped his father against one of the stacks and helped Macy search.

They found his mother huddled in a corner shivering.

"Mom?" Tolen touched her cheek and she shrank back.

"No, no. Please no more. I can't take it. Please, stop torturing me." She covered her face with her hands and sobbed.

Tolen dropped beside her and forced her to look at him. "Mom, it's me. It's Tolen. I've come to save you. I have Dad." He ran his fingers across her forehead. "*Lon'adras.*" She stopped crying and though her eyes still held a hint of disbelief, she reached out to touch his face.

"Not a nightmare? Real?" Desperation laced every syllable. She grabbed the front of Tolen's shirt in her fists.

"Yes. I'm here, Mom." Tolen's eyes filled with tears as he wrapped his arms around her and she clung to him.

A lump lodged in Macy's throat. They didn't have time for a long reunion. She swallowed. "I'm sorry, Tolen, but we've gotta go."

He turned to look at her. His mother still clung to him, her face buried in his shirt.

Areen looked up at the sound of Macy's voice and hid under Tolen's arm like a scared child.

Tolen whispered, "Her mind isn't right, Macy. I'm not sure what to do."

"Let's just get them out of here. You can figure out how to heal them later."

"You?" Areen said from beneath Tolen's arm, pointing a shaky finger at Macy.

"Yep, me. Can you walk? We've got to get out of here now and I'm not sure I can keep carrying you."

She huddled back into Tolen and he lifted her face. "Mom, we have to go. I need you to walk, okay?"

Areen took a shaky breath and nodded.

Macy blew out a breath, trying to work out a possible escape. "Okay, Tolen, I've got an idea."

Tolen walked back to his father, his mother holding onto his arm the entire way. He lifted his father over his shoulder; his mother didn't even seem to notice he was there. "Great, let's hear it."

"We'll put you and your parents in one of the carts. I'll put on the clothes from the Ookra I killed earlier. I'm short enough I should be able to pull it off. I'll push the cart out of here and hopefully we can get to the door without being stopped."

He looked around the dungeon and she knew he had as many doubts as she did. "What about a distraction?"

Macy shrugged. "If we need it, we'll figure it out."

He shook his head, but they had no choice but to keep going with the current plan, no matter how risky.

"Okay."

"Okay." She squeezed his hand, ran back into the passage, and dragged the two bodies back with her.

"Who's that?" Tolen pointed to the little Doogar man as Macy hid the bodies behind the stacks.

"Kelner." She came back around, carrying the Ookra's cloak. "Long story. I'll tell you later." She quickly pulled the cloak over her head. It reeked of the dungeons. She gagged and switched to breathing through her mouth.

"I'll be right back." She peeked outside. The guard who'd been leading the DéHool was nowhere in sight.

A lone cart stood near the corner of the building. She ducked down and walked as fast as she dared over to it. The reason behind its abandonment was apparent instantly. One of its wheels was near falling off, the wood cracked and full of termite holes, but she didn't have time to be picky.

She gritted her teeth, whispered, "*Mig'nata*," and pushed the cart back to the entrance of the dungeons, trying to mimic the slow, jerky movements of the Ookra.

When she pushed back through the door, Tolen popped out from behind a stack of bags.

"Any trouble while I was gone?" Macy tossed the smelly hood back off her hair.

He shook his head. "Nope."

She raised her eyebrows. "Let's hope your luck holds." She grabbed a couple of the maggot bags and tossed them into the cart. "After you climb in I'll put a few more over you." Tolen wrinkled his nose and she shrugged. "You might need the cover. It worked last time."

"Last time we were hiding in bags going in. If someone sees us taking these out, we're in big trouble," he said, but climbed the side of the cart with his father over his shoulder. Macy could hear him situating Daedal on the bags.

He stood up and held out a hand to his mother. Macy waited below, ready to help her if she needed, but Areen managed to get over the side on her own.

Tolen's whisper to her carried through the rotting wood. "Stay down, Mom. I'll be right back."

Macy stepped back as he jumped over the side. He pulled her into his arms and kissed her in a way that made her forget for a moment where she was and what they were doing. He pulled back and touched her lips with his finger. "Stay safe." His eyes held hers for a split second, long enough for her to see the worry pooling there before he jumped back on the wheel and scrambled over the side of the cart. She stuck her fingers through one of the holes and felt Tolen's big hand cover them.

She leaned her head against the side. "Don't worry, Tolen. Everything's going to be okay." She gritted her teeth. It was going to take a miracle.

Macy covered the cart with one of the moldy tarps lying on the floor, took a deep breath, and allowed her Kuna to rush to her hands. "Just in case," she whispered as she pushed the cart toward freedom.

She was halfway through the doorway before the first scream erupted. She spun around looking for the culprit, only to realize the screams were coming from inside the cart.

"Mom!" Tolen's muffled cry came through the tarp.

"Tolen, shut her up," Macy called through her teeth.

"I can't. She's screaming and thrashing around. It's like something's hurting her."

"That is because she cannot leave." The male voice was deep, cold, and full of malice.

CHAPTER 25

FIGHT FOR LIGHT

MACY'S KNEES BUCKLED UNDER THE WEIGHT OF THE EVIL ENTERING the room and she fell forward.

Tolen peeked out the top of the cart.

"Hello, Tolen." The voice was louder. Whoever he was, he was getting closer. Macy could hear his feet crunching on the dirty floor.

Tolen jumped out of the cart and landed beside her. She tried to stand back up.

"Tolen, I—I can't move." Panic ripped through her chest. Why couldn't she move? She'd never felt anything like this before.

Tolen pulled her to his side, leaned against the cart, tried to push it and hold onto Macy at the same time. Areen screamed louder.

"I wouldn't do that if I were you. You'll kill her." The voice sounded amused—as if this idea wasn't at all unappealing.

Tolen stopped and spoke in a trembling voice. "You *will* let us go."

"No, I'm afraid I won't."

"You will!" Tolen pulled the Glockshaw from his pouch and threw them. "*Mi'no ha!*" They burst into flame and shot forward. The passage lit up in the light of the fireballs and Macy got the first glimpse of the creature coming for them.

He was huge, red-skinned, with yellow eyes. Black horns erupted from either side of his head and curved down to his chin.

Daemon.

He flicked his hand lazily at the Glockshaw. They blew out in a puff of smoke, and the hall fell into darkness once more.

His laughter echoed through the dark—the sound hurt Macy's ears and reverberated through her skull.

"Is that all?" He continued to laugh. "I thought the Ninth would actually pose a threat. But you are nothing—nothing but a weak, simple-minded child."

He stepped from the shadows. His grotesque form was worse than she could possibly have imagined.

"How disappointing." His voice lowered to a deadly whisper.

Tolen trembled beside her. The smell of cloves and earth swirled around him.

Why did his gifts work and she couldn't get her Kuna to respond at all?

"Let my mother go."

"My dear boy, I couldn't even if I wanted to. You see," he stepped closer, "her soul belongs to me. She gave it to me long ago. Her life…" he pointed a long red finger at Tolen's chest, "instead of yours."

"You lie!"

"Oh no, I do not. Your mother is not the person she's made you think she is."

Macy glanced at Tolen. He was lost, entranced by the Demon Master's words. She wished she had the strength to do *something*, anything!

Daemon circled closer, his yellow eyes mocking. "Oh yes. Long before you came along, she was far more powerful, far more important, far more…interesting. She loved a far greater man than your pathetic father. I'll never understand how Daedal managed to get her to fall for him, but I warned her she would one day pay for the mistake of leaving. She begged and pleaded the day I found you both hiding in some two-bit town. You were nothing but a sniveling little brat back then." He looked Tolen up and down. "Not that you've changed much." His lips curled back over black pointed teeth.

"She swore that she would come back to me if I spared your life. Had I known you were the Ninth, I wouldn't have been so generous." He tipped his horned head. "Areen entered into the pact before they rescued her, the stupid earth-men. But then fate gave me a gift—none other than her one true love." Daemon flicked something off his dark cloak. "I must say it has been most rewarding torturing the bane of my existence." He leaned forward and glared in Tolen's eyes. "Funny…you seem shocked. Your mother never told you—"

"Enough Daemon." Areen leaned over the side of the cart. "You have me. Let my son go."

"Mom?" Tolen twisted to look at his mother, his face ghostly white in the blue light.

Areen didn't look at him, her lip trembled, but she kept her eyes on Daemon. She seemed to be back to herself—the childlike fear gone from her face and replaced with revulsion and anger.

Daemon answered Tolen's plea with an evil sneer. "Oh yes, she once loved me, before the Dark made me into the god I am now. And she will be with me again."

Areen's voice shook. "I will stay with you, Daemon, but I will never be what you want."

Daemon's face twisted. He paused inches away.

Tolen lowered Macy back to the ground gently without looking at her—she could do nothing to stop him—stepped forward and bridged the gap between them, his nose wrinkled in disgust. "I will fight you for them."

"What?" Macy yelled.

"No, Tolen!" Areen shouted.

Daemon laughed. "You dare challenge me?"

Tolen's jaw clenched. "Yes. If I win, you sever the pact, she goes free, you leave my parents alone, and we all leave in peace. If I die—" he swallowed loudly, "then nothing changes."

"No, Tolen don't. You don't know what he's capable of," Macy pleaded, fighting against the invisible bonds holding her captive.

Tolen looked down at her and whispered. "Macy, I have to. It's our only chance. I have to try."

Terror ripped through Macy's heart. "Tolen, please. Remember who you are. The whole world needs you. You can't risk that for three people."

Tolen squeezed his eyes shut. "Macy, I do know who I am. I'm the Ninth Chosen and I am responsible for the three of you." He dropped to his knees beside her, and ignoring their audience, cupped her face in his hands. She shook from the effort to move as he placed his lips at her cheek and whispered so softly she could barely hear. "I'm the distraction. Get out of here. Save my parents if you can, but if you can't," his voice cracked, "just get yourself out." He pulled away and looked in her eyes. "I love you, Macy. Whatever happens, that will never change."

Daemon growled impatiently. "Ah, young love. So…nauseating."

Macy barely heard the demon's cruel words through her pain.

Tolen's jaw hardened and he jumped up. "Let's do this."

"Tolen, no!" Macy tried to hold on to him, go after him, force him to stay with her, but she had no strength. Angry tears burned in her eyes.

Areen, screaming and sobbing, rushed forward and grabbed Daemon's long black cloak. "No, Daemon, please, spare him. Spare him!"

Daemon laughed and flicked his fingers. Areen's hands flew behind her back as if tied with ropes, and she fell to the floor with a huff. She opened and closed her mouth, but no sound came out. Daemon cast her a hateful glare before turning back to Tolen. "Into the courtyard, young one. I want a more enthusiastic audience to watch you die."

○○○

Tolen's head throbbed as he followed behind Daemon. He barely cast a glance at his sobbing mother, her pain too unbearable. He couldn't see his father, lying unconscious inside the cart, maybe already gone. He didn't look at Macy as he tugged out of her grasp, but he did touch the top of her head as he walked by. The love he had for her rushed through his hand, into her body and somehow he knew, once he got Daemon away from here, Macy would be able to move again.

She would find a way. She would survive. He hoped telling her he loved her wouldn't make it harder for her to move on if he didn't succeed. He'd meant his promise that he would do all he could to stay alive, to keep them both alive, but he'd be an idiot if he didn't accept the real possibility that *none* of them would survive this. He swallowed the pain of this thought. *I'm so sorry I didn't do a better job protecting her, Bastian. Please, if there is some way for the Light to help her to escape this place, please guide her. Save her. Please.*

He could feel something tugging at his life force, something different from the darkness here. Something elusive, sensing him, sizing him up, trying to find his weaknesses—Daemon? With effort, he focused on tightening his shield. He may not be strong enough to beat this monster, but he wasn't about to give him additional weapons.

Focus on the vibrations surrounding you; you will know the extent of their power by the strength of the darkness flowing from them. Call your gifts to the forefront of your mind, balance the warmth, sense the instant that each gift will be needed, and call it forth at the right moment.

Bastian?

I am here, Tolen. You are not alone.

With each step his heart pounded out a disjointed rhythm like the melancholy beat of the executioner's drum. He closed his eyes and swallowed hard. *What am I doing? You were right. I'm not ready. I'm not strong enough.*

Do not underestimate the power of pure love, Tolen. Sacrifice for the right reason brings strength the Dark cannot understand or contend with. Bastian's deep voice resonated warmth through Tolen's mind and body, but fear still clouded his heart.

Bastian, I don't know how to do this. I don't know how to be the Ninth. I'm just a freak from a small town in the middle of nowhere.

Tolen, if that is what you truly believe, then that is all you will ever be. Believe in yourself as I believe in you, as Macy believes in you, as the Light believes in you.

Daemon stepped out into the gray light and silence filled the area as if a switch had been flipped to turn off the wind and murmuring crowd.

The tall, hairy guards leading DéHool, Raksasha, Ookra, and a number of other creatures Tolen couldn't name, stopped what they were doing and began to gather.

Daemon walked into the wide circular space surrounded by the hideous statues Tolen had glimpsed from inside the cart.

He cast a quick glance behind him to see Macy dragging a tarp into a shadowy area beside the entrance to the dungeon—the bulge at the middle must be his father. Pride swelled within him.

His mother shook in the doorway, her hands clasping the rocky frame, anguish etched in every line of her face. She seemed to be trying to walk through the door despite the pain. Macy would have to leave her. The knowledge cut through his heart. He met his mother's eyes for a brief moment and he could tell she knew she would not leave this place, but her fear was for her son, not herself. He hoped she knew how much he loved her.

Daemon began to speak and Tolen turned his attention back to the Demon Master, his heart hammering, head pounding, chest heating up with Kuna while at the same time constricting with sorrow.

"My people…" Daemon threw off his dark cloak, revealing a heavy sword sheathed to his back, and lifted his arms to the growing crowd. "I have before you the last hope of the Light." He pointed mockingly at Tolen. "The last shred of possibility for their success against us," his lips curled into a disgusting grin. "The *Ninth* Chosen."

Murmurs echoed through the crowd. The DéHool snarled, saliva dripping thickly from their razor-like teeth, and stamped their monstrous paws.

Tolen's hands started to shake and the Kuna became uncomfortably hot.

"You will watch as I kill him and your hearts will never more be afraid of the Light's power. Without the Ninth, nothing can stand in our way."

Tolen closed his eyes. *Bastian…if I die…I'm the Ninth—all hope will be lost for everyone else.*

Put your trust in the Light. Bastian's voice carried strong and clear. The Watcher's presence felt so real in that moment; he swore he stood right beside him.

Open your eyes see what is there.

Something Evrah said came rushing back to him. "*The gifts of the Hidden are exactly that—gifts from the Light. We do not have magic powers or potions. Everything we are, everything we can do is because of the Light. You must remember this. Without the Light, we would have nothing—be nothing. The Light has chosen you, Tolen Daedal Téloran.*"

Trust the light. *Believe* …. Bastian's voice trailed off, but Tolen could still feel his presence there with him.

He opened his eyes.

He could not do this alone because he was just a boy, just a life force in a mortal body. *I am who I am because of the Light.* The words filled him suddenly, rising from deep within him. *I am more than just a freak from a small town. I am more than my mistakes. I am the Ninth—I trust in the Light.* Macy's voice cut into his thoughts. *Show the Dark what you are made of Tolen* … He took a deep breath. *Please guide me, show me. Help me use my gifts. Whether I die today or not, please, help me save them.*

A surge of blessed warmth filled him from head to toe and the despair of the Shadow Realm lifted from his mind. He still had no idea how to fight Daemon and win, but fear no longer had hold of him, his mind was incredibly clear.

The Light had come.

Heat surged to his palms, ready for release, his Watcher's eye went berserk behind his lid, and he saw seconds into the future.

Macy rushes to stash Daedal behind a pile of boulders, and Areen collapses in the doorway as Daemon raises his giant sword high in the air dropping it over Tolen's head in one fatal stroke ….

"Tin'ruhl!" Tolen shouted and a twelve-foot high wall of gray dirt shot up from the ground, knocking Daemon's blade out of his hand.

Daemon growled, dove for his sword, and flipped back to his feet in one lithe movement—the mammoth steel blade glinting wickedly in his monstrous grip.

Tolen twisted his hands in the air, the wall of dirt fell, the ground shook under Daemon's feet, and the Demon Master stumbled. *"Mi'no ha!"* Tolen shot a burst of fire from his hands, twisted his fingers until it formed a flaming spear and forced it toward Daemon's heart.

Daemon dove out of the way, but the flaming spear turned to follow. His eyes widened. *"I'kashti!"* A giant moss covered, wooden shield appeared in his clawed fist and absorbed the spear, leaving nothing behind but a trail of smoke and the smell of singed flesh.

"Walkarna!" Daemon screamed and hundreds of crows and other

horrid massive winged creatures spiraled through the air toward Tolen—talons out, black eyes wild.

"*Vin'akra!*" Tolen shouted. A whirlwind curled up from the ground creating a swirling barrier, blocking him from the attacking flock

He cast half a glance over his shoulder to see Macy behind a huge boulder, her face torn, her knife out as if ready to rush to his aid. "No Macy! Go! NOW!" He twisted the vortex until it covered Daemon from head to toe.

The flock dove toward Tolen, their path now clear. "*Den mea tin'ruhl!*" Huge rocks rose from the ground and rocketed into the pack, knocking them one by one out of the sky.

He couldn't watch to see what she was doing, but he could feel Macy's inner struggle as she dragged his father out of harm's way back toward the door. She did not want to leave him, but she would do what they'd come here to do.

His shard pulsed with energy, and his eye showed him a flash of the future. He barely rolled out of the way before a huge, black root broke free of the ground right where he'd been standing, twisting and curling like the many tentacles of an octopus seeking him out.

He pushed back against the tree with his own thoughts, focusing on the gift that was born with him. The tree became still, but he could feel his strength waning quickly, the darkness in the Shadow Realm tugged at him body and soul, seeking his weaknesses, fighting to put dark thoughts and fears into his mind.

Daemon laughed as Tolen panted.

They were running out of time.

Tolen looked right into the hateful yellow eyes and shouted. "*Den aktra!*" His voice didn't frighten him as he took on the power of his subconscious and sent his will to several dozen Kreydawn standing motionless nearby. The Kreydawn ran at Daemon, their pick axes held high over their heads.

Daemon's laugh cut off and he raised his sword, struck down the throng of Kreydawn as if they were nothing, and turned back to Tolen, his chest heaving, his eyes full of poisonous malice.

"You have the Dreamer gift." He tilted his horned head mockingly. "Interesting. There is *darkness* within the Ninth."

Tolen's chest tightened, but he ignored Daemon's frightening words, preparing himself for the next attack, hoping against hope that Macy had escaped.

"Let's see how you handle the ultimate weapon of evil, *Dark one*." Daemon's lips twisted into a wicked grin. He threw his hands up in the air. "*Kindrak' al' duberio!*""

The sky instantly darkened. Tolen could barely see through the thick gloom.

The cries of the Wraiths circling the Prison grew louder. Their dense mists formed into a black cloud and hurtled toward the ground, descending over Tolen before he could move or speak.

Their oily heaviness layered over his skin like a cloak of darkness and evil, suffocating him, sucking the life from him. The cries of lost souls echoed through his skull, piercing his heart.

Pain—pain more excruciating than breaking his bones a million times, heart wrenching pain, ripping his soul in half. The black dreams were back, but this time they were real, tangible, horrifying, everyone he loved was dead, he'd failed them all....

"TOLEN!" Macy's voice carried through the mist and his Second Sight kicked in again. *Macy rushes toward him her knife out, her Kuna building, returning to her despite the power of the realm. Daemon steps in her way and lifts his sword.*

Tolen was going to die and Macy was going to die trying to save him.

His heart thundered in his ears. *No!* He fought against the power that held him, but it was too powerful, he couldn't stop it. They were going to die.

"*Mi'no ha!*" Macy shouted and heat seared over Tolen's body, cutting through the wraiths, but the flame didn't burn him, it cleared his mind and pushed the darkness of despair from his heart.

Light's Aid had come.

He saw Macy through the reforming Shadows, twisting a fireball toward Daemon who again had conjured his shield. She blasted fireball after fireball, but he was advancing, his sword within inches to strike.

"NO!" *It can't end this way. She will not die for me.* Tolen pulled what strength he had left deep into his body, let it build in his chest, and shouted toward the sky, focusing everything into his gifts. *"Y'NA TO'CON-CHLA MINDRA! RADI'NON! ODRA AKTRA DEN! VAST DóN AKTRA!"*

I AM THE NINTH CHOSEN! LIGHT COME FORTH! BRING US AID! FIGHT FOR US!

Pure-white, beautiful, warm light engulfed his body.

The Shadows screeched and writhed away from him, scattering into the wind. Creatures nearby hid their eyes and dove for cover. Daemon howled in pain and dropped to the ground, throwing his shield over his head.

Macy turned to Tolen with wide eyes.

Tolen looked up as the light gathered into a huge ball and shot up through the thick, gray murk above, creating a bright hole in the sky.

Winged, human-like figures descended from the hole and swept toward the ground.

As they landed in a circle surrounding them, Tolen's jaw dropped. The winged men were not alone—each of them carried one of the Radia Warriors.

Incrah stepped from the arms of one and sidled next to Tolen, his eyes never leaving Daemon's inert form. "You picked a good place to practice your gifts Tolen, but how about some help?"

"How did you—?" Tolen stuttered, failing to form a coherent sentence.

Incrah raised his sword to the side as Daemon stirred. "No idea. We wanted to come after you as soon as Ras'met received the message from the trees, but we had no idea where to find you. We'd almost given up the search when suddenly the Guardians came and told us to come with them. They heard your call to the Light. You somehow created a link straight to the citadel." Incrah glanced at Daemon who started to stand as the light faded. "We need to hurry; their power can't last long here."

Tolen looked at the winged men—*The Guardians?*

Macy moved to Tolen's side and squeezed his hand once before letting go—he could feel her Kuna in her warm fingers.

Did they have enough strength left to survive this? The call to his gifts had taken nearly all he had left. He didn't have time to look around to see if someone had found his parents before the first surge of Dark servants recovered.

The hairy guards released the DéHool and the wolves launched forward, their red eyes full of bloodlust. Seconds later throngs of nightmarish creatures—hunger for death on their malevolent faces—followed.

Tolen's Second Sight flashed too fast for him to understand. He couldn't see if they would survive.

Everything seemed to move in fast forward as he glanced at the people he couldn't stand to lose—the Radia Warriors, the Guardians, *Macy*.

His eyes darted to the sky; the hole was slowly closing. "*Mi'no ha! Vin'akra! Ma'sha! Win'tashta! Tin'ruhl! Nit'ahai!*" *Life to fire and wind! Hear me animal, water, Earth, nature!*

The last of the strength within him released as a rushing wind, pushing toward everything that could side with them outside the hole in the Shadow Realm.

Eagles, hawks, and owls shot through the door in the sky, carried by the wind he called. Great fires started around the courtyard—the light and warmth sent hordes of small lizard-like creatures cringing away from the battlefield. Rain—crisp, warm rain—poured down and tall, grayish monsters shrieked in agony as their skin sizzled and burned; they dove for cover beneath the rocks and statues. Thick, dark, roots snaked their way up from the hard ground, and wrapped themselves around every evil servant they could reach.

The Radia Warriors raised their weapons with wicked precision against Daemon, the DéHool, and their masters. Several wolves lay dead or dying on the ground.

Hope filled Tolen's heart, even as his knees shook with exhaustion.

BOOM!

The ground shook beneath their feet.

BOOM!

All light vanished, and they were suddenly bathed in darkness.

All fighting stopped. All sound stopped.

Thick blackness—heavy and putrid—fell upon them.

Evil, merciless, horrifying laughter filled the void, resonating off the wall of black.

Tolen covered his ears in pain, but it did no good. The laughter echoed inside his head, in his bones, everywhere.

Darsapean had come.

CHAPTER 26

THROUGH THE TUNNEL

"Come on Tolen, time to go," an unfamiliar voice whispered in his ear. Someone wrapped their arms around his waist and he had the sensation of being lifted upwards. He had no idea if it were friend or foe, he could no longer fight; he couldn't do anything.

Just before the blackness consumed him, he was lifted out of the Shadow Realm and into the light.

The horrible, agonizing laughter slowly faded into silence and he finally had control of his thoughts again. Up ahead another man carried Macy, his vast wings beating the air in swift, smooth movements.

They were mere minutes into the trip when the tunnel opened to a breathtaking scene where the sun rose majestically, liberatingly above a range of lush, green mountains.

The darkness in the Shadow Realm had drained him body and mind, but the light here uplifted and energized him, brought peaceful warmth that went beyond the body and reached into his soul. All the fear he'd felt evaporated, replaced with pure serenity.

The nightmare was over.

The winged men set them down in the center of a huge amphitheater next to a white marble building.

"Wait here. Your parents are safe." They took off quickly, leaving Tolen and Macy to stare around in awe. Tolen took two strides and pulled her into his arms.

"We did it," Macy whispered against his chest, relief echoing through every syllable.

"We did." He buried his face in her hair. She was alive. His parents were alive. They were alive. They'd done it. Euphoria made his head swim. He relished her warmth as his eyes took in their surroundings. Tall walls made of clear glass separated by great marble pillars enclosed the room. A raised partition along the circular walls housed twelve huge chairs—or maybe they were thrones—made of white-blue crystal.

Everything glittered brightly, the floor, the walls, the thrones, the white-marble pillars. It was the most beautiful place Tolen had ever seen.

"Thank goodness the Radia warriors showed up with the Guardians," Macy whispered as she turned to lean against him and look around. "I wonder where the Radia Warriors went…"

Tolen sighed. "That's the *second* time my Sight showed me I might lose you." He squeezed her tighter and kissed the top of her head. "Please don't do that to me ever again."

She chuckled softly. "No promises, buddy."

Tolen rested his chin on her hair, the euphoria and relief was beginning to trail off, leaving him feeling sleepy. "I didn't know the Guardians could fly." He said with a yawn.

"That's the first time I've seen them, but I've—"

"—heard the legends," he finished and she glanced up and smiled. "What is this place?"

She looked out the glass walls at the beauty outside. "I think we're in the Light Realm, at the Citadel of Light."

"Do you think my parents are really okay?"

Macy wrapped her arms over his. "I hope so."

"Your parents are in the place of Healing. You will see them shortly."

They turned to see a tall, elegant woman wearing a floor-length white dress. Her soft brown hair waved down her back.

She held a thick book bound in tan leather and a long gleaming silver pen. "I am Keytleen." Her soft, chocolate eyes were kind. "Will you come with me please? There is someone who wishes to speak with you."

Tolen looked at Macy and she shrugged. He took her hand and they followed the woman out of the room.

Keytleen led them down a long walkway made of more marble and glass, open to the sky above, that led into the large marble building. Statues of beautiful men and women stood sentinel every few feet. Gold name-plates were mounted on their pedestals, but most of the names Tolen couldn't pronounce if he tried.

Keytleen stopped before a majestic door carved with flowers and trees that seemed to move within the wood. The door opened without her touch and they followed her inside.

Tolen had no words to describe the beauty of the citadel. Its beauty surely surpassed the Taj Mahal, the great cathedrals, the castles of England, all the Seven Wonders of the World. It was breathtaking. Every surface gleamed. Vast murals covered the walls and high ceilings, showing incredible scenes of things Tolen had always believed to be myth. Now he wasn't so sure. Intricate furnishings adorned the halls that opened every twenty feet or so. Every now and then elaborate tall doors materialized out of the walls, camouflaged by the murals.

Keytleen soon stopped at one of the doors and a deep voice issued from the other side. "You may come in."

"You have ten minutes." Keytleen held open the door and motioned them inside.

It looked like some type of fancy hospital room. Hidden partially from view by a white curtain, a huge marble bed was piled with fluffy white blankets. Various monitors hung on the walls, but they weren't beeping with pulse rates and oxygen levels. Tolen had no idea what they were reading, but as they came around the curtain his eyes were no longer on the monitors but drawn to the old, white-haired man lying on the bed.

"Jonas?" Tolen and Macy said at the same time.

Jonas motioned them forward and pointed to two cushioned chairs beside his bed.

"Hello you two." He waved his wrinkled hands. "It's so good to see you."

Macy smiled wide. "And you! How are you? Tolen said Nova poisoned you."

Jonas nodded. "Ah, yes, she did. I am mending."

Tolen clenched his fists by his side. "And the camp?"

Jonas nodded again. "They are all well. We evacuated the families and the warriors defeated the Dark army. The Protectors safely returned the Dominants here, to the citadel. Incrah and the others have returned to help rebuild the camp in a new place and the Guardians have provided them with another Sphere for the time being."

Tolen leaned over the side of the bed. "I am *so* sorry, Jonas. It's my fault Nova poisoned you. She wanted to get me away and knew she couldn't do it if you could sense where I was."

"I know, my boy. But, she has paid the ultimate price."

Tolen ducked his head and Macy squeezed his fingers.

"Don't feel bad, either of you. Nova chose her fate when she made a deal with the Dark." He patted their hands. "I must congratulate you both. You discovered that light and beauty can be found even in a place as evil as the Shadow Realm. It isn't just to be found around us, it is within us. Wherever light is, darkness cannot be. You brought your light with you and you survived. You rescued two important people, and you discovered something about yourselves and your intertwined destinies that I believe you would not have found any other way."

Tolen looked out the window at the beauty beyond—his relief mingled with new doubts. "Jonas, can you tell me—? Is it true? What Daemon said about my mother?"

Jonas sighed. "The Guardians have told me a little about your parents, Tolen. It is a long and sad story, much of which I think should be told to you by them…but yes, your mother has been involved with Daemon in the past. He was your father's brother."

"That demon is my uncle?" His voice shook.

"*Was* your uncle, Tolen. There is nothing left of the man once called Daemon Téloran."

Tolen put his face in his hands. Macy rubbed his back, but even her touch couldn't drive away the horror of the truth. "I never really won the fight, how did they get my mom out of there? Daemon had some kind of control over her."

"She endured intense pain until she passed into the kingdom of the Light. He only has power over her within his own realm."

"Is she okay?"

"I believe she will be. She has been through much, her mind and her heart need time to heal."

"And my father?"

"Keytleen informed me that he has not yet regained consciousness, but the Healers are very good here. He is an incredible man. I believe he will recover in time."

They were silent for several minutes. Everything had happened so fast it was hard to believe it was real.

Tolen shifted in his seat and squeezed Macy's hand, needing the comfort her touch could give. "Jonas? Who was behind that painful laughter? And how did I create a link just by asking the Light for help?"

Jonas took a deep breath and glanced out his window. "There are many laws that govern our worlds, Tolen. It is a lengthy and deep course of lessons that take time to learn and understand, but I can tell you that being the Ninth Chosen gives your life force the ability to bend certain laws as the need arises. Such as in the case of you holding the Dreamer gift, an ability that is boundless and incredibly dangerous…" his voice trembled, as if speaking of the Dreamers weakened him. Prickles ran down Tolen's spine.

"As for the voice you heard, it belongs to Darsapean. The reason it caused you so much pain is because he is the master of *Fear*, the co-creator, and though he is still locked in Misery he has somehow found a way to use his strength in his own realm."

Tolen sat up straighter. "No, not just in his own realm. He has power on Earth too." He told Jonas about what happened when he was held under the Shadow veil and Darsapean had spoken to him—without the details of what he'd seen. When he finished, Jonas looked exhausted.

Macy cleared her throat. "There's more. When I was searching for Tolen's mother, I came across a Doogar prisoner by the name of Kelner. He said the Dark is planning something. They kidnapped him and his family four years ago." She put her hand in her pocket. "Back before Tolen's shard came to Bastian, we were spying on a group of Kreydawn who were mining something in Nevada, but we never got a chance to discover what. Tolen and I saw the same group hauling the rocks into the Shadow Realm." She pulled a strange silvery chunk of rock from her pocket. "It was this—Kelner gave me a piece. He said to give it to the Guardians—he said we had to stop the Dark, but he was murdered before he could tell me more. He said the word 'gateway' as he was dying." She dropped it into Jonas's open palm.

Jonas rolled the stone between his fingers. It seemed to glow brighter with his touch. "This is one more piece of disturbing news to have reached me. I will speak with the Guardians and we'll pray that my fears aren't correct."

"What fears?" Tolen and Macy asked at the same time.

"That Darsapean has figured out a way to escape from Misery."

Tolen shivered and Macy squeezed his fingers so tightly they started to throb.

Jonas ran a gnarled hand over his eyes. "I have council with the Guardians in the morning. I will pass along this news."

Keytleen peeked around the curtain. "I'm sorry, but Jonas's readings are low. He needs to rest now. I'll take you two to your rooms where you can eat and get some sleep."

Tolen stood and squeezed Jonas's hand. Macy leaned down and gently gave him a hug.

"See ya," she whispered and they followed Keytleen out of the room and back down the hall.

She showed them two rooms side by side. "The left is Tolen's, the right is yours, Macy. Someone will be in to bring you some dinner and a change of clothes." She bowed her head and turned to leave.

"Excuse me." Tolen cleared his throat. "When can I see my parents?"

Her eyes softened. "As soon as the Healers give the okay, I will take you to them." She bowed again and left.

Macy peeked into her room. "Wow." Tolen followed her without pausing to look at his own. He didn't want to be away from her yet.

Her room looked like a grand master suite Tolen had only ever seen in advertisements for fancy hotels—decorated in shades of soft coral, sky blue, and cream. A large bed with a white marble headboard almost completely filled one wall, the opposite held a beautifully carved dresser and gilded mirror, a door next to the dresser revealed a gigantic bathroom with a white claw-foot tub and separate shower, more of the bright murals colored every wall. A vase overflowing with at least a dozen different varieties of flowers sat on a tiny breakfast table beside the bed, its aroma filling the room.

Macy collapsed on the chair beside the table. "If I wasn't so tired I'd feel guilty for being so filthy in a place like this." She waved her hand at the luxury and grinned. Then she looked at him, her grin faded, and her eyebrows wrinkled in concern. She got back up and wrapped her arms around his waist.

"What's wrong?"

Tolen sighed. "It's hard to explain. It feels so…unreal. I've spent the last several weeks thinking about how to save my dad, and now that it's done I'm not sure what I'm supposed to do next."

Macy stood on her toes and kissed under his chin. "Whatever it is, we'll do it together."

CHAPTER 27

THE GUARDIAN COURT

Three days later…

TOLEN HATED WAITING.

His father slept fitfully in the bed beside Tolen's chair. It was not a fun pastime, watching his father sleep, but Tolen knew that given his Sight he would be the first person to know when his father really woke up and he wanted to be there when it happened. As of yet, he had no indication it would be any time soon.

Daedal's face abruptly shifted from the usual mask of pain and fear to a blank stillness so eerie that Tolen panicked, jumped off the chair, and put his head on his father's chest to make sure he was still breathing.

He relaxed when his ears detected the faint thump-thump of Daedal's weak heart and the shallow whoosh of air moving in and out of his lungs.

Tolen took a deep breath, sat back in the chair, and reached over to squeeze his father's long fingers. They were cold and clammy. He could just make out the scars on the right hand from his attempt to give his son's shard back to the Guardians.

"Come on, wake up, Daedal."

"Tolen!" Daedal whispered hoarsely. His eyes flashed open, bright with worry, searching until they found his son's face.

Would he really wake up this time? "I'm here Dae—Dad."

Daedal's eyes closed and his face relaxed. "Tolen…" he mumbled, the fear in his voice replaced with obvious relief. But within seconds the mask of pain was back and Tolen knew he was lost in dreams that no one seemed to be able to pull him back from.

Tolen sighed, so much and so little had happened in the last three days.

Dane's father had arrived on their second day, along with Kiad and Deegan. Hank received special honors from the Guardians for his son's sacrifice, and the Doogar warriors received the Fallen Warriors Blessing for their loss of Elryn, as well as awards for their own bravery. Tolen had stumbled out apologies and thanks—but it felt nowhere near enough for all his best friend had done for him or for what the Doogar had sacrificed for him. Hank had seemed to appreciate the gesture, and Kiad and Deegan had said it had been an honor, but Tolen vowed someday to do something that would repay all the Doogar people. He owed them so much.

Tolen spent nearly every waking minute with Macy, but since that first day, neither Jonas nor anyone else had talked to them. They were awakened each morning for breakfast, left to wander the grounds by day, or spend short, one-sided visits with his father, and then they were escorted back to their rooms at night.

His mother remained in a "Healing Sleep" with no visitors, and his Second Sight wasn't helping him with her, either. His father would say random things, but his thoughts, for the most part, remained clouded and dream-like. The Spheres kept saying that his mother would wake up when she was ready, and his father's mind would heal with time—the Tormentors had done their job well—but Tolen felt impatient to get to know the man who had risked so much to protect him. It was hard to think of him as "Dad" when he didn't even know him.

The corrosive anger he felt toward Daemon and the forces of the Dark had taken root in his heart. He wanted desperately to make them pay for what they had done to his family, to Macy's family, to Nova's family—to so many innocent people.

Daedal's fingers twitched again and he mumbled something unintelligible.

The door opened. Keytleen stepped into the room. "Sorry to disturb your visit Tolen, but someone wishes to speak with you."

Looking forward to seeing Macy, Tolen turned with a smile. He almost fell out of his chair when Keytleen wheeled his mother through the door.

She looked healthier, physically, than Tolen had seen her in years, but here in the bright light of the citadel he could see how much the emotional strain had aged her. She had more streaks of gray than red in her hair now, and the worry lines had deepened beside her eyes and mouth.

Keytleen slipped out quietly and closed the door.

"Mom, are you okay? I've been so worried. I haven't even been able to sense your thoughts or anything." Tolen hugged her gently.

"I'm sorry, Tolen. The Spheres have been keeping a powerful shield around me to prevent Daemon from discovering where I am. I guess it's blocking your Sight as well." Her voice was back to the harsh whisper he remembered all too well from their days in hiding. "I am mending." She looked down at her blanketed legs. "Slowly."

Tolen shook his head. "I'm so glad you're awake." He sat back in his chair, but pulled it closer to her.

She looked over at Daedal. "He looks better than he did when we escaped." Her voice sounded sad, almost guilty.

Tolen nodded and pulled the blankets back up to his father's chin.

Areen reached over and squeezed his hand. "Thank you for saving us, Tolen," she paused and Tolen looked up, "but you really shouldn't have."

"What?"

She sighed and twisted her tiny hands in her lap. "You should have left us there."

"And let you both die?"

She closed her eyes. "It is a fate we both deserved for what we've done. We defied the Guardians. We kept you from your destiny. My promise to Daemon has given the Dark power over me. I have become too weak to fight. I will forever be a burden to my people. You would have been so much better without us."

Tolen's anger turned to pain. He touched his mother's chin and forced her to look at him. "Mom, I understand now why you did it. Is it going to make my job harder? Yes. But I've learned how easy it is to be irrational and stupid when you're worried about the people you love."

A question rose in her eyes, but before she could wonder who he was referring to he went on. "You were just trying to protect me from a fate that, honestly, terrifies me. I completely get it."

Her eyes filled with tears and spilled down her cheeks. "How can you ever forgive me?"

Tolen leaned over to hug her again. "I've already forgiven you." He swallowed the lump in his throat.

She clung to his neck like a small child. "I love you so much, Tolen."

"I know, Mom. I love you, too."

The door opened and Keytleen stepped in. "I'm so sorry to interrupt again, but the Spheres are worried about your mother. They have asked me to bring her back to the Healing room, and, Tolen, you have been summoned. The Guardians wish to speak to you and Macy in the throne room immediately."

Tolen nodded and started to sit up.

His mother touched his face and cleared her throat. "We'll talk again soon. I know I have a lot of explaining to do. No more secrets, Tolen. I promise."

Tolen squeezed her hand. "Just get better, okay? Everything's going to be fine." His voice cracked.

Keytleen walked toward his mother's chair and Tolen's heart throbbed. He hadn't realized how much he loved her, how grateful he was for her, until he thought he'd lost her. He never wanted to feel that again.

He slid off the bed to his knees and dropped his head in his mother's lap. He forgot about their audience as he twisted his fists into the blanket over her legs and his anguish and worry spilled over. He knew he needed to be strong, but in this moment, he needed her. He needed his mother to know how important she was to him.

"Mom, I missed you so much. Knowing you were alive…I had to come for you. Saving you and Dad is the smartest thing I've ever done. It *was* the right thing to do," he bit back a sob and pushed his face into her blanket.

She ran her fingers through his hair, soothing him with the same non-sense words she'd used when he was a small child. Only now he knew they weren't nonsense.

"Fear not my son. You are Light, you are Truth. You are strength, you are goodness. Tolen, I love you."

Another hand began patting his back softly. He looked over to see his father lying on his side watching them, one arm dangling over the side to pat Tolen's back. His eyes were still slightly dazed, but it looked as though the real Daedal was trying to see out of the pain-riddled mind. "Tolen, Areen…I love you," he whispered in a raspy voice. A single tear ran down his cheek before his eyes closed once more and his shallow breathing resumed.

Areen took her husband's limp hand. Tolen sat up and wrapped his hands around theirs, his heart swelling with overwhelming gratitude for this short reunion with his parents. No matter how bittersweet it might have been, it gave him a glimmer of real hope for the future of his family.

Tolen walked to the great glass amphitheater to find Macy pacing outside the closed doors. Keytleen told them they were to wait outside until the Protectors let them in, before she went back the way they'd come.

Macy looked beautiful. Her blond hair glistened in the sunlight. The slight breeze swirled the gauzy white material of the traditional citadel dress around her bare ankles.

She looked like an angel.

She belonged here, surrounded by peace and light. How could he take her back into a world of fighting and pain? Yet, how could he face the challenges of his destiny without her? A smile lifted his cheeks—not that she'd let him anyway.

"Hello, beautiful." Tolen wrapped his arms around her and kissed her cheek.

She leaned into him with a sigh. "I hate these stupid dresses."

"I know, but you still look beautiful."

She pulled back slightly to look him up and down. "You don't look so bad yourself."

Tolen tugged on the collar of his white button down shirt. "I'm not a big fan of the clothes here either."

"You look good in anything." Her cheeks turned pink and Tolen grinned. "How's your father doing today?"

Tolen shrugged. "Same. How was your walk?"

Macy touched his face. "Short, but beautiful." She squeezed him tighter and added, "I'm sorry about your dad."

He brushed his lips against hers and murmured. "It's okay. He sort of woke up when my mother came in."

"What?"

He sighed. "Keytleen brought my mom in to see me."

"Really? That's great she's finally awake."

He nodded.

"So, your Dad sort of woke up with your mom there. How'd that go?" Her voice was sympathetic.

He shrugged. He didn't know why he didn't really want to go into details about the visit. Maybe it was because he didn't have time, or maybe it was too painful.

"No answers then, I take it."

Tolen swallowed. "No. But we really weren't given time to talk—"

The doors opened and they stepped apart, ending their conversation. The two Protectors motioned for Tolen and Macy to go inside before closing the doors behind them.

On the thrones sat twelve men with long, white hair, but youthful faces. Their white robes seemed to reflect the light from the sun.

Macy let go of Tolen's hand and took two steps forward.

"Bastian?" She took off at a run toward the man at the far end.

Tolen paused. The man didn't look much like the Bastian he remembered, yet there was something familiar about his eyes. It wasn't just the fact that they were Watchers' eyes, there were—he noticed with a start—several pairs in the room, this man's eyes held a depth and a sparkle that was achingly familiar.

Macy flung herself into Bastian's arms and he swung her around, his wings tucked tightly to his back. She clung to him sobbing while he rubbed her back and sang softly in her ear.

Tolen couldn't stop the tears from gathering in his eyes.

Bastian sat down and grabbed Macy's hands. "*LaUnahi*, I am so proud of you. And you, too, Tolen." He motioned Tolen forward.

"Bastian, what happened?" Tolen forced a chuckle over the lump in his throat. "You were um…dead."

Bastian laughed lightly. "Not dead, just finished with my mortal duties. The Light accepted my sacrifice and I was allowed to join the Guardians. Now I will be with you both wherever your destinies lead you."

"So, it really was you I heard." Macy grinned through her tears.

Bastian nodded with a smile.

Macy lifted his shard from her shirt and started to pull it over her head, but Bastian put his huge hand over hers.

"No, *LaUnahi*. It belongs to you now. Protect it. It will serve you well."

"Did you know, Bastian? Did you know that Tolen's shard, my shard, yours—that they were all part of the same shard?"

Bastian closed his eyes and sighed. "I did."

"Why didn't you tell me?"

"Timing. I felt it was something the two of you needed to figure out on your own." He lifted his eyes, chagrin in his half-smile. "Can you forgive me?"

Macy threw her arms around his neck. Tolen smiled and nodded. Remembering their audience, he looked around and cleared his throat. "So, um, you're the Guardians."

"We are." They spoke in perfect synchronization, their voices deep, melodic.

Tolen shifted his feet. "I'm sorry, I don't know what I'm—am I supposed to bow or something?"

The first man on the left spoke softly. "No, young man. We are but the Light's humble assistants. We serve the Light and its people. Our position is one of respect, earned after a life of unselfish service, but never one of worship. That belongs to the Light and the Light alone, for only *They* are perfect enough to be worshipped."

He inclined his head and his thick white hair fell over his shoulder. "I am Zarin, leader of the Guardians. You have succeeded in your quest, Chosen ones. You have passed the test. You have discovered your combined destiny and accepted your duties.

"We have counseled with Jonas and the Radia Warriors. We know that Darsapean has found a way to smuggle creatures out of Misery, but we have yet to learn how he is managing it. Our power remains intact over *him* for now, but we must discover what he is up to and soon. Darsapean must not escape." He leaned forward. "We will speak with you alone Tolen."

A Protector stepped up to the platform and led Macy back outside. Tolen's heart pounded in time with her footsteps. She cast him a tiny smile before the doors closed behind her.

Zarin sat back against his throne and looked Tolen up and down. "We are aware of your feelings for Macy."

Tolen's heart kicked up even faster. He swallowed loudly. *It's right. I know it's right.* He glanced at Bastian who offered him a sad smile.

"There is much to do, questions we must ask, histories we must search. Your birth was the result of a broken law, yet here you stand as the Ninth Chosen. The depth of your feelings for the girl and your resultant actions also go against ancient law. Should you continue on your current path there is something you must know. Hidden laws are different from human laws. Hidden laws are connected to the life force that breaks them and the consequences are different for each soul."

Tolen cleared his throat. "I have a choice then, to be—to be with Macy?"

"Choice is a gift of the Light, Tolen. You can choose what to do, but you cannot choose the consequences the Balance will issue. I cannot tell you what may happen, but I offer you a warning. Tread carefully and be aware of every choice you make."

Tolen nodded and looked at Bastian. The Watcher's eyes were shifting, his expression unreadable. Zarin started speaking again and Tolen turned his attention back, trying not to think of the consequences that could lay in store for them.

"You will remain here until the eve of your eighteenth birthday. The Dominants will continue your training until that time."

"What happens the day before my birthday?"

The Guardians' eyes all locked on Tolen's face. "When you turn eighteen you will transcend and reach the full potential of your gifts. Your life force will become too strong to shield. We cannot allow you to stay here, for fear your presence will give away our location to the Dark. You will go to the Zenith. There you will complete your training." Zarin leaned forward again and the gravity of his next words sent a thrill of danger through Tolen. "The Final Battle is near at hand. The time for the Gathering of the Chosen has come."

∘ ∘ ∘

Macy stared out across the beautiful grounds of the citadel as Tolen led them to their favorite spot. The golden leaves of Ardia's tree shimmered brightly above them in the warm light—the Guardians had placed her here after she returned Bastian's body to them—creating a peaceful spot to talk and be alone together.

She had been so happy to see Bastian, and to learn he had never really left her. The shards beneath her shirt pulsed gently and she smiled.

Tolen wrapped his arms tightly around her and rested his chin on top of her head. She leaned into his chest, listening to the gentle rhythm of his heart. The warmth of his touch sent trickles of pleasure along her skin and did enticing things to her Kuna.

There was a lot they needed to discuss. She didn't want to be the one to bring it up and ruin the mood, but she was worried. "So, what did they want to talk to you about?" She squeezed his arms.

"The usual. My destiny, my future. Something about the Gathering of the Chosen…" He trailed off running his fingers through her hair. She sensed there was more, but he didn't want to talk about it. She took a deep breath and closed her eyes. There'd be time later. Right now it was okay to just enjoy the moment, together in the safest place in the world.

They were silent for a time before Tolen broke the stillness. "It's funny to think about how much has changed. It wasn't that long ago I was dealing with school and bullies and wondering what sort of experiment went wrong to make me what I was. Now here I am, standing in another dimension, the most beautiful girl in my arms, and the fate of the world in my hands." He sighed and trailed his fingers from her hair down her arms. "It seems so impossible."

His touch made it hard to concentrate. Her Kuna heated up and her skin tingled. "I don't remember enough of my human life to relate to anymore, but even with all I've seen and done as a Chosen, I never imagined that I would one day be standing in the *citadel* with the *Ninth…*" *wanting him to kiss me…*

Tolen squeezed her more tightly and leaned over her neck to kiss her before burying his face in her hair.

"Do you know what the Guardians were talking about?" she asked needing the distraction. "The Gathering of the Chosen?"

He took a slow breath. "No clue."

Macy twisted in his arms, and reached up to trace her finger along the crease between his eyebrows. "The Chosen are scattered around the world. Before we can lead them in battle against the Dark, we have to find them and bring them together."

"And I need to train and transcend and all that important stuff before we do that." He said it casually, but she could see the apprehension in his eyes, the fear that he wouldn't be enough.

She tapped his chin. "Hey, you know what?"

His eyes were still far away as he answered. "What?"

"I think you have officially won the bet." She forced a playful smile.

"What bet?" His eyes narrowed, but the corner of his mouth lifted a tiny bit.

"Remember the bet we made in the Binithan? The one where we decide who's the coolest by the time you finish training? Winner chooses the prize?" She wiggled her eyebrows.

He chuckled. "I'm not done training yet and you are still cooler than me—by far."

"Finished training or not, you kicked butt in the Shadow Realm. You win. Deal with it." She held his gaze and whispered seriously. "What *do* you want, Tolen?"

Tolen ran his thumb across her lips. Warmth pulsed through her body and she trembled beneath the heat of his touch. His Watcher's eye flashed and his brown eye seemed to be on fire, the depth of the love she saw there made her insides ignite.

They were meant to be one despite the rules. She knew this with every part of her, every particle of her life force. Had Tolen's parents not messed with his destiny and kept them apart, maybe things would have been different, maybe they would have grown up and only loved each other like siblings. But that path of fate had changed. Instead they met as two people with broken hearts and clouded futures, and in each other found comfort, peace, and hope for more. They were a team for the good of all mankind, but they loved each other because it gave them both balance and hope, because *they* chose this path and they would make it work. She'd thought the prophecy disproved the rightness of their relationship, but as Tolen had said, this was outside the prophecy. They may have been chosen to fight for Light, but it was their *own choice* to be together. The Balance brought them together for a reason, and she no longer felt that the only reason was Chosen duty and sharing a prophecy.

It was to give them a gift of love. Pure, perfect love. Their lives had been filled with heartache and struggle. The Light knew their hearts, their needs, their hopes and dreams, and it used the Balance to guide them to each other so they could really understand the only reason to fight and keep fighting. The solid truth that would keep them moving forward in their destiny despite the hardships they would face.

Love.

Jun'tar had been right. Love *was* so much more powerful than anger.

Her Kuna rushed to the surface as if to confirm this truth; she controlled the power, held it, let it burn the feeling into every cell in her body.

Tolen lifted her chin and his deep voice seemed to resonate down into her bones. "You, McLacy Allicandra. I want *you*, always and forever.

Wherever I go, whatever I do, I want to do it with you. I can face any challenge, any destiny, as long as I have you by my side."

She touched his face. "I love you, Tolen."

The smile that blossomed across his face chased away the fear and doubt from his eyes. His hand moved to her hair and then he was kissing her in a way that seemed to take them out of the world and drop them into an impossible fairytale. Nothing else mattered in that moment, not destiny, not war, nothing except them.

EPILOGUE

To'Conchla Mindra…

Tolen opened his eyes to see his reflection staring back at him from the large mirror above the dresser. His blue eye slowly dilated and shifted; his brown eye mirrored the confusion he felt as jumbled pictures flashed through his mind.

It had been the same scenario every morning for the past week. He woke up to the whispered voice saying, "Watcher…Watcher…The Ninth Chosen…" And then his head was filled with a rush of images too blurred to make any sense.

He thought of the strange voice and blurry images. The voice seemed to be getting louder, and if he really concentrated, he could remember seeing faces in the hazy images and…feeling what they felt.

He took several deep breaths while the images slowly faded and the soothing tranquility of the citadel calmed his racing thoughts. The view outside his window alone could make him forget evil even existed, but it was out there—he knew it, he'd felt it, and he'd fought against it. Here, surrounded by light and goodness, where even the buildings themselves radiated peace, it was easy to ignore the truth. He watched the golden lip of the sun slowly brighten the tops of the Mountains of Promise. Everything was so vibrant here, as if the colors themselves were alive.

The day he would leave fast approached. He would be eighteen in four days—a day Tolen was not looking forward to. With all the warnings and the fearful looks being thrown his way everywhere he went, he actually dreaded his transition to adulthood, his *Transcendence,* and all its impending consequences.

As easy as it was to get lost in the peace here, the breaking of dawn always brought with it the truth of why he was really here.

He wasn't Tolen Daedal Parks, weird-eyed town freak with no friends and no father. He was Tolen Daedal Téloran, Ninth Chosen, and gifted follower of Light, with a destiny so huge that if he thought too deeply about it his untrained gifts would go berserk. Bastian and the Dominants had been trying to train him to govern his emotions in order to better control his gifts, but it was still so new to him. For years he'd been avoiding the power he could feel growing within him. Fearing it even. It felt like a growth, a tumor, something he could neither stop nor control.

He no longer felt that way about his gifts and for the past several weeks, first in the Binithan with the Doogar dwarves, then at the Radia Warrior training camp with Jonas, and now here in the Citadel of Light with the Dominants, he'd been trying to learn to connect with that power, harness it, use it, understand it, and let it free. And for a while he had been confident in his efforts. He had learned much and was doing well.

He'd learned how to shield his life force from affecting the Balance and drawing the Dark to wherever he was. He'd discovered the element within himself that connected him to his gifts, his *trigger.* But the closer he got to his Transcendence, that moment when his gifts and his physical body would fully unite, the more he felt like he was moving backward instead of forward in his progress.

His thoughts turned back to Macy and he couldn't stop the smile that lifted his cheeks. Because of her, he'd accepted who he was and knew with her by his side, he could face the clouded future ahead. With her strength, knowledge, and help, he'd been able to save his parents from the Shadow Prison.

He shivered at the memory.

That wasn't entirely true. If the Guardians hadn't shown up with the Radia Warriors, they would have failed, and not only would he have been responsible for his parents' deaths, but Macy's death as well. Every time this thought came, he relived the moment when he'd seen into the future and watched Daemon kill Macy—a future that had come way too close to being real.

He pushed his fists against his closed eyelids.

It hadn't happened. She survived. We all survived…

Barely.

His breathing increased and the light scent of cloves and earth swirled from his hands. He pushed them through his soft brown hair, took two deep breaths, threw off the covers, and stumbled over to the glass doors leading to the balcony, his movements harried, jerky. He pushed through the doors into the warm light spilling over the mountainside and turned his palms toward the sun. His heart slowed from a gallop to a trot and the Kuna slowly left his hands. Moments like this told him the warnings were real. The closer he came to his birthday, the more his gifts thought for themselves—overcoming his self-control. Sometimes even his slightest emotional reaction caused strange things to happen. Just two days ago, all he'd been doing was standing on the balcony thinking about the afternoon with Macy, and all at once the entire rim of the Forest of Grace had sprouted a new row of trees, and fields of wildflowers cropped up all over the realm. He didn't know he'd had anything to do with it until Keytleen, his assigned messenger for the citadel, showed up at his room moments later and told him the Guardians wanted to see him.

He'd then spent the next three days working with a group of Spheres who tried to teach him how to recognize the shifts in his own gifts. It was pointless—they'd already told him once he was eighteen he wouldn't be able to hide anything from the Dark anyway. He'd be too…powerful.

He closed his eyes. That was why they'd made him train with the Spheres—those who possessed the ability to shield not only their own life force from affecting the Balance, but also the life forces of others. It wasn't really to train him, but to calm the fears of those who lived here, those who were afraid his presence would bring harm to the realm.

He opened his eyes and looked up at the sky. Something cut through the fluffy clouds, headed in his direction and became larger every second. He stepped back as soon as he realized who it was, and moments later Bastian landed lightly beside him. His white robes emitted a pale glow that softly mimicked the sun rising behind him. His bright sapphire eyes glittered like crystal, the dark pupils dilating and contracting slightly. Tolen wondered what he was seeing with his Second Sight.

A slight smile touched the Watcher's lips, but something behind the smile didn't help Tolen's anxiety.

"Are you all right, Tolen?"

Tolen looked away from Bastian and leaned on the marble railing. "Yeah. Just the usual—oversensitive gifts and weird dreams."

Bastian leaned beside Tolen. "You will learn to control your gifts. I have faith in you." He sighed and folded his hands in front of him. "As for your dreams…do you know what they really are?"

Tolen dropped his head and nodded. "I think—" he met Bastian's knowing look. "Okay…I'm pretty sure I'm getting glimpses of thousands of different lives. Human, as well as Hidden-kind. It's mostly hazy, but sometimes their faces are clear and I can feel what they're feeling."

Bastian stroked his beard. "Your life force is awakening to the calling of the Ninth. The visions will continue to increase in frequency and intensity, so you may be led where you are needed." He gave Tolen an understanding smile. "I know it can feel overwhelming."

Tolen snorted—a trait he'd picked up from Macy. He smirked. She'd be up and waiting for him to get his butt out of bed. The thought of seeing her pushed a tiny bit of the anxiety away.

Bastian chuckled, but it was tense, almost forced. "She *is* up," he responded to Tolen's thought and looked back out toward the mountains. The muscles in his jaw twitched and Tolen sensed that the real reason he'd come was not to talk about Tolen's visions—it was something else. Probably something Tolen really didn't want to know, but needed to know. The seconds ticked by and still Bastian said nothing.

A hundred inquiries wouldn't get Bastian to talk before he was ready, so Tolen stepped back into his room and walked behind the deep-blue dressing screen. He ignored the tan uniform slacks and instead took down his jeans. Today was his weekly free day, no uniforms, no training, just time for him, Macy, and the usual visit with his parents. He pulled a white t-shirt over his head, and moved out from behind the screen to see Bastian sitting in the chair beside the breakfast table and staring out the window, his eyes still shifting.

Tolen sat down in the opposite chair and stepped into his sneakers, counting in the Hidden tongue in his mind. This was a calming distraction that Kyndras, the one Dominant he could honestly say he liked, had taught him to use when he needed to ignore the things that were upsetting his emotions. Counting in Hidden wasn't easy and required a lot of concentration.

He'd just reached fifty-two when Bastian finally spoke. "Tolen, there are a few things I need to discuss with you."

Tolen swallowed and absently scratched the back of his arm. "About my visions?"

"Partly. I also want to talk to you about your training, and a few other things."

Tolen sighed and glanced up at the ceiling. "I don't think I'm doing as well as they'd like."

Bastian shifted in his seat. "On the contrary, the Dominants informed us that you exceed their expectations."

Tolen looked at Bastian in surprise. "Huh. That's not the way they make it sound. I was sure Dunrath wanted to bury me under the Mountains of Promise. I never realized someone so old could scream so loud."

"As you first noticed in Jonas's camp, the Dominants are not gentle in their training methods, but regardless of what you may think, they are very impressed. O'shae believes the wind has claimed you; it will follow and obey you at first call. Took'rah said the animals speak to you as to one of their own. Kyndras is very fond of you, and she assures us that the water will bend to your will. Dunrath, despite wanting to bury you under the mountain, said that you have the Earth's acceptance and she will listen without question. Nephen told us what we already knew: you have the Light's allegiance. Jun'tar was one of the first Dominants you worked with and he absolutely beams whenever he speaks of your Kunamin abilities. Ras'met said there is nothing he can teach you that you do not already know in the Nature Speak. He has simply been fascinated watching you. And Vindi…well…"

Tolen tried not to roll his eyes. Vindi was the smallest Dominant, bald, wiry, with translucent, paper-thin skin. He looked as if the tiniest wind could carry him off. But what he lacked in height and substance, he more than made up with attitude. He was by far the most ill-tempered man Tolen had ever met. From the very beginning, he hadn't been afraid to say he didn't like Tolen.

Bastian nodded knowingly. "Vindi has his own way of doing things, but he, too, has said your ability to blend in with your surroundings and settle the Balance around you rivals an Unseen with years of training."

Tolen shook his head in shock. All of the Dominants except Kyndras were so gruff it was hard to believe they'd actually said anything good about him. "They couldn't tell me that themselves?"

Bastian cleared his throat. "They have already left for the Zenith."

"What? Why?"

The Watcher sighed. "Things are developing faster than we imagined. They want to get there ahead of you—make preparations—"

"My presence at the Zenith is going to endanger everyone there, just as it does here. Isn't it?"

Bastian looked away and nodded.

"Bastian, I can't keep doing this. The Doogar, Dane, you…Macy." His voice cracked and he cleared his throat. "It's not right, putting everyone around me in danger because I don't know enough." He sat up taller in his seat. The time had come to let Bastian in on what he'd been contemplating the last few days. "I've been thinking—"

Bastian cast him a humoring look.

"You already know?" Tolen tried not to feel irritated.

"I am sorry. I know it frustrates you that I can sense your thoughts, but I am still your Watcher.…" He sighed. "Tolen, I have been impressed by more than just how well you have done with the Dominants. Despite your doubts and your fears, you are determined to follow through with your destiny. You have grown in the last few weeks. But, no, you are not ready to face what is out there on your own. Not yet."

Tolen shook his head. "Look Bastian, I know I'm not as strong as I need to be and I don't know enough, but Macy…Macy can teach me all

I need to know about the Hidden world. You taught her. She's my trigger. I'm in better control when I'm around her."

"Tolen, you are forgetting that once you reach eighteen you will no longer be able to shield yourself from the Dark. Do you really want to put her in that kind of danger?"

"I'll learn to control it. I-I'll figure it out…." His desire to stay close to Macy warred with the panic he felt at putting her in danger.

Bastian's eyes softened. He knew the chink in Tolen's armor. He knew Tolen wouldn't intentionally do anything that could hurt Macy. "Your thoughts are deep, Tolen. Your compassion for others is one of your greatest gifts, so I know you will understand what I have to say, even if you do not like it."

Tolen's palms turned slick with sweat.

"We are out of *time*. Maybe had things begun differently your plan would have worked. I could have trained you, but that is not how it happened. Things have been set in motion that we have no control over. You know you cannot succeed in your destiny if you do not learn to balance your power correctly, and the world cannot survive without you. The danger that exists because of your lack of knowledge is something we must all accept, and we will help you where we can. The people here, though afraid, realize this. Those preparing for you at the Zenith are ready. They know what to expect. They are ready to do whatever is necessary to help you, to help the Light. And the Light…the Light will do whatever is necessary to save us all."

Bitterness fought for place in Tolen's heart. If only his mother hadn't tried to hide him from his destiny. So much would be different. Bastian continued to speak, unaware or maybe just so involved in his own thoughts that he wasn't paying attention to Tolen's.

"The Zenith is one of our oldest and most protected strongholds." Bastian took a deep breath and closed his eyes. "They will be prepared for your arrival. They *will* be ready. You will grow in strength and confidence. You will succeed, Tolen. We must have faith…" His hand twitched.

Tolen pushed up from the table and turned to the window.

"Forgive me."

Tolen looked back to see Bastian's eyes glistening. "I know this is difficult for you. The expectations, your parents…" he trailed off. "You are doing remarkably well, Tolen; do not be too hard on yourself. Your weakness will become your strength in time." He met Tolen's eyes for a brief moment. "But we must pray it will be soon. Darkness is spreading. Their numbers are steadily increasing. Dark servants are everywhere. The world has changed a lot since you came here. Your visit to the Shadow Realm has set things in motion. Creatures that previously cowered from our Radia Warriors have become more brazen—attacking small settlements of Hidden-kind. The Dark is moving its pieces. It is setting the board."

Bastian sighed. "There is a crack in the connection between Misery and Earth that Darsapean exploited under our very noses. It was a tiny flaw that the Guardians were aware of, but believed it was too minor for him to manipulate. Once again, we underestimated the strength of the Dark.

"Before we came for you, Macy and I were tracking a small band of Kreydawn in the Nevada desert. They were mining something. It is not unusual for Kreydawn to be miners and gatherers, so their movements were not that suspicious—until the two of you discovered what they were mining. That Doogar, Kelner, gave a piece of it to Macy when you were in the Shadow Realm. That rare metallic rock contained traces of the same metal used to fashion the first gateway to Misery. Darsapean's minions have been mining it. He has found a way to widen the crack."

Tolen folded his arms across his chest. "You're not talking size when you say widen, right?"

"Correct. The metal within the stone harnesses the power of Light. Movan use them to make Light Spears and other rare weapons."

"Are you saying it can harness the power of the Dark as well?"

"Yes. We believe Daemon found enough of the metal to create a gateway from his side in the Shadow Realm to the crack in Misery. From there he smuggled creatures from Misery into the Shadow Realm where Daemon has been releasing them into the earthly realm. As the world is filled with more Dark creatures, the Dark's power grows. As its power grows, it can allow darker, more powerful creatures to escape Misery.

Once the world reaches a certain point in darkness, or Daemon finds something powerful enough to overcome the remaining Light imprisoning him within the walls of Misery, Darsapean will be able to escape."

Tolen dropped back in his chair. "If we hadn't gone after my dad—"

"If you and Macy had not gone into the Shadow Realm to save your father, we would not know any of this. It seems there are many reasons the Light wanted you to save your father. You have given us a chance to prepare, to plan."

Tolen pushed his hands through his hair. "Okay, so what's the plan?"

"Radia Warriors have been out fighting, spying, and gathering information. Notice was sent to Watchers to prepare their Chosen for the Call. All over the world the Hidden will be preparing for battle…and for the Ninth to lead them."

Tolen stood up and started pacing.

"Tolen, the army will gather to you at the Zenith. Once the word reaches the colonies and Hidden settlements, the planning can begin. Darsapean's escape may be imminent, but we are more prepared now than we would have been. Because we have been forewarned, we believe the Dark will lie low for a while, giving us more time to prepare you for battle."

Tolen tried not to be angry that he'd been left out of the plans. It was his own fault. He hadn't learned enough; despite Bastian's praise he knew he was far from where he needed to be. He lacked suitable control over his emotions—the effect they held over his gifts frightened more than just him. He took a deep breath and counted to ten in his head. "Okay. I'll go to the Zenith. I'll train hard."

Bastian didn't respond and Tolen paused to look over his shoulder. Bastian's eyes reflected the sunlight and burned with an intensity that made Tolen's insides turn. There was more, and it was worse, and a growing dread inside him said he knew what was coming. He dropped back in his chair, his hands shaking.

Bastian nodded sadly. "I am afraid it *is* much, much worse. We believe Daemon has left the Shadow Realm. Our warriors captured a group of Ookra who told us he is in the earthly realm, but they did not know where. They were not given his exact location."

An image of the seven-foot-tall Demon Master stalking toward him in the dungeons of the Shadow Prison flashed across Tolen's mind. The blood-red skin, the hate-filled yellow eyes, the huge black horns erupting from the sides of his head curving down to his black pointed teeth. His deep, cold voice. The frightening strength of his power.

Tolen took a deep breath. "How do you know that the Ookra weren't lying? I thought he couldn't survive outside his own realm anymore."

"That was true when we first won the war, but as the world increases in evil the Dark's power grows, allowing evil to more easily survive here. We believe the Ookra because of an attack on a village of Kunamin. Daemon left no survivors and his symbol was burned into the foreheads of the bodies. His way of sending us a message."

Tolen pushed his fists into his eyes.

Bastian shifted. Tolen could hear the fabric of his robe rustle. "You saw it. Did you not?"

Tolen's stomach twisted. "Yes. I'd hoped it was only a nightmare."

"It was not." Bastian released a slow breath. "You have seen more," his voice cracked, "concerning Macy, yes?"

Tolen nodded slowly, his fists still over his eyes. His breathing increasing, the heat returning.

Bastian spoke softly. "Your birthday is in four days."

"Yeah, and I leave in three."

"Yes."

The words burned as they left Tolen's throat. "And Macy won't be going with me."

He felt Bastian's hand touch the top of his head and he looked up into the Watcher's eyes to see the same anguish he'd felt every time he'd seen the vision of two forests, one where he was, and one where Macy was—nowhere near each other.

"Why…?"

Bastian lowered his hand and his eyes turned to the open window. "We cannot always understand the desires of the Light, Tolen. We must simply trust that whatever path they guide us to is the one we are most needed upon. We must trust that whatever mission the Light has in mind for each of you will deal a heavy blow to the Dark."

Tolen followed the Watcher's gaze out the window as something Macy once told him came rushing into his mind. *Following the wishes of the Light is not always easy, just worth it in the end.* "Does Macy know?" he whispered.

Bastian looked back into Tolen's eyes and slowly shook his head with anguish in every line of his face. He closed his eyes briefly before he spoke in a trembling voice. "Your parents wish to speak with you. Macy is waiting. Tell her what you feel she needs to know, as the Ninth you are meant to watch over her more than I, but be wary of your emotions that they do not sway you or cause her to doubt. The details of where she must go will come to you once you accept the truth." He turned and jumped over the railing, extended his wings full span, and soared into the sunrise.

Tolen watched him fade into the distance and the weight of their situation fell over him. Just two weeks ago he'd promised Macy that *together* they would work through the challenges of their destiny. She'd already feared that his training would pull them apart for who knew how long. He had just ignored the idea that it could happen so soon. The pain in his heart made him suddenly very weak. The fire left his chest and he buried his face in his hands.

BOOK THREE

A CHOSEN PATH

CHAPTER 1

THE KEEPER

The moment of his death drew near.

He could hear it in the echo of paws thundering toward him across the forest floor, and in the shrieks of the demon Raksasha carried on the winds of the Shadow storm.

Eamun Woodlore, Watcher and Keeper of the Last shard did not have long.

He dropped from his vantage point in the trees and glanced up at the darkening sky as tears splashed onto his cheeks.

There would be no stars this night.

He crushed the herbs between his palms, blew them into the wind, and closed his eyes to Watch them trickle into every footprint he had left behind. With his eyes closed, the nightmare became too real. The echo of terrified screams filled his ears and his eyes snapped open. He pushed his feet forward, his own sobs mingling with the howl of the wind.

He could not save them, but at least Sashan had escaped. His entire family would not die in vain.

He paused beside a towering pine. His fingers trembled as he tugged the blood-red shard from its cradle within the scepter. It glowed red-gold in the dim light. He knelt at the base of the tree, and tears dripped off the end of his nose as he dug his hands into the cold earth, deeper and deeper. With a silent plea, he gently dropped the shard beneath a thick root, placed his hand on the rough bark, and whispered so that only the tree could hear. He pulled his hand away and a gleaming, golden symbol burned brightly for a few seconds in the wood and then disappeared.

With a surge of fierce relief, Eamun pushed the dirt back into the hole and waved his hand over the mound of earth. Thick grass sprouted around the tree until the ground surrounding it appeared undisturbed. He sprinkled another handful of herbs through the grass. His waist-length gray hair whipped around him as he paused to listen.

The shrieks of the Raksasha and the DéHool's howls were too close. He couldn't lead them here.

He waved his hands behind him as he ran back, careful to match each step. The grasses stood upright as he passed, hiding his footprints.

The howling grew louder and he felt an unnatural cold layering the air around him.

The Shadow Wraiths were almost upon him.

He emerged from the thicket to see the first line of DéHool. Their red eyes flashed to the trees behind him.

He clenched his teeth and dropped to his knees in front of them.

The wolves howled in victory and flung themselves on him.

Eamun threw his arms up toward the sky. *"Radi! Y'na hi y'takra!"* A burst of white-hot light engulfed him, and then all was silent.

The fire burned out as quickly as it started. The black, skeletal Raksasha uncovered their yellow eyes. The second pack of wolves rushed forward, but where Eamun had been, nothing remained but a dozen dead DéHool and a pile of ash.

A long, mournful cry echoed through the sky as the clouds released their rain and washed away the grisly scene. A silvery great horned owl circled low over the destruction before spreading its vast wings and soaring through a hole in the clouds.

○ ○ ○

"Eamun is dead."

Forrest Bastian looked up at Zarin as he scanned the scroll in his hands, his wings dragging on the ground behind him as he paced.

"I am sorry, Bastian. Word has just reached the citadel. His village was attacked." The leader of the Guardians—those charged with watching over the affairs of earth—sighed. "Our Sight over the village has dimmed, but as far as we can tell, there were," he gulped, "no survivors."

Bastian tugged on his long, white ponytail, his sapphire eyes bright with worry. "The Last?"

Zarin shook his head. "No sign. I am certain we would know by now if the Dark had it. Eamun must have hidden it before he died. The owl tells us he sacrificed himself before the DéHool could take him."

Bastian stood and began to pace. The other eleven Guardians watched him with concern. He stopped mid-stride and turned to face them.

"The Last shard is powerful enough to create a rift in the Balance that could allow Darsapean to escape Misery. This is what he has been searching for. Someone must find it before he does."

Zarin took a deep breath. "Sit down, friend." He waved his hand toward Bastian's chair and waited for him to sit before he continued. "Even if the Dark somehow gets the Last before us, they will only have access to a fraction of its powers. You know the legend. Threefold protection. A Treasurer, a Seeker, and finally a new Keeper. Only with the three united can the Last reach its full strength—and only then can the Keeper wield it."

Bastian's eyes narrowed. "If I remember correctly, the legends also suggest that with the death of the Keeper, the power of the Treasurer and the Seeker are also lost and the Last must choose anew. What if the Dark discovers who they are before we do?"

"We will do all we can to find them first, and protect them until the Last chooses the new Keeper." Zarin placed the scroll on the table in front of him and sat down, his face strained, his eyes weary.

Bastian shook his head and started to stand again, but Zarin met his gaze with enough pain in his expression to push Bastian back into his chair.

"Bastian, what more can we do?" Zarin looked at each man in the room. "This news has hastened our need for the Ninth. It is time to talk to the children."

ACKNOWLEDGEMENTS

Every time I type the words *The End* at the finish of a manuscript, I feel three distinct emotions: a kind of sadness at the close, an excitement for what's to come, and an overwhelming amount of gratitude toward those who've helped me reach The End. I've said it many times, and I will continue to say it, I could never follow my dreams if it weren't for the incredible team I have in my corner.

First and foremost, my Father in Heaven and His Son Jesus Christ, for their guidance and love. My incredible family—my husband Brent, my boys, my parents and siblings, and my in-laws—for standing behind me, supporting me, and loving me despite my craziness. My friends for their advice, faith, and encouragement.

I would also like to thank the team at Snowy Peaks Media. Especially, Heather, for working so hard and being the sweetest editor a writer could ask for, and Kirk, for your dedication, enthusiasm, and hard work.

Staci, thank you for continuing to help me with social media.

Thank you to my Beta-Readers for your advice and excitement: Mom, Angie, Tricia.

KayLynn, the interior rocks, again. Thank you. You are truly talented.

Deborah, your cover design is perfect. I am your forever fan. Thank you.

Teyla Branton, talented author and incredible woman, thank you for your awesome endorsement.

Huge thanks to my loyal readers for continuing this adventure with me.

And finally, to the incredible individuals who continue to fight their battles to become who they were created to become, and to the youth who continually inspire me, each and every one of you, I thank you.

ABOUT THE AUTHOR

K.A. PARKINSON WAS RAISED IN A SMALL SUBURB WHERE SHE SPENT most of her time hiding under her bed with a book, a bag of cookies, and a flashlight. She currently resides in Utah with her husband and two children. If you would like to learn more about K.A., and the world of the Hidden, please visit www.kaparkinson.com.

CHARACTER INDEX

FOLLOWERS OF LIGHT (BY ORDER OF APPEARANCE)
Tolen (Parks) Téloran—The Ninth Chosen (Hidden-kind)
    Parents: Daedal Téloran (Protector) Areen Téloran (Sphere)
Jonas—Sphere and shield to the Unastra training camp
Macy Allicandra Burdow—Chosen (human)
    Parents: Max and Alli Burdow
Forest Bastian—Watcher
Incrah—Radia Warrior Captain
Jeno—Radia Warrior
Kapha—Radia Warrior
Rada—Radia Warrior
Denhon—Radia Warrior
Sernad—Radia Warrior
Beyn—Radia Warrior
Evrah—Incrah's mother and camp linguist
Lafar—Light elves
Dane Smithy—Doogar
    Father: Hank Smithy—Doogar
Hander—Doogar
Kiad—Doogar Warrior
Deegan—Doogar Warrior
Elryn—Doogar Warrior

THE DOMINANTS:
O'shae—Arwah

Took'rah—Animashta

Kyndras—Leenwa

Dunrath—Télora

Nephen—Lóklana

Jun'tar—Kunamin

Ras'met—Honitahai

Vindi—Dicernan

SERVANTS OF THE DARK

Shadow Wraiths—Thick, black, oily mist-like creatures who hide in storm clouds

Raksasha—Blood Trackers. Main purpose is to track and kill the Chosen

Night Demons—Blood drinking demons who pull themselves up from the ground to feed on the death of the battlefield. Their decaying flesh is covered with maggots and bloody scabs. They are bald, have no eyes, or legs…Night Demons are one of the most grotesque creatures born of darkness

Divinators (crows)—Their eyes have been replaced by Oracle stones. Whatever they see, their masters see

Reconn—Chameleon type creatures used mostly as scouts

Phantoms—These mist-like creatures are placed within the dead or dying to reanimate and control them

Ookra—Demon servants

DéHool—Giant demonic wolves. Their sole purpose is to hunt and destroy Watchers

Darsapean—Lord of the Dark, currently imprisoned in Misery

Daemon—Demon Master and High Captain of the Dark

Daklafar—Once Lafar-Light Elves, but now serve the Dark

Tormentors—Tall women with gray skin, lifeless black eyes, and floor length orange hair. Their screams cause unbearable pain. The dark uses them to extract information from their prisoners

Kreydawn—Mindless creatures controlled by Suppressors

Suppressors—Single-eyed creatures with the Dreamer ability, they control the services of the Kreydawn

Thrundoon—Huge men covered with black fur. Extremely strong. Masters of the DéHool

Sundrák—Sentry's posted outside prison cells. Bald, translucent skin, no eyes,just an overlarge nose in the center of their face set above blood-red lips

Shrieg—Gigantic, venomous, bat-like creatures

Kinchomen—Lizard like creatures, more of a nuisance than dangerous

Gungruin—Tall gray skinned creatures that can take on the appearance of anything they touch. Water is the only thing that can melt through their disguise

CHOSEN GROUPS/ABILITIES:

Honitahai—Nature speakers: have the ability to speak with all plant life and ask for aid

Kunamin—Fire wielders: can create, manipulate, throw, and snuff fire with their hands

Télora—Earth Movers: can ask the dirt to do their bidding

Arwah—Wind Shifters: can use the power of wind to aid them

Dicernan—Unseens: can become invisible

Leenwa—Water Callers: can call water from anywhere and ask it to help

Animashta—Listeners: they understand animal's thoughts and communicate with them. They can project their own thoughts and desires into the animal's minds, as if they are sharing thought. It enables them to work together as a flawless team—so long as the animal is listening and willing. The animal always has a choice—it is not forced the way the DéHool are.

Lóklana—Radiance: they can call light in darkness from within the life that stores it

HIDDEN LANGUAGE DICTIONARY

Ladonradi—The Light

Degani—The Dark

Liosladon—May the Light lead and protect you wherever you may go

Ladon—Light. Light come forth is Radi

To'—The

Y'na—I am

Hai—Here

Mindra—Chosen

Vast—Fight

Pench Ni'yā àlo—Be still

Lon'adras—Heal

Dón—For

Y' takra—Take me

Da'bay—Friend

Ke'ay—Help

Mea—Me

Chan'ta—Please

Mah'ne—Journey

I'kashti—Summon

Walkarna—Servants come

Minradak-con-siadras—This ground is sacred and protected. The words spoken to bless the earth and make it burial ground, protecting those buried from the Night Demons

To'conchla serith hune doocrah—The Ninth shall lead them.

Den aktra—Aid us

Kindrak' al' duberio—Shadows heed me

Den mea Tin'ruhl—Aid me Earth

Y'na to'Conchla Mindra! Radi'non! Odra den aktra! Vast don aktra!—I am the Ninth Chosen. Light come forth. Bring us aid. Fight for us!

CHOSEN TERMS

Mi'no ha—Life to fire

Vin'akra—Life to wind

Ma'sha—Hear me animal

Win'tashta—Water hear my call

Tin'ruhl—Earth hear my call

Radi'non—Light come forth

Los'lon—Nature hear me

Vel'don—Veil me within

To'Conchla—The Ninth

Mindra—Chosen

Words said to increase the body's natural abilities. Each word when said with intent has the power to speak to the life force and ask it to enhance that body part:

Konsh'la—Makes your hearing stronger. "The ears""

Inreedo—Makes your eyesight stronger. "The eyes"

Mig'nata—Increases strength. "The body"

To'—The

Lon'adras—heal, repair, return

Places of Interest

Green River Utah: Areen chose to hide Tolen here because of its proximity to a deserted Sphere settlement that would enable her to ask for aid from the Doogar

The Binithan: Doogar settlement hidden deep within the caves beneath The Lava Beds National Monument in California

The Unastra Training Camp: Located in the mountains bordering California and Oregon, the Unastra camp is home to many followers of Light

The Shadow Realm: The Dark dimension. Nerve center for all creatures of Darkness and the location of the Shadow Prison

The Light Realm: The Light dimension. Sanctuary for followers of Light. Home of the Citadel of Light—headquarters for the Guardians

Misery: A phantom dimension housing Misery, the prison built by the Guardians